Stealing Roses

By Heather Cooper

Stealing Roses

Stealing Roses

HEATHER COOPER

Allison & Busby Limited
11 Wardour Mews
London W1F 8AN
allisonandbusby.com

First published in Great Britain by Allison & Busby in 2019.
This paperback edition published by Allison & Busby in 2019.

A CIP catalogue record for this book is available from
the British Library.

10 9 8 7 6 5 4 3 2 1

ISBN 978-0-7490-2402-4

Typeset in 11/16 pt Adobe Garamond Pro by
Allison & Busby Ltd.

The paper used for this Allison & Busby publication
has been produced from trees that have been legally sourced
from well-managed and credibly certified forests.

Printed and bound by
CPI Group (UK) Ltd, Croydon, CR0 4YY

For Terence

Cowes, Isle of Wight

1862

Chapter One

Eveline is Late for Luncheon

Eveline was making her third attempt to sketch the scene before her: the great cedar tree, the four grey walls that surrounded the garden, the huddle of roofs sloping down toward the shore, and the sea beyond. The two drawings she had made already – neither of which captured the magnificence of the tree, or the light glancing from the water – had floated away from her lap, and eventually the third was discarded also. Somehow she could not bring the sketch to life. She turned to the book, and, reminding herself of her resolution to learn some lines of poetry every day, began to murmur those she had chosen as today's task.

On either side the river lie
Long fields of barley, and of rye . . .

Eventually, as the warmth of the spring day, and the distant rhythm of the waves, and the lullaby of the words, all combined, her eyes began to droop and the book fell from her hands to join the crumpled sketches lying on the grass below, waking her as it landed. Since she was in fact sitting on the broad branch of a beech tree, and was some twelve feet above the ground, there was nothing for it but to climb down the usual way (this involved the edge of the inner wall, which enclosed the rose garden, the roof of the old potting shed – carefully, here, since there was a glass panel to avoid – and an upturned wheelbarrow) to rescue the book and the unsatisfactory sketches, and once on the ground it occurred to her that she might be wanted indoors. As though to confirm that prickle of conscience, she heard the faint familiar chime of the luncheon bell, and with a small sigh of exasperation, which originated more from her own unproductive morning than from its interruption, she slipped back through the low door in the wall, climbed the steps to the lawns, and crossed the terrace to the house.

Within, all was bustle and energy. Eveline could hear her mother's and sisters' voices even as she entered the dining room, raised in animated discussion of whether a cold soup should be served for the dinner tomorrow evening, and if pineapples could be got at this late stage, and if they could how they should be prepared. Her two brothers-in-law were engaged in a good-tempered argument over the merits and demerits of a pair of carriage-horses, which Arthur had recently bought, as his wife had taken a fancy to them, and Bevis suspected of having been less of a bargain than Arthur believed; Daisy and Kitty were whispering together; and her aunt and Miss Angell were engaged in trying to persuade six-year-old Henry that he must eat some bread and butter, and some cold chicken, before he could have any hope of the trifle, which was already on the sideboard in all its alluring splendour of cream and cherries and angelica.

'Eveline, at last!' Her mother caught sight of her youngest daughter as she tried to seat herself unobtrusively next to Aunt George. 'Wherever have you been?'

Eveline knew that this question was largely rhetorical, and she remained silent.

'Well, it is a cold luncheon today, so there is no harm done, but really, Eveline, your hair!'

Eveline's hair was, she knew, a source of constant sorrow to her mother. Mrs Stanhope had been famous in her youth for the fair ringlets, which framed her heart-shaped face so becomingly. Her hair was a little faded now and there were streaks of silver among the gold beneath her cap, but even in middle age she was a remarkably pretty woman. Her two elder daughters had inherited her looks to a large extent – Louisa, in particular, as lovely as her mother had once been, and Beatrice, although a little less classically beautiful, possessing the same white sloping shoulders and rosebud mouth – but Eveline had taken after her father. She was taller than her mother and sisters by a head, with dark unruly curls that sprang from any attempt to confine them, and unfashionably strong features: a wide mouth, a straight nose, and heavy brows. She had been miserably conscious of the disappointment this caused to her mother since she was twelve years old, and still occasionally felt awkward and clumsy beside her sisters; but she had talked herself out of minding this very much some years before, and now felt there was something of a relief in not being a beauty. She did not expect compliments; she did not spend hours with her hair twisted into painful rags; she did not feel alarm in walking out without a sunshade; and in all this there was a freedom that she would not now have traded for her sisters' anxiety about their porcelain skin and smooth shining hair.

'Your mother is a little anxious about tomorrow's dinner, my dear,' said her aunt quietly.

'Of course. It's no matter, Aunt George. Although I don't know why Mama is in such a state; she loves to give dinners, as a general rule.'

'I think,' said her aunt carefully, 'that she is concerned about her mix of guests. She has invited Mr Watson, and the young man who works for him, and she worries that the Sandhams may feel they should not be asked to meet them.'

'We are a small town here, Aunt, of course we must all meet each other! And the Sandhams are not so very grand.'

'They are large fish in this small pond, my dear, and they think themselves so. But I have always found Mr Watson's company more to my taste than that of the Sandhams; he is thoughtful, and has seen a great deal of the world, besides, which is more than one can say of Augusta Sandham, whose horizons are bounded entirely by the stout walls of her house and her estate.'

Eveline sighed. 'As are mine, Aunt George, are they not?'

Her aunt regarded her gravely. 'Anyone who reads widely is a citizen of the world, my love, and you are a reader.'

'I love to read, indeed I do, but that will not do for me. It cannot be enough. I have seen so little. I have been to so few places; hardly beyond this town, and when I do it is to visit other people whom I already know, who have houses very like ours, and eat dinners like ours, and listen to the same music after dinner, and – oh! It is so . . . confining!'

'Then you will have to make your own adventures, my dear,' said her aunt calmly, and turned her attention back to Miss Angell and Henry and the trifle.

Eveline's plan to spend the rest of the day reading was thwarted by her mother's saying that she would need her for the afternoon; there was so much to be done for the next day, and Eveline could help her check through the lists of food to be ordered and prepared and decide on the flowers.

'The roses are not in bloom yet, but jonquils will be perfect. And primulas, perhaps, for the table?'

'Shall I go and gather them now?' asked Eveline, seeing a chance to escape from the house presenting itself.

'No, the morning will be better – and I need you to help me with the seating plan now. Can we put Mr Watson next to Lady Sandham? Will that offend her?'

'I hardly see how she could be offended by being seated next to a sensible, interesting man.'

Her mother regarded her crossly. 'You know perfectly well, Evie. Mr Watson is a director of the Railway Company now; and he made his money in shipbuilding. Augusta Sandham thinks herself a great deal too grand to mix with people in trade as a general rule, and only his wealth reconciles her to meeting him at all; and then, he asked me so particularly to invite his young friend who is something clever in the railways, too, that I could not say no.'

'Are the railways trade, exactly?'

'Worse than trade,' said her mother briskly. 'And the railway is to run alongside the Sandhams' park, and ruin their peace and spoil their view.'

'As it will for many people. And Arthur's fortune came from trade, and they have never minded Arthur; who could?'

'That is two generations ago, and Arthur is a gentleman; anyone may see that. And then, Evie, although I have invited Mr Watson's young friend, I do not know him at all, and I understand him to have come from the north – Yorkshire, or some other very cold, bleak place. Heaven knows what Augusta will make of him. She will put on her grandest airs, you may be sure.'

'Well, put Lady Sandham next to Bevis; he will charm her. And I think if you seat Mr Watson next to Aunt George, he will have a much pleasanter evening.'

'Are you trying to match-make, Evie? Mr Watson and your aunt?'

'Of course not, Mama! Aunt George would not marry.'

'She is not so old – a few years older than me, and Mr Watson is a pleasant man, and rich. Would it be so very shocking?'

'No, not shocking, exactly; but' – she stopped to consider why the idea was so unwelcome – 'Aunt George belongs here.'

'If it is only our wishes that keep her here, then that is a selfish reason. I do not see why she should not have a home of her own, and a husband, if she wishes it.'

'I think it is you who are matchmaking, Mama.'

'Nonsense, Evie. It is only that Mr Watson is such a dear friend, and it is so many years since his poor wife died, that I do not like to think of him alone.'

Georgiana was Mr Stanhope's only sister, his elder by two years, and had come to live with her brother's family a few years after his marriage. Louisa and Beatrice were very small, and a maiden aunt was certainly a great help to the family in caring for and entertaining two little girls so close in age. Georgiana was too much of a mouthful for the children, and she soon became Aunt George to everyone. When the girls were old enough to need a governess, Miss Angell had arrived; but Aunt George had stayed, and was able to enhance their education by adding Latin and mathematics to Miss Angell's repertoire of history, French, and watercolours. There seemed to be no rivalry between the two ladies as to their teaching territories, and when Eveline arrived (perhaps a little unexpectedly, for she was born some ten years after Louisa, and nine years after Beatrice) she was duly educated by both as her sisters had been. Miss Angell was much beloved by all the girls, and Aunt George, though she could be acerbic, was a teacher and a companion full of wisdom and merriment in equal measure. When Louisa married at nineteen, and Beatrice the following year, the household seemed quiet and a little melancholy; yet Beatrice was now living only a few streets away, and Louisa, though further off, was a still frequent visitor to her parental home; and the relief from the talk of wedding dresses and lace, which seemed to have obsessed her mother and sisters for so long, was felt by Eveline to be an advantage, at least. She continued to read, to study, to walk with her father along the river learning the names of the flowers and birds, and occasionally she contrived to escape to climb trees, undetected by her mother.

On the eve of Eveline's thirteenth birthday, however, her life changed. Mr Stanhope had taken his youngest daughter walking along the river path, which led away from the little town, as he so often did, and on their return to the house he had felt tired, and had gone upstairs to rest before the evening meal. At six o'clock Mrs Stanhope had gone to wake him and remind him to dress for dinner – he was inclined to be absent-minded, and to neglect the formalities on which his wife placed a good deal of importance – but he could not be woken, and when Dr Pearson arrived he could do nothing but shake his head sadly and give his opinion that Mr Stanhope's heart had failed, very suddenly, and in all probability with little pain.

The memories of the year following her father's death were as blurred as imperfectly remembered dreams: the rustle of the black silk dress her mother wore; the twilight gloom of the house with the blinds all drawn; the falling apart of the household routines, so that meals were forgotten and lessons neglected. Yet, as time passed, her mother began to wear lilac ribbons, there were new curtains in the morning room, and order returned. Eveline still spent her mornings learning whatever her governess and Aunt George had decided to teach her, but the dancing and music teachers who had been engaged when Louisa and Beatrice were growing up were somehow forgotten. Eveline missed most bitterly the walks she had been used to taking with her father – the river path, the sandy flats by the estuary, and the seashore; instead she spent long afternoons curled in the chair in her father's study where he had used to sit. No one took a great deal of notice of her in there, which suited her very well, and she read her way indiscriminately through her father's books: Shakespeare and Milton and Shelley and Byron; atlases and herbals; medical textbooks; maps and charts; great tomes with engravings of scenery from Italy, and Egypt, and the Lake Country; treatises on the rotation of crops and diseases of cattle; books with coloured pictures of birds and animals; and tucked away on the higher reaches of the shelves, reachable only by the use of the library steps, a beautiful book with pictures of men and women from the East, naked or in exquisite dress, in gardens full of flowers and on silken cushions, with golden bells on their ankles and jewels about their necks, entwined gracefully together in all sorts of interesting and astonishing ways.

This afternoon, however, there would be no chance to retreat to the sanctuary of the study. After the seating plan was done to Mrs Stanhope's exacting standards, Eveline was required to mind Daisy and Kitty and Henry while her sisters walked into town in search of shoe roses and scent – Louisa a little condescending now about the shops, which she once found enchanting but compared unfavourably with those in Newport, the town nearest her new home – and Beatrice anxious to learn from her sister what the latest fashion dictated in the wider world. Eveline was fond of her nieces and nephew, but two hours in their company were enough to make her very glad to see her sisters returning. They were delighted with their purchases.

'New lace gloves, Eveline, look, how pretty! Although a little delicate for you, perhaps, but there were some red silk roses, which might become you,' said Beatrice.

'And what will you wear for the dinner tomorrow, Evie?' asked Louisa, admiring the lace against her wrist.

'I had not thought,' said Eveline.

Louisa shrieked at this. 'Come upstairs – the Angell will take the children now, and we will see what might be suitable. I must say that green thing you have on now does nothing for your looks. And you really must dress well for tomorrow: Charles Sandham will be there, and he is a man of taste, I know.'

Eveline regarded her sister with suspicion.

'You know him, then?'

'We met him in town, with his uncle, and were introduced – just back from a grand tour, you know, Italy, Greece, Vienna; oh, wonderful places! He is full of the most interesting stories.'

'And handsome, too,' added Beatrice.

Eveline recollected the seating plan for tomorrow's dinner, and her mother's insistence that Charles Sandham be seated next to her.

'Are you and Mama conspiring to marry me to Charles Sandham?'

'You would be extremely lucky if Charles offered for you, Evie,' said Louisa briskly. 'But if you would make an effort – here, sit down, let me try to do something with your hair – one never knows.'

Eveline sighed and submitted to her sister's ministrations.

Chapter Two

The Dinner Party

The guests were seated. Lady Sandham, as Eveline had predicted, was being charmed by Bevis, who was listening with apparent fascination to her strictures on how a new parlourmaid should be trained. All his attention was focused on her; had she been the most entertaining and beautiful woman in the world, he could have hardly looked more rapt in admiration. This, thought Eveline admiringly, was the secret of Louisa's husband's charm: not that he himself was particularly clever or amusing, but that he could make anyone he conversed with feel that they were clever and amusing themselves, because he listened with such attention, and responded so admiringly, and smiled so readily. Mr

Watson and Aunt George were engaged in a lively conversation about the latest of Mr Dickens' novels, and Arthur, seated on the other side of Charles Sandham from Eveline, was engrossing him in the ongoing tale of the carriage-horses. Louisa and Beatrice were either side of Sir William, who looked very well pleased with the arrangement; and their last guest, Mr Armitage, the young man who worked with Mr Watson, although his looks were somewhat forbidding, was listening to Miss Angell's talk of a design for a new herb garden with no apparent impatience. Mrs Stanhope felt the dinner was going to be a success.

Arthur, having exhausted the carriage-horses once again fell silent, and Charles Sandham turned to Eveline. A nephew, and the sole heir, of Sir William, Charles had been talked of in the neighbourhood, since Eveline could remember, with much interest: said to be a fine boy, and then a handsome man; rumoured to be a little wild, and then forgiven on account of his youth; spoken of variously as cultured, and clever, and sophisticated. Despite all these interesting speculations, however, he had not visited his uncle and aunt for any extended period until this spring, when his university education and subsequent travels abroad had ended. He had come into a modest fortune on attaining his majority, it was said, and lived in London in some style; and he had the expectation of a very substantial fortune from his uncle in the future. Mrs Stanhope's dinner was, in effect, in his honour, for the Stanhope family had not previously met him, apart from Louisa's chance encounter, and the Sandhams were among their closest neighbours, and certainly the most important in Mrs Stanhope's eyes. The estate marched with their own –

although the Sandhams' park was very much larger, and their house very much more grand, and their drive was so very long and sweeping that the two families always paid their visits to each other by carriage, even though Eveline had often thought that, had there been a gate in the high walls that separated their ancestral acres, the distance could have been covered on foot in a great deal less time.

'The views from this room are very fine, Miss Stanhope,' Charles began. He gave her a smile, which seemed to combine an acknowledgement of his own good looks, with a slight ruefulness that he should have been so blessed. 'I see that you look across the lawns down to the sea, and your gardens are most delightful. The prospect puts me in mind a little of Italy. I was there, you know, for some weeks last summer.'

'I should so love to see Italy, Mr Sandham! But I cannot believe that this view of ours bears any resemblance to the places you have seen.'

'Oh, of course it is not so fine as the views across the bay of Spezia, for example, or as truly dramatic as those from Ravello.'

Eveline felt all the inadequacy of the very view she had tried to draw yesterday, and how dreary it must be in comparison to the grandeurs he had seen.

'I should very much like to hear of your travels,' she said. 'I understand you have seen a good deal of Europe?'

'Indeed.' He flourished his knife and fork expansively. 'Where shall I start? Well, Miss Stanhope, we crossed to France on a rough sea, to begin with; it was a dangerous beginning! Paris was our first stop, of course, and I spent a month there. We lodged very near the Opera . . .'

Eveline was entranced by these traveller's tales. Charles Sandham spoke well, and described the scenery, the fine buildings, the paintings and sculptures, the galleries and gardens, in much detail. He and his party had visited Versailles; crossed the Alps by a high pass; braved the catacombs of Rome; sailed along the Italian coast. She observed his profile as he spoke: fine features, fair curls, hazel eyes. Certainly he was a handsome man. The evening was passing in a far more agreeable way than she had thought possible.

In the drawing room afterwards, however, when the gentlemen had been left to the port and the brandy, the conversation became a great deal more difficult. Lady Sandham, a little deaf and therefore prone to speak more loudly than she was aware of, was seated by Eveline on a small sofa, and taking up a good deal more than her share of the space.

'This is a very small party, Miss Stanhope. Some of the respectable families are out of town, of course; I suppose the Debournes are gone up to London, so you could not get them.'

'Mama prefers smaller parties, Lady Sandham,' said Eveline.

'Small select parties are always preferable, of course, but it is odd to be meeting these men connected with that dreadful railway. We have known Mr Watson for some time, of course; he was mayor of the town, I recall, years ago, so of course one meets him everywhere, and yet he is not quite . . .' She let her voice trail away, as though lost for an exact description of what Mr Watson was not. 'And the young man with him – your dear mama is so generous in her invitations, is she not? But really, is he, do you think' – she lowered her voice a fraction, although it retained its general stridency – 'a *gentleman*? The way he speaks – so very curious to hear – not quite what we are used to, perhaps . . .'

'Mama is indeed hospitable, Lady Sandham,' said Eveline carefully, 'and no friend of Mr Watson can ever be unwelcome here; Mr Watson was a dear friend of my father, you know, long before he became a director of the railway, and he speaks so highly of this Mr Armitage, who is the chief engineer, I believe.'

'Engineer? Indeed,' said Lady Sandham, raising her eyebrows. 'How very original. I am quite sure I have never met anyone of that type before.'

'Well,' said Eveline firmly, 'I think we are fortunate in all our guests.' She caught Aunt George's eye, who was listening with interest and some amusement.

Lady Sandham began again.

'And how odd that you should have your old governess to dine with you! In my day the governess would have dined with the other servants.'

Eveline flushed scarlet with annoyance at this, hoping very much that Miss Angell had not overheard.

'Miss Angell is no longer our governess. She is a dear friend and we are honoured that she dines with us.'

'You are a very modern young woman, miss.'

'I hope I am. I would not wish to be an old-fashioned one.' Eveline stood up. 'May I fetch you some tea?' Eveline walked away towards the other side of the room. Aunt George no longer looked amused; she was white with rage.

* * *

The gentlemen's entrance was a relief. Eveline hoped for a further chance to hear Charles talk of Florence and Venice, but his uncle had engaged him in discussion of a yacht he was minded to buy – sailing looked set fair to become Sir William's latest enthusiasm, for he had heard a rumour that the Prince of Wales was to become a member of the yacht club. She walked to the window; the light was almost gone, and the trees were black silhouettes against an inky sky. The guests would be leaving soon, and she might, she thought, make a sketch from the window of her bedroom of the trees against that sky. Suddenly she was impatient to escape from the chatter and the teacups and horrible Augusta Sandham. She might perhaps plead fatigue, she thought, and took a step towards the door, hoping to steal away unnoticed.

'You were admiring the night sky, Miss Stanhope?'

She turned, and to her annoyance, found that Mr Armitage was standing at her side, regarding her intently. He had a strong, angular face, with a mouth that looked rather hard and stern. She swallowed her impatience.

'I was, indeed, admiring it – I was thinking that it would make a fine picture, if I could draw it.'

'You are an artist, then?'

'I try, Mr Armitage, but alas, my skill is not what I would wish it to be. I see scenes that I wish to sketch, scenes such as the twilight out there, with the light fading, and the trees so dark and dramatic, but I never quite seem to capture on paper the *essence* of what I see.'

He seemed to mull this over in silence for a few moments, and then said, 'I have no such talents, but I admire those who have.'

'You have other talents, though, Mr Armitage, I understand. Mr Watson has sung your praises to us all. You are a very skilled engineer, he says.'

Mr Armitage nodded briefly, but did not speak.

Eveline sighed; here, it seemed, was a man with even less taste for small talk than she had herself. She cast around for something to say.

'I hope you are enjoying this evening?'

'Yes, well enough,' he said shortly, and then added, 'but you are perhaps not, Miss Stanhope? I had the distinct impression you were about to leave us.'

'No, of course not – that is, I have a slight headache.'

'Then of course you must go.' He bowed slightly; she could not read his expression. Her mother, however, was regarding her from a few feet away with a very readable face – Mrs Stanhope was all too aware that her youngest daughter was prone to escape from social gatherings on flimsy excuses, and she had seen Eveline's surreptitious move towards the door.

'Oh, it is nothing,' said Eveline reluctantly. She searched afresh for a topic of conversation, since he still gave no indication of doing so. 'Is the new railway progressing as it should, Mr Armitage? Will we have an end soon to all the digging and noise?'

'If all goes well, the line will open in under two months. You will be able to travel to Newport with a journey of ten minutes. I hope you will be among the first of the passengers to do so?'

'Ten minutes?' She thought of the journey as it was now: the rattle and creaking of the old carriage, the horses tiring as

26

they tackled the long hill, the jolting, the cold in winter. To reach Newport, the town some five miles away, which, a great deal larger than their own little seaside town, could boast finer shops, and a concert hall, and all manner of amusements, was an hour's journey on a fine day; more when rain and mud prevailed; a whole day when a horse went lame or a wheel came loose.

'Indeed. And ten trains a day. You will be able to stay there for your shopping and gossiping all day, or just for a half-hour.'

'Shopping and gossiping, Mr Armitage? Is that your view of women's occupations?'

'Or whatever else you may choose to do, of course.'

'So much destruction seems a high price to pay for such trivial pursuits.'

'Destruction?'

'Yes, destruction, of our paths and woodlands and meadows! The walk along the river, so peaceful and beautiful, is all lost now; explosions, great scars across the meadows, the trees felled, a tunnel being gouged out of the hill, and the countryside quite spoilt.'

He looked unconcerned. 'You want a railway. There is a price. But the countryside will mend.'

'I am not at all sure that I do want a railway! In fact, I am very sure that many people do not.'

'You feel much as Lady Sandham does, I collect.'

Eveline, furious at being supposed to think as Augusta Sandham did on any subject at all, promptly lost her temper.

'You cannot possibly know, Mr Armitage, what effect your railway will have on the people who live here. It may bring advantages for men, and business – although the poor fishermen who live by the river will be ruined, I dare say, now their cottages are quite cut off – but as you have already suggested, it cannot benefit women except by enabling them to be useless and stupid in a wider sphere than before; and the countryside will never again be as it was. You come here from the *north* and when you leave again you will take no responsibility for what you have inflicted upon us!'

'I am sorry you should feel so, Miss Stanhope, although it is not *my* railway. I am an engineer, not the owner of a railway company. Nevertheless, I believe you are wrong, and that it will benefit both men and women. Travel and commerce will be open in a way none of us could previously have dreamt of, and not just to the rich, but to all. It will make a difference to the working people of this country, for the good – it is already happening in other parts of the country – I have seen it.'

He paused, and looked at her sardonically. 'Although, of course, you are right about one thing; I am from the *north*, and I will leave again when my work here is done.' He nodded his head at her, turned, and walked away to where Arthur and Bevis were proposing a game of billiards, which they cordially invited him and Charles to join.

When the guests had gone, and Eveline at last reached the sanctuary of her bedroom, it was past midnight. Jennie, the new maid, yawning and half-asleep herself, jumped up guiltily from the chair by the dying fire.

'Don't worry, Jennie, I can manage perfectly well,' she said. 'Go to bed. I'm sorry to have kept you up so late.'

She undressed, and prepared for bed, and then wrapped a blanket around herself and sat in the window seat to gaze at the darkness and indulge all her feelings of outrage. Augusta Sandham's unkindness about dear Miss Angell was horrible; and then that tall man, with his cold gaze and his lack of understanding about what the coming of the railway meant to her, to her family, to their town! She thought of the walk by the river that her father had so often taken with her: her earliest memories were of the sunlight on the water, the coolness of the shade beneath the woods along the banks, and the wild roses towering high above her infant head. In the autumn, they would pick blackberries, and at this time of year, there would have been primroses in great pale drifts beneath the hawthorns, and she would pick bunches for her father, burying her face in the fragrant petals as she gathered them. Next month the May blossom would be out, and the Queen Anne's lace frothing beside the path, and the bluebells with their ravishing scent. Now that was all torn away; gangs of men had dug and laboured and shouted, rock had been blasted so that the noise echoed over the town, trees had been felled, and the whole glorious stretch of land laid waste. She closed her eyes and leant her head against the wall, trying to take refuge in her memories. Drowsing, she was again by the river with Papa, listening to his voice – 'and here, Eveline, this is willowherb; the great willowherb, I think, rather than the more usual variety, the rosebay; the dog roses are very fine this year, I notice,' and he had stopped to write in the notebook he always carried, while Eveline ran ahead, having spotted a red squirrel on the branch of an oak tree ahead. Was she six, or seven? It was midsummer, and so hot that petticoats and stockings and boots and a dress and a bonnet all were encumbrances, and her skirts had wrapped themselves around her ankles as she ran. She came to a break in the trees where there was a little wooden jetty overhanging the water and stopped. A group of boys – a dozen of them, some no older than her, some perhaps ten or twelve – were swimming. Some were splashing in the limpid shallows; some jumping from the edge of the jetty where the water was deep and green; some running down the grassy bank below the path to hurl themselves into the delicious coolness. All were entirely naked.

Eveline had stopped and gazed at the boys. Their thin, pale bodies were foreign to her. Their shouts rose to her ears as her father caught up with her, and they stood together, silent and unseen, watching. She wished with all her heart that she too could take off her clothes and feel the water on her hot skin, could dig bare toes into the soft mud at the water's edge, could jump and let the river close over her head, and rise up laughing and spluttering and gasping with the cold. No sooner had those wishes formed, however, than she knew, somehow, that she would not be allowed to do so; that Mama and her sisters and Miss Angell and even Aunt George would all regard such a thing as shocking, not to be thought of, forbidden, although she hardly knew why; and she looked up at her father, and knew that he too wished, for a moment, that to swim naked on a summer's day was not forbidden, while accepting that, for his daughter, it was impossible. They had turned then and walked back, hand in hand, both silent.

30

Eveline had soon forgotten the scene, or thought she had. Now, though, half-dreaming, she saw again the dimpled water and heard the shouts of the boys by the river. They would be grown, now, those boys; they would be young men – perhaps they were working to build the railway. There had been an accident a few months ago, when part of the new tunnel being driven through the rock had collapsed and a young man working there had died. She had read his name in the newspaper – she had forgotten it now – but he had lived in the town. He might have been swimming in the river on that long-ago summer's day. She found she was shivering, and climbed into the high bed, but she did not draw the curtains, and she lay awake for a long time watching a crescent moon, sharp and clear and remote, move very slowly across the sky.

Chapter Three

The Professor of Photography

'Louisa and Bevis are walking into town this morning,' said Mrs Stanhope, 'to have their likenesses taken, and Beatrice and Arthur have decided to join them. It will be delightful to have their portraits, and you must not be left out, my dear. Perhaps you could change your dress, Evie; that blue walking costume would look well, I think.'

'Their portraits? Surely that would mean hours of sitting for the painter, and are they not travelling back tomorrow?'

Mrs Stanhope laughed. 'Not painted, silly girl! Have you not seen the new establishment in the high street – the Professor of Photography? They are to sit for photographs. I would like all my daughters photographed together – it will be a charming group.'

'Oh no, really, Mama, I cannot possibly – I have promised to help Aunt George this morning, with . . . with her plans for the garden, and in any case Louisa and Beatrice will look charming enough without me.'

'Nonsense, Eveline.' Her mother could be implacable on occasion. 'I should like all my daughters photographed together. Now run upstairs, and put on something elegant instead of that green thing.'

Beatrice and Arthur's house was a handsome villa, much embellished, since their marriage, with stucco columns, and a porch, and a veranda. It was in a less elevated position than the Stanhopes', and closer to the high street. Louisa, Bevis and Eveline called to collect them on their way to the photographer, and there was a great deal of talk about the previous evening.

'I thought Charles Sandham delightful,' said Beatrice. 'Such an air, such manners! Evie, he talked to you a good deal.'

Louisa and Beatrice exchanged speaking glances.

'He did seem to like you, Evie,' said Louisa. 'And he spoke to me after dinner, at great length – told me of Venice, the palaces and churches built practically in the water, everything just as one has imagined! He certainly is most entertaining.'

'I liked him very much,' added Bevis. 'I have invited him to stay whenever he should care to.'

Louisa looked pleased at this news, although she chided her husband a little for his not having consulted her before issuing an invitation.

'Really, Bevis, you know we agreed that we should have new furnishings in the drawing room before we have any guests!'

'Perhaps he will advise us on our choice; he seems to have a fine eye for such things – all that talk of art and so forth! Still, he says the card table and the races are more to his taste, if the truth were known, and we are to play a few hands sometime.'

'You are not to keep him away from us, Louisa,' said Beatrice crossly, 'we are far more in need of entertaining company here than you.'

'Mr Watson is always a delightful guest, I think,' said Eveline. 'He seems almost one of the family, after so many years as a friend. He is glad, I think, that the railway is nearly complete, for he has been so busy as its director, and once it is done he intends to devote his time to reading and fishing.'

'Oh, he is a dear man.' This from Louisa. 'But the young man who accompanied him – what can Mama have been thinking to invite him? He was so unsmiling – hardly said a word – and when he did, that voice! I declare I could hardly understand him. No graces, no compliments – whereas dear Charles was most effusive about my new lilac satin, and said he had seen gowns of a similar cut in Paris, but none so exquisitely displayed! He quite made me blush.'

'Yet he was very attractive, I thought,' said Beatrice. 'Mr Armitage, that is. Not handsome, exactly, but tall and striking. A pity that he speaks so oddly.'

'He comes from Yorkshire,' said Eveline, 'how should he speak? I suppose he thinks the same of us.'

'He played a good game of billiards, at any rate,' said Arthur.

* * *

34

They had arrived at the studio of the Professor of Photography, a gentleman from London who had set up his shop a few months ago and had become something of a craze for the people of the little town. Louisa and Bevis were photographed first; Louisa seated on a white wicker chair, with Bevis leaning against a painted column behind her, and a huge palm providing an exotic touch.

'Now, perfectly still, please!'

Minutes passed as the Professor disappeared beneath the black tent behind the camera tripod, and Louisa's and Bevis's faces assumed a kind of desperate glare with the effort of not moving a muscle. After that, Beatrice and Arthur were arranged in identical poses; then the two couples together, with the ladies seated and the gentlemen standing behind their wives, against a painted landscape of improbably dramatic mountains and a balustrade; and finally, Louisa, Beatrice and Eveline in a group. For this, the Professor – a portly man with a fine moustache, who was quite possibly not a professor at all – placed Louisa and Beatrice on a seat with baskets of flowers beside them, and Eveline standing behind them holding a bunch of lilies of the valley. ('Really?' said Eveline when the flowers were proposed, but her sisters agreed with the Professor that they would add a maidenly note, which would perfect the scene, and she was overruled.) As the long minutes stretched by, Eveline felt first that she might scream, then that she might faint; her very eyes seemed to hurt with the effort of keeping them open, while the back of her neck developed an excruciating pain that radiated through her shoulders. The relief of being allowed to move at last was intense.

'Wonderful, ladies, gentlemen, thank you! Perfect subjects, youth and beauty combined!'

Eveline, although with no very warm feelings towards the Professor after the torture he had made them endure, would have liked to know what the next part of the process would be. Although the Professor was a large, untidy man, his clothes and hands stained with inky blotches, it was with infinite delicacy that he removed the glass plates from his camera to carry them away to another room, from which emanated strong smells of something metallic and harsh.

'How is the image formed?' she asked him, as the others were putting on capes and coats and hats.

He smiled at her; he had a kindly, crumpled face. 'Next, the plates will have a developing solution poured over them. One must be very gentle with that: too heavy a hand will blur the image. Then—' but Louisa and Beatrice were impatient to leave the dark, stuffy rooms, and Eveline learnt no more.

It was arranged that the photographs would be sent up to Mrs Stanhope as soon as they were ready; within the next few days, the Professor assured them. On leaving the studio, by now giddy with relief at their liberation, the party decided to walk along the seafront, where there was always something new of interest. And today was no exception, for a small crowd had gathered to watch half a dozen horses dragging carts, on which small painted wooden huts were balanced, down to the water's edge. It was soon discovered that these were new bathing machines, and very superior models at that.

'I believe the queen herself uses a bathing machine,' said Louisa. 'I really do not think I could do so, however – the cold! And then getting in and out of one's clothes in a little wooden box – too, too fatiguing!'

Beatrice agreed, but Arthur and Bevis were much in favour.

'Swimming is a fine sport,' said Arthur, 'and I was reckoned something of a champion at Cambridge.'

'I should like to learn to swim, Arthur,' said Eveline. 'Could you teach me? Is it hard to learn?'

'No, after a little while it feels perfectly easy,' Arthur assured her. 'The water supports you, you know, and with practice you can float, or—'

'Arthur!' His wife stopped him. 'You know perfectly well that you could not teach her to swim, and Eveline, really, what a thing to ask! Gentlemen and ladies cannot bathe together – what an idea! How . . . indecorous!'

'Then how am I to learn, Beatrice?' asked Eveline impatiently.

'I don't think you should learn at all.'

'But the queen may swim? And I may not?'

'Oh, well, Mama will have something to say, I imagine. I cannot think she would agree.'

Mrs Stanhope, however, to the surprise of all her daughters, did not immediately rule out the idea of Eveline's learning to swim. When Beatrice and Arthur had walked back to their house, and the rest of the party had returned, Eveline broached the subject, and her mother said merely that if a respectable bathing-woman could be found to attend Eveline she would have no objection.

'Although, Evie, you will need a proper bathing dress, and as you have so little inclination for going to the dressmaker as a general rule, I do not know how you are to get one.'

'I would go to the dressmaker if it were for a bathing dress, Mama, of course. It is only the hours one has to stand about being pinned into things and deciding on stupid bits of satin and ribbon that make it so tedious.'

Louisa rolled her eyes.

'Really, Eveline, you are a peculiar girl! How are we to get you a husband if you do not take an interest in such things?'

'Please do not feel that you have to get me a husband, Louisa. I am very happy without one, and I certainly would not want one that had to be procured for me by my sister.'

'Eveline, you will apologise to Louisa for that remark,' said Mrs Stanhope sharply. 'She is trying to help, and she is quite correct in what she says. You can be very provoking in the way you affect this disdain for pretty clothes.'

Eveline bit her lip.

'Very well, I am sorry. But really, I cannot see why I have to—'

'That will do,' said her mother. 'And in fact, you will need a new dress before long, something very smart, for we have an invitation here to the grand opening of the railway in June. All the town will be there, and I know the Sandhams are to cut a ribbon and make a speech, and there is to be a luncheon afterwards, with everyone who is anyone attending.'

'I thought the Sandhams were set against the railway, for bringing noise and spoiling the view across their park,' said Eveline. 'Why are they now so ready to cut ribbons and make speeches?'

'Oh, Augusta would not stand upon her principles if it meant missing a chance to play the *grande dame*,' said her mother. 'And Sir William will always do as his wife wishes. He is too sensible to do otherwise.'

'Are Bevis and I included in the invitation, Mama?' asked Louisa. 'For we can quite easily make another visit, you know – we need not bring the children.'

'Yes, you are included, my love – all of us are, George and Miss Angell too, I am happy to say. And you must of course bring the children. Eveline can mind them, you know.'

'Oh, delightful! I shall certainly need a new costume,' said Louisa, 'and I have seen the very thing, I believe, at my dressmaker's; a crinoline skirt, very full, in peacock blue, with pagoda sleeves.'

'That does sound very lovely,' agreed her mother. 'Now, Eveline, what about you? It is not too soon to think about it, you know. A pretty apricot, perhaps, or a soft primrose?'

'I do not wish to attend the opening of the railway,' said Eveline. 'How can we, Mama, when it has spoilt all those places which Papa loved so much, and caused so much destruction?'

'If your father were here,' said Mrs Stanhope, 'I feel sure he would be interested in the railway – the engines, you know, he would have been fascinated by those! And the idea of travelling in ten minutes a distance which now takes us for ever!'

'He would have hated the ugliness of it all. The quiet walks, all gone, and the horrible brick houses that have sprung up everywhere.'

'You will allow me to differ,' said her mother. 'And we all miss Papa, Eveline, but we must live our lives without him now, and this event is important for us and for the town. He liked Mr Watson, too, and the invitation is from him. Papa would certainly have wanted us to attend.'

Eveline struggled with her feelings for a moment. There was much truth in what her mother had said, for her father would have been most interested in the railway, she knew. Yet surely Papa would have wished her to stay true to herself, and to her principles?

'Did Mr Watson call himself to bring the invitation?' she asked, cautiously.

'No, it was Mr Armitage who brought it. He did not stay; merely thanked me for a pleasant evening last night, hoped that we would all be able to attend, and left. He does not have a great deal of small talk, I must say.'

Eveline, promising to cut flowers for the dinner table, escaped from the house that afternoon, taking an old satchel to hold her sketchbook and pencils and a volume of verse, and made her way through the rose garden to the door in the far wall. With practised ease she climbed once more into her beloved tree, and settled on the broad smooth branch, which formed a seat. This time she hung her satchel firmly on a convenient spur. The new leaves, a sharp fresh green, screened her now from any but the most observant passer-by; she was safe. She could, however, see out; to the north was her favourite view, and she renewed her attempt to sketch it; and this time, she felt, she was happier with the result:

the cedar of Lebanon, its dark branches sweeping outwards in horizontal planes, the houses of the little town, and the glimpse of the sea. And yet the light was elusive, and she felt all her inadequacy as an artist as she watched the cloud shadows make changing patterns across the waves, turning the blue to indigo. At last she decided to read a little, her back against the trunk of the great tree; and then, closing her eyes, she pictured the walks of her childhood. She thought of the river as it curled away from the estuary, its surface rippled by the wind, and the scudding clouds turning it grey. On the east side of the river, the fields stretched away, cattle in the nearer meadows clustering beneath the willows, while on the higher ground the young corn showed fresh and soft. The western bank, however, along which the little path had used to run, was, she knew, now ravaged by the railway workings. A broad gash had been carved from the gentle wooded slopes, leaving a scar of raw earth running as far as one could see, with rocks piled either side and the metal rails gleaming dully. The track had been raised in parts on vast banks of stone and soil; a shanty town of huts and shelters for the workers sprawled along the side. On the outskirts of the town, new roads had appeared, with rows of terraced houses all built of the same harsh new brick; and there were gangs of men working, wielding pickaxes and shovels, leading in horses and wagons with the next section of rails. The few little cottages by the water's edge, belonging to fishermen, were now cut off by the railway, stranded, their old pathways sliced away. The little wooden jetty would be tiny and forlorn in the distance.

A breeze was rising from the shore, and at length the chill drove her to prepare to climb down once more. All at once, she made a decision: she could not, would not, go to the opening ceremony for this railway. It would be a day of formal clothes, stilted conversation, and ridiculous pompous speeches, all to celebrate this monster that was to invade their peaceful world. Whatever her mother might say, she would not go.

Chapter Four

A Meeting

The photographs had arrived. Mrs Stanhope, Eveline, Aunt George and Miss Angell gathered round the dining-room table, where the prints had been carefully laid, to view them.

'Louisa looks very lovely,' said Miss Angell. 'Dear Beatrice, too. All of you. Charming.'

Aunt George looked at her affectionately.

'Really, you are absurd, Angell! Louisa as always manages to look perfect, but Beatrice looks terrified, as though she were facing a wild animal. Bevis looks as though the cares of the world were on his shoulders, and in this one Arthur very much as though he might be sick.'

'And Evie, your face is somehow blurred,' added Mrs Stanhope.

'It was very hard to keep still,' explained Eveline. 'We were all practically shaking with the effort.'

They all surveyed the prints again.

'Well, I think Louisa and Bevis will wish to have their portrait, at least. And when you look carefully, Beatrice and Arthur's is not so bad. But Eveline, you will have to go back.'

'Oh, no, Mama, surely not! It was agony. Really, will this one not do pretty well?'

'Eveline, you do nothing but contradict me these days. I would like to have portraits of all my girls, and this one could be of the Queen of Abyssinia for all one can tell. You will have to go back to the studio. It will be good practice for you; any lady needs to know how to look elegant and to stand still.'

Eveline was about to protest when it occurred to her that she might get a chance to learn more about the mysterious art of photography if she visited the Professor again.

'Very well, Mama,' she said meekly. 'I can walk there this afternoon, perhaps, and see if I can have it done straight away?'

'You cannot go alone, Eveline. And I am not free today; I have a thousand things to arrange. Tomorrow you and I can take the carriage down.'

'If Jennie walks with me, I can go today, though.'

'Very well. Yes, go today, and take Jennie. But do not wander about the town, just to the studio – and take the high street – do not be roaming about the back lanes.'

Jennie had been with the Stanhope household for only a few weeks, hired when Martha, the lady's maid who had been

44

with them for almost as long as Miss Angell, had given in to rheumatism and gone to live with her sister in the town. Martha had recommended Jennie – 'A good girl, ma'am,' she had assured Mrs Stanhope. 'My own niece, hardworking and cheerful. She can sew and mend lace, and she knows how to dress hair; I've had the teaching of her, you see, and you won't do better.' So Jennie had joined them, and was living up to Martha's promise splendidly. On their walk towards the town that afternoon, Eveline learnt a little more about her: her mother, Martha's sister, had been widowed young, and Jennie scarcely remembered her father; times had been very hard when Jennie was small. Her mother had taken in laundry, and minded children, and just managed to scrape a living for herself and her little girl; but later in life she had married a kind, respectable man, a local shopkeeper, and now she lived in a more comfortable way.

'Do you remember your father, Jennie?' asked Eveline.

'Scarcely, miss. I was four years old when he died. He was a fisherman and drowned at sea. I can recall waiting for him by the harbour wall, and him sitting by the fire, mending nets, and pulling me onto his knee to tell me stories of mermaids, but nothing more.'

'I am sorry. I lost my own father when I was scarcely more than a child, you know, but I do at least have many memories.'

'You are fortunate, then, miss.'

'I am, I know. In many ways.'

Just as Eveline and Jennie reached the door of the studio, a tall figure came towards them, and she recognised the forbidding young man from the evening party, who had been so abrupt, and made her so cross. She drew herself up a little, prepared to be very distant.

'Miss Stanhope.' He gave a very slight, stiff bow. 'Jennie.'

'Mr Armitage.' Eveline regarded him with some distrust. 'Are you about to have your likeness taken by the Professor?'

'What? Oh, good God, no, what an appalling idea.' He grinned, looking suddenly younger. 'You, I take it, are?'

'Yes, I fear so. It is not a pleasant experience, believe me. You are wise to avoid it.'

'I intend to avoid it, you may be sure.'

'Well, we must not detain you, then,' she said. 'Jennie, we should go in . . .'

'As I have seen you, Miss Stanhope,' he said, 'I have some news that might interest you. We are to build a bridge across the line – linking the high road with the river path, you know. The fishermen who live along the riverbank will have a route to get to and from their cottages and their boats. You were concerned, I recall, about such things. I hope you will feel reassured.'

She considered this news.

'Yet that will hardly help them if the smoke and the noise of the engines disrupt their fishing.'

'The men I have talked to are very glad at the prospect of getting their fish to market by rail in so short a time.'

'Oh. You have talked with them yourself?'

'Naturally I have.'

'I see,' said Eveline, 'well, the bridge may be useful, certainly.' She sounded, even to her own ears, ungracious. His face resumed its closed, unsmiling look.

'I thought you would wish to know, Miss Stanhope, that is all. I am sorry to have kept you from more important matters.' He touched his hat to them both, and strode away, looking distinctly stormy.

'Goodness, Jennie,' said Eveline, trying to laugh, 'how very odd Mr Armitage is. He looks so cross, so quickly!' For some reason she could not account for, she felt rather shaken by the encounter.

They found the Professor arranging a display for the window, which consisted of a large framed print supported on an easel and surrounded by potted palms (the print featured a fat baby in a lace dress). The Professor welcomed them; hoped Mrs Stanhope had found the photographs to her taste? Ah, alas, yes, there had been some blurring of Miss Stanhope's face – regrettable, but so easily done! Of course he would take another likeness; yes, he was free now, and happy to do so, no charge, naturally, if Miss Stanhope would just care to hang her cloak here?

While he set up the tripod and adjusted the camera to his liking, Eveline looked about her. A stack of business cards lay on a table: *Theodore Fry, Professor of Photography. Portraits of the Gentry*. There was an assortment of furniture and objects crowded to the side of the room – velvet drapes, painted landscapes, a Grecian urn – all seemingly chosen for their dashing theatrical flair and classical allusions, but on closer inspection all a little shabby. Lamps were set around the little stage area where the subjects posed. A heavy curtain screened a doorway through which the Professor bustled to and fro, but Eveline could not see into the dark recesses.

'And now, dear lady, if you would take your position?' He was sliding a rectangle of glass into the wooden camera box.

'Could I perhaps be seated, this time?' she asked. 'I might find it easier not to fidget.'

'Of course, of course – the very thing – or we do have this, which some people like to help them stay perfectly still,' and he produced a wooden contraption, which looked vaguely as though it might be a medieval instrument of torture. 'It is concealed behind the back, you see, and this part supports the head and neck.'

Eveline looked at it in horror.

'Oh, no, thank you,' she said. 'I will just sit down, and concentrate on not moving.'

'Indeed, as you wish, dear lady – now, if you would look towards me, so – and please, as still as you can . . .'

Eveline looked into the camera, and tried to concentrate on being perfectly motionless. She let her thoughts float away from the stuffy studio and the heat of the lamps, away to the river, and the bridge that was to be constructed over the railway line. The fishing families who lived along there, taking their boats down to the estuary and out to sea for mackerel and gurnard and herring, and rowing upstream for trout and grayling, had already had their peaceful lives disrupted by the construction of the line, the months of digging and explosions, the wagons rolling in with their vast loads of stone and metal, the gangs of men who shouted and cursed and toiled. Their peace would be gone for ever once the railway was open and the trains ran so close to their cottages. And yet, she reflected, they would be able to get their fish to the market in Newport so much faster, fish which could lose its value on a hot day if the carts were slow; and there were fishermen who lived along the seashore, too, so many of them, who sailed out to catch bass, and sole, and smooth-hounds, and whose livelihoods depended so entirely upon a good price for their catch. Eveline and her father had often walked along the shore beyond the town, and seen the boats hauled up onto the sand, while the men unloaded the heaps of fish with rainbows gleaming on their scales. She heaved a tiny, imperceptible sigh. Next time she saw Mr Armitage, she would acknowledge that, in this case, he might be right, and she would be perfectly gracious about it. Although, of course, the wider point remained that the wanton destruction of a beautiful landscape was still a terrible thing, a cataclysm that would remain long after she, and he, and the fisherfolk, were all forgotten.

'Miss Stanhope?'

The Professor was smiling and bowing before her; the minutes had passed more swiftly than she had thought possible.

'Oh, forgive me; my thoughts were miles away!' She smiled. 'It did seem a great deal easier, this time.'

'You were an admirably poised subject, dear lady. The print will be ready in a day or two, unless you would care to wait now, to see the plate? With just one, it should not take long to develop. It will not be ready to take away, of course, but you will see the fruits of our labours.'

'Oh – yes – I should like to wait. Jennie, let us see how

it has turned out. And Mr Fry – Professor – might I look through the camera?'

'Please do, but take care, Miss Stanhope.' He raised the black cloth that shrouded the machine. 'You look through this aperture – here – and you can move the lens, thus, to reach the sharpest focus.'

Eveline peered through the darkness, and suddenly she saw the scene before her: the chair and the silly painted backdrop, upside down, tiny, yet magically exact in every detail. She gave a cry of delight. As she emerged from the darkness of the camera cloth, the Professor was smiling at her.

'You find it interesting?'

'Wonderful!' she said. 'Extraordinary. Would you explain to me, Mr Fry, how it works?'

'It would be my pleasure, my absolute pleasure. But first I must take the plate into the dark room. The developing solution must be poured over it, you see, before the image has time to deteriorate.' He lifted the plate away from the camera with the utmost care, his long fingers holding the extreme edges, and bore it away reverently. While he was gone, Eveline and Jennie took turns to gaze through the camera lens, both enchanted by their new view of the world.

'Would you sit on the stage, Jennie?' asked Eveline. 'Then I can see what it would be like to take a portrait.'

Jennie obediently took her place on the seat. Her face, framed by the black straw bonnet that was her outdoor hat, somehow took on a new aspect, as the effort of keeping still took away the sweetness of her natural expression, and she looked sombre, and older.

'Would you take your bonnet off, Jennie? I should like to see what it might be like to make a photograph of you without a hat.'

Jennie untied the strings beneath her chin, took off the bonnet, and removed the pins which held up her hair. Eveline realised suddenly that she had never seen her maid without either a plain cotton cap or the black straw bonnet encasing her hair entirely, framing the pale face that bore a scattering of freckles like brick dust. Now Jennie shook her head and waves of corn-coloured hair shot through with reddish lights rippled down over her shoulders, falling almost to her waist. She was transformed.

'Oh, Jennie, how wonderful! What a beauty you are. You would be a marvellous subject for a photograph – or a painting – I should love to draw you.'

Jennie blushed and laughed. 'Draw me, miss? Why, of course, if you wish to.'

'I do, although I should never capture you as a photograph would; and indeed, if I were a photographer, I would make your portrait this minute.'

A slight cough heralded the return of the Professor. 'Ladies, if you would not object to stepping into the dark room, you can see the plate; it is still wet, but the image is fixed.' He caught sight of Jennie, then, her bright hair glowing against the faded drapes behind her. 'My goodness, dear ladies! What a vision! Remarkable!' He stared with frank admiration.

'She is a vision, indeed,' said Eveline eagerly, 'and, Mr Fry, I should like you to take Jennie's portrait too. Can you do that today? Have you time? I shall pay, of course, myself,' she added, guiltily aware that this was not a project that her mother was likely to approve, let alone to fund.

'Indeed, I do not have another client this afternoon; I would be delighted, truly delighted. Now, if you would step this way; take great care, do not trip on the step here, and best not to damage those pretty hands by touching anything, you know – the chemicals we use are very strong, very strong indeed!'

He swept aside the heavy, dusty velvet that hung across the doorway at the back of the studio, and led them along a narrow corridor. It was almost totally dark here, lit only by a weak gas lamp glimmering from the ceiling. Opening another door at the end of the passage, he ushered them into a tiny room bathed in a dark red glow from another lamp within a crimson shade. The fumes that had been detectable in the corridor now caught in the throat, sharp and astringent. Rows of bottles were ranged on shelves, labelled Silver Nitrate, and Fixative, and Varnish. A glass plate was propped above a wide sink, and the Professor lifted it so the light shone dully through it.

'This is a negative image, you see, so the dark areas will be light, and the light dark, when we make the print,' he told them. 'I think we have a good likeness, this time. The image looks sharp.' They stared at the curious picture, enthralled; it was an other-worldly, looking-glass image, ghostly and strange.

Back in the studio, Jennie was seated, and her hair arranged so that it fell around her face. Eveline watched intently as the lights were set up, and the camera plate put in, and the lens adjusted. Jennie managed to keep still for the required time, and the Professor was hopeful that they would have a fine portrait.

'Shall I send both prints up to your house, Miss Stanhope?' he asked as they were leaving.

'No, thank you; we will come back to collect them, if we may,' said Eveline.

'Of course, of course,' said the Professor, 'it will be my pleasure to welcome you. I can make sure they will be ready tomorrow, if you care to call in.'

'That will be perfect – and, Mr Fry, do you think,' she said, 'that if I could spend some time with you, you would be kind enough to show me how to take photographs?'

Chapter Five

The Art of Photography

Mrs Stanhope did not approve of young women walking about the town, or still worse in the countryside, by themselves. She herself had no taste for walking, and Georgiana and Miss Angell, who could have been ideal chaperones for Eveline, were forever in some remote part of the garden, devising new planting schemes, or conniving with the gardener to order new exotic species for the conservatory, or drawing up extravagant ideas for a palm house, or even, outrageously, actually digging or weeding or setting out seedlings. She was not entirely sure, when she reflected upon the subject, how it was that Miss Angell had become not just the governess, but a member of the household; but it seemed to have been a natural process, for the girls had all been very much attached to her, and by the time Eveline was too old to need a governess, it had come to seem as though Miss Angell were an unofficial extra relation. In the difficult dark days and months that followed John Stanhope's sudden demise, both Georgiana and Miss Angell had proved an unexpected source of strength and comfort, attending to the practical matters and all the melancholy duties that his wife was in too deep a state of shock to manage. She was glad, of course, that they were able to offer Miss Angell a home, for where else was the poor woman to go? Besides, she was a companion for Georgiana, and the two of them were practically obsessive about the garden, which was useful, as Mrs Stanhope was thereby relieved of that particular care.

Mrs Stanhope had married her two elder daughters very satisfactorily. She had launched them both into society, held a modest ball for each, dressed them exquisitely, and given them sensible advice on how to behave; their beauty and good manners did the rest. Louisa's Bevis was charming, and courteous, and rich; and Beatrice's Arthur was amiable, and gentle, and comfortably off. Both weddings were delicious confections of orange blossom and lace. All was as it should be, and within a few years the babies arrived, Louisa's Henry, and then Beatrice's Kitty, and then Louisa's Daisy – really, she was very blessed, she thought. Her successes should equip her perfectly for carrying off a similar triumph with her youngest daughter.

And yet she did not recall having any battles of will with the others in the way she seemed to, almost daily, with Eveline; Louisa and Beatrice had not wanted to be always running about, or disappearing for hours at a time, or disregarding their appearance so that they looked like scarecrows. The latest whim was that she was walking into town every five minutes to visit the Professor of Photography, which would have seemed most improper had not all Mrs Stanhope's acquaintance been swept up in the craze to have their photographic likenesses taken. Eveline had explained that Mr Fry was teaching her a little about photography – 'just so I have another accomplishment, Mama, for you know I never learnt to play or sing like Louisa or Beatrice, and my drawing is nothing outstanding' – and although her mother felt that, for some reason, photography was not nearly as elegant an occupation as music or watercolours, she did not want to make everything a cause for conflict, and she had found herself agreeing to Eveline's scheme, with the proviso that Eveline must always be accompanied by Jennie on her walks to the Professor's studio. Mrs Stanhope had a high regard for Jennie, who seemed a very sensible young woman, and, moreover, Martha had recommended her, and Martha had been a most intelligent and respectable servant for so many years.

So it was that Eveline found herself able to arrange with Mr Fry that two or three times a week she would come to his studio to learn about photography. He seemed delighted to teach her – and Jennie, who was to Eveline's pleasure eager to learn too – what he knew, for he had a genuine enthusiasm for his art, and since his customers were generally coming at a fashionably late hour of the day, he could devote time in the morning to her.

Nine o'clock, would that be too early for Miss Stanhope? No? Then indeed, he would be most happy – and Mr Fry was sensible enough to know that in this small town, the patronage of the Stanhope family was valuable. The first lesson was to have the workings of the camera explained, the advantages of the Rapid Rectilinear lens, and what the focal length should be, and how to adjust it; and then it was the preparation of the plate, and she and Jennie watched Mr Fry polishing the glass to a perfect clean surface, and then pouring the collodion over the plate with the utmost care, delicately tilting it to achieve an even coating. An hour flew past, and Mr Fry's first client of the day was due, and so they must leave; and so thrilled were they with the knowledge they had gained, and the prospect of how much more they had to learn, that they very nearly forgot to take with them their portraits from the previous visit. Eveline barely glanced at her own (except to check that her face was in focus, lest she should have to undergo a third session before the camera), but she studied Jennie's with great interest.

'You look very romantic, Jennie,' she said, admiringly. 'A Guinevere, or the Lily Maid of Astolat, perhaps!'

On leaving the studio, Eveline calculated that they might steal another half-hour of freedom before they need return home. Along the seafront, they stopped to admire the new bathing huts, and then walked on a little to watch the fishing boats leaving the harbour.

'You will know many of the fishermen, Jennie, since your father was one of their number,' said Eveline. 'It must be a fine life, to be out on the ocean, in all weathers.'

'Not so fine in the winter, Miss Eveline; there is no certainty that they will make a catch, and it is cold, and dangerous.'

'Oh – of course – forgive me, Jennie. How stupid I am.'

'Not at all, miss. But it is a hard way to earn a living. I have a . . . a friend, who was a fisherman, but now is working for the railway, and it is a far better way of life – hard, still, but with good pay, and prospects of being promoted in time, and even a house one day.'

'Yet working on the railway is a dangerous occupation, too, is it not? Do you not worry for your friend?'

'I do,' said Jennie, 'but life is a risk, miss; and I would rather Ned were not out at sea, as my father was, though he has a boat still, and goes out night fishing now and then. But he likes the work on the railway. The man who directs them is a fair master, he says.'

Jennie's conscious look and blush seemed to indicate that Ned was more than just a friend.

'Then I am glad for him. I hope Ned keeps safe.'

'I hope so too; and he is learning about the way the railway is planned, and built, so that one day he may rise in the company.'

'Mr Watson, then, is teaching him these things?'

'Oh, no, not Mr Watson, miss; he is a good man, but he leaves all the real work to his friend, the man who is the chief engineer, Ned says. The gentleman we met in the street, outside the Professor's shop,' she added. 'Mr Armitage.'

'Mr Armitage?' Eveline considered this news. 'Well, I trust he will prove a good friend to Ned, Jennie, for your sake.'

Chapter Six

A Thunderstorm

Mrs Stanhope was pleased with Eveline's new photograph.

'Now, that is very much better!' she said, examining the print. 'You must have managed to keep perfectly still for this one, Evie dear.'

The portrait showed Eveline with her face turned slightly away, and a pensive expression.

'I look faintly tragic, I think.'

'Thoughtful, perhaps. What were you thinking of, I wonder?'

'I was thinking of how long it would be before I was able to move,' said Eveline untruthfully.

'In any case, it is a great deal better than the last one, and I shall have it framed and put it in the drawing room,' she said briskly. 'And Evie, something delightful! The Sandhams have asked us to dine – you, me, and Beatrice and Arthur too, I gather – on Thursday week.'

'Is that delightful? We have been dining with the Sandhams for ever, and it is not usually a particularly wonderful experience.'

'Delightful because Charles Sandham will be there, of course! I do not know when I have met a more charming man.'

'They haven't asked Aunt George?'

'They always ask Aunt George, as a matter of course, and she always declines. You know Aunt George gets a nervous headache if she dines away from home.'

'I think she is very sensible.'

'Whatever do you mean? You do talk nonsense, Evie, sometimes.'

It was a fine, warm day. Eveline wandered into the garden, finding her aunt and Miss Angell, as usual, busy among the plants. They were kneeling before a fine herbaceous border, trowels in hand, vigorously attacking a plague of ground elder which had invaded the columbines.

Aunt George stood up as her niece approached, groaning a little as she straightened her back.

'Eveline, darling girl. How nice. Come to help us?'

'I'd love to.' She took the trowel and began to dig at the stubborn roots. 'Sit down for a while, Aunt George. You too, Miss Angell, do take a little rest.'

Both ladies subsided onto the garden seat that stood nearby, while Eveline dug for a while in silence.

'We have a plan for a change to the rose garden in the autumn, Eveline,' said her aunt. 'Something less formal, and perhaps underplanted with catmint and lavender. We have heard of some new Bourbon roses which sound delicious. Which was the one we particularly thought of, dear?'

'*Souvenir de la Malmaison*, was it?' said Miss Angell, absently. 'We have a list, Eveline, with descriptions that really make one's mouth water! They can be ordered by post, you see, from a grower in the Midlands, and they will come by train, and then the packet steamer: isn't that a wonder?'

Eveline sat back on her heels. 'It is, indeed. I am sure your new roses will be delightful. You are both true artists in the garden.'

'Well, thank you, my love,' said her aunt. 'That is a serious compliment. You could not say anything that pleased us more.'

Eveline resumed her digging at the ground elder. 'We are to dine with the Sandhams,' she said gloomily. 'There will be more fuss about what I have to wear, and how my hair is dressed. Really, Aunt, you are very lucky not be obliged to go to these dinners and parties and tea-drinkings.'

'One of the many advantages of being an elderly spinster is that one may please oneself a great deal,' said her aunt. 'I have managed to acquire the reputation of being an eccentric, and it is extremely useful. People just shrug and regard me as an oddity, I fancy.'

'And yet you enjoy company, sometimes, Aunt. You like talking to Mr Watson, and to the rector, I know.'

'Your aunt likes only the company of sensible people who can converse on interesting topics,' said Miss Angell, smiling at them both. 'That does limit things somewhat. I shall go and find our hats, I think, George; the sun is quite strong now. Eveline, dear, I shall bring yours too . . . now where, I wonder, did we leave the hats?' She wandered away in the direction of the house.

'Angell by name, and angel by nature!' said Aunt George. 'Now, leave that blessed ground elder, my love, and come and sit down. Your mother would be horrified if she knew I was allowing you to do that; you know she is forever telling me that we have a gardener to do the work, and it is not ladylike to be grubbing about in the earth.'

'I know, Aunt George, she has told me that too, a thousand times. But you and Miss Angell love to garden, do you not? And you have created such delights!' She looked at the great bank of flowers before them: tall elegant white tulips with fluted petals, velvety purple irises, and pale-blue Veronica. Later, she knew, there would be the deep blues of hardy geraniums, the soft creamy lilac of phlox, the pinks with their heady clove scent. 'You choose the colours, and the shapes, and the fragrances, and make a work of art.'

'It is our passion, indeed.' She looked with satisfaction at the border. 'And, Eveline, you know, to return to why I do not accept invitations: I am perfectly content, you know, to meet just a small circle of friends. I do not care for too much society. But also, you know, I would not care to leave Maria alone for evening after evening; and she, absurdly, is hardly ever invited. People are such snobs, and the Sandhams are quite the worst. I am very well contented with the way things are.'

Maria! Eveline had forgotten, almost, that Miss Angell had another name; but there was an austere edge to her aunt's voice that discouraged further discussion.

Eveline had planned to spend that afternoon sketching and reading, if she could; but she was thwarted by her mother's announcement over lunch that she had ordered the carriage to take them to the dressmaker's.

'For you must, positively must, have another evening gown, Evie,' she said firmly. 'The Sandhams will think I am a shockingly uncaring mother, for I am sure you have worn the same one for the last three times we have seen them.'

'You are very kind, Mama, but I am sure the Sandhams pay no attention whatsoever to what I am wearing.'

'But I do, Eveline. And,' she added cunningly, 'you wanted a bathing dress, I thought? So we could have you fitted for that at the same time.'

They were to take up Beatrice as they passed her house, for Beatrice too was in need of a new dress, it seemed. The journey was slow, as the horses laboured up the long hill in the heat, and a wagon in front of them lost a wheel, which delayed them further, and by the time they arrived at the establishment of Madame Delphine (whom Eveline suspected of being no more French than Mr Fry of being a professor) they were glad to be welcomed in and offered tea and almond biscuits while they looked through books of the latest styles. Beatrice, who was acknowledged even by Louisa to have an unerring eye for choosing clothes that became her, found a dull rose satin, which perfectly complemented her fairness, and explained in exact detail to Madame Delphine how she would like the gown trimmed – 'a band of lace here, Madame, cream, *not* white, and bunches of silk rosebuds just at the shoulder.'

Attention now was turned to Eveline; Mrs Stanhope suggested a pale-yellow figured silk that had caught her eye, and Eveline was by now resigned to acceding to her mother's wishes, although she protested vehemently against the idea of a crinoline skirt.

'How can one even get through doorways in such a contraption?' she demanded. 'We are not going to a grand ball, that I know of. Louisa and Beatrice look pretty in great hooped skirts because they are little and delicate, but I am too tall. And I do not think I could even walk properly in such a thing!'

Beatrice, rather to her surprise, came to her rescue.

'You know, Mama, I do not think the yellow would suit Evie. She is too sallow, you see, and I think she is right about the crinoline. I have seen a new style – where was that book from London, Madame? Ah, thank you, yes. You see, Mama, a skirt looped up at the back to form a little bustle, quite elegant, and see this dark red, which would suit her far better.'

'I am here, you know, Beatrice,' said Eveline, but she submitted to having the red silk draped around her, and tugged, and pinned, on the grounds that at least a pale-yellow crinoline had been avoided. A bathing dress was added to the order – 'No, two bathing dresses, I think,' said Mrs Stanhope, 'if you are to persist in this swimming idea, we had best have a spare to be in the wash' – and Madame promised that everything would be delivered as soon as the designs could be made up.

Outside, the heat of the morning had turned sultry, and there was a distant growl of thunder. Before the carriage had gone very far, rain started to drum on the roof, and the wheels were soon slowing in the mud of the roads.

'At least we will be able to get about without all this nonsense when the railway comes,' said Beatrice. 'I shall be able to visit the dressmaker as often as I like, without Arthur grumbling that he needs the horses, or that I am gone out of the house for ever.'

'If the only advantage of the railway is to enable us to visit the dressmaker more frequently, then I do not think it a great leap forward,' said Eveline.

The horses laboured on, and the wheels creaked and groaned, and it was well over an hour before they entered their familiar streets, and Beatrice was impatient to be home – 'for Kitty is with the new nursemaid and there is no telling what she may be up to,' she said.

'What Kitty is up to, or the nursemaid?' asked Eveline.

'Either, or both. They are as bad as each other, I suspect,' said Beatrice. 'What can be taking us so long?' The rain was so heavy now that it was obscuring the windows, and its noise drowning all other sounds, and the carriage seemed now to have stopped completely. Eveline lowered the window and leant out to see what might be preventing their progress.

It was a scene of chaos. A great wagon lay on its side at an angle across the road, with its load of metal rails spilt around it, and its team of horses struggling against the harness as their driver cut at their reins with a knife to try to free them and quiet them a little. A dozen or so men were clustered round the wagon, and shouts filled the air. A few of their number had their shoulders against the side of the wagon and were straining to lift it.

'It is an accident, a wagon overturned,' she said. 'I will see if there is anything we can do.' She opened the door and scrambled down from the coach before her mother could remonstrate with her. The rain soaked her in moments as she made her way towards the men. As she drew nearer she could see that beneath the overturned wagon a figure lay, immobile, as the men above him tried to move the great wooden side of the cart. She could see only his head and shoulders, his face white, as beneath him blood streamed into the road, mixing with the rainwater in rivulets that sank into the mud and mire. With painful slowness the men inched the wagon up, lifting it enough for others to pull him from beneath the cart. The men who had raised it let it fall again, gasping for breath, their clothes and hair plastered against them in the deluge. Others were leaning over the fallen man, who was now hidden from Eveline's sight.

One of those who had been lifting the wagon sank to his knees beside the man on the ground, turning to speak to those around him, and then shaking his head. At last he rose, and as he did so caught sight of Eveline. He strode towards her; and Eveline realised with a slight shock that it was Mr Armitage, hatless, soaked, in his shirtsleeves, and streaked with mud.

'Get in the carriage,' he said to Eveline, abruptly. 'You will not want to see this.' He turned and spoke to the coachman, who perched above them, hunched beneath his wide-brimmed hat. 'The road will be blocked for some while, I fear. You had best turn and take the lower road. I'm sorry.'

'Can we not help?' asked Eveline. The rain struck, cold and relentless, through her clothes.

'Thank you, but no. Getting your carriage out of the way is the best help.'

'But a doctor, have you called for a doctor?' she asked.

'He is beyond a doctor's help.'

'It – it is not Ned? Jennie's young man?'

'What? No, it is not Ned Fox. But he is someone's sweetheart, I suppose, and someone's son.' He looked stricken, the rain running in rivers down his face. 'Eveline, please, you should not see such a thing. Get into your carriage, for God's sake. Go.'

He turned and walked back to the group of men. Eveline stood in silence for a moment, looking at his retreating figure, and then climbed back into the carriage.

'Really!' said her mother. 'Look at you, perfectly drowned, Eveline. As if it is not tiresome enough to have to wait about like this, now you are a complete scarecrow and probably about to catch your death of cold. Whatever is happening?'

'Someone is dead.' Eveline found it hard to get her breath. 'A man – crushed beneath the wagon.'

Mrs Stanhope and Beatrice exclaimed in horror that Eveline had witnessed such a thing.

'Poor girl,' said her mother with unaccustomed gentleness. 'A hot bath for you at home, and a cordial for the shock. And your bedroom fire lit, in case you should have a chill.' Eveline said nothing; she found she was shivering, and cold to her very core.

The coachman was turning the horses by this time, and their carriage began to move. The rain was easing a little, so that they could see from the carriage windows that they were driving down the streets they would never normally take – narrow, with little huddled houses, the tiny passages between them leading back to dank yards where more ramshackle buildings could just be glimpsed. Two women, black shawls held above their heads against the rain, stopped to watch their passing; a child's face, as pale as a ghost, was framed in a grimy window; a thin ginger cat stared at them from a doorway. Rubbish and filth lay in the gutters, and a vile stink rose from the torrents of water washing beneath their wheels. The carriage lurched painfully along the cobbles and broken stones that formed the street, emerging at last onto open ground. A whole cluster of the dark streets had been razed to the ground, it seemed, for signs that advertised a slaughterhouse now lay discarded, and a wide gravel road had been made. On one side there was a sea of mud, where heavy wheels and hooves had churned and ramped the soil, and on the other rose the newly constructed railway station building, its red brick harsh against the grey skies. The rails, either side of a central platform, lay almost complete.

To Eveline, now, it seemed a vision of hell: ugliness, devastation and death. All that evening, the white face of the man beneath the wagon, with his blood seeping into the mud beneath, was before her, and neither cordials not hot baths could drive it away. When at last she slept, her sleep was troubled and anxious, and her dreams were haunted. Again and again she saw the dead man, lying so still upon the ground, and a tall figure walking away from her in the cold hard rain.

Chapter Seven

Dining with the Sandhams

The parcels from Madame Delphine arrived on the morning of the Sandhams' dinner party. Eveline was eager to see the bathing costumes, and bore them away to her bedroom to examine them. Each consisted of a dress with short sleeves and a wide collar, the full skirt reaching to her knees, with a pair of wide trousers to wear beneath. The fabric was a heavy serge; one dress dark blue, the other crimson, trimmed with rows of white braid. She surveyed them doubtfully.

'How will I keep afloat in this, Jennie? The sheer weight will drag me under, won't it?'

Jennie tended to agree.

'It does seem a lot of stuff, miss, to wear in the water. But you will be a strong swimmer, I dare say, once you have learnt.'

'I hope so.' She held the bathing dress up against herself and turned to the looking glass. 'Heavens! I suppose I should be glad I am not expected to swim in a crinoline, however.'

'Will you be learning soon, miss?'

'I long to start. But apparently I need a respectable bathing-woman to teach me, and Mama has to ask among her friends for a recommendation, and most of her friends think swimming is rather decadent, so it will probably be winter by the time I can begin.'

Jennie nodded sagely. 'That would be a pity, miss. Swimming in the summer is a fine thing.'

'Can you swim, Jennie?' asked Eveline idly, still holding up the ridiculous bathing dress against her.

'Oh, indeed, miss. I swam always as a child – we lived right on the shore, then, you know – and still do, when I have the chance.'

Eveline spun round.

'Oh, Jennie, then you could teach me! What a wonderful plan! I could swim every day if you were with me. How long does it take, do you think, to learn?'

'You would learn fast, I am sure, Miss Eveline.' Jennie looked doubtful. 'But would Mrs Stanhope agree?'

'Why should she not?'

Mrs Stanhope, however, did not approve of Eveline's plan at all.

'A respectable older woman teaching you is one thing. But Jennie is no older than you are, Eveline, and what people would see would be two young women swimming together unaccompanied.'

'How can that matter? I can walk with my maid – why cannot I swim with her?'

'It is quite different. Swimming involves – well, changing in those ridiculous huts into bathing dresses – any passers-by able to see you in the water – ankles, shoulders, all exposed! At least an older person with you would lend a modicum of decency.'

'That is absurd,' said Eveline. 'I have no freedom! May I do nothing at all that is not confined to a drawing room, and hedged about with rules, and small talk, and nonsense?'

'I have allowed you to be out learning this photography nonsense; I give you an inch, and you immediately take a mile! You will have to learn to live by the rules of society, Eveline, or you will be an outcast and then you will have a great deal less "freedom", as you call it.' Mrs Stanhope swept from the room; the conversation was over.

The carriage ride to the Sandhams' that evening was, as a result of this discussion, made in a frosty silence between mother and daughter. It was, fortunately, a very short journey. Beatrice and Arthur had already arrived, Beatrice resplendent in her new rose satin dress.

'You do look very lovely, Beatrice,' said Eveline warmly. 'You are so clever with clothes!'

'Thank you, Evie,' said Beatrice, genuinely pleased, and conscious that her younger sister was no threat to her own status as the belle of the gathering. 'And I am so glad that I chose that red for you. It becomes you very well indeed.'

There were other guests to greet – the Debournes, and the Goodwins, and the Seymours – before they went in to the dining room, where the table blazed with candles, the glass and china sparkled, and a heavy scent of lilies hung over all. Eveline found herself seated at several removes from her mother, for which she could only be grateful, with her brother-in-law on one side of her, and Sir William on the other. Charles Sandham, whom she had rather hoped to talk to, was across the table from her, but seemed to be devoting all his attention to her sister. Eveline, however, was content to be next to Arthur, of whom she was very fond, and they chatted amiably over the soup. She led him gently to the topic of his time at Cambridge, and how he had bathed in the very pool Lord Byron had been said to favour, and how he had been challenged to swim all along the Cam to Grantchester and had very nearly drowned when the river plants had become tangled around his feet.

'You are fortunate, Arthur,' she said wistfully. 'How delicious it sounds! I can picture the green water, just as you describe it, so cool and deep.'

'Well, dashed cold, I should call it,' said Arthur, 'rather than cool.' He leant across the table to his pretty wife. 'Bea, did I ever tell you about that time I swam up the Cam and nearly went under?'

Beatrice, however, was listening to an anecdote of Charles Sandham's about his sailing exploits in Italy; and something about the flush in her cheeks, and the way she was leaning towards Charles to catch his words in the general hubbub, made Arthur look away, and turn back to Eveline with another story of a walking tour of the north when he and some friends had dived into the lake at Windermere, and how that really was cold, by Jove! – but splendid just the same – and how magnificent the scenery was there, quite as grand as anything Italy could offer, he would swear. Sir William then claimed her attention, full of the outrage that was the new railway and all its works, and how their own view, which his ancestors had looked on for hundreds of years, was changed utterly, and how the abominable noise from men and machines was likely to spoil his sport for ever, come the shooting season, for the birds would be scared away and very likely fly off to the estates of his neighbours from sheer spite. In this way the dinner was eaten, and the ladies withdrew, and the gentlemen joined them half an hour later, mostly a little flushed and all very jovial. Charles came over straightaway to where Beatrice and Eveline were sitting.

'I have some fine pictures from my grand tour, which you ladies may like,' he said. 'Engravings, and sketches, and watercolours, and even some photographs; the French are rather in advance of us there, you know, and I have some fine views of Paris.'

The ladies expressed themselves very eager to see them.

'Come along, then, to the library,' said Charles, 'there are too many to bring out here.'

'Arthur will wish to see them, too,' said Eveline hastily, seeing her brother-in-law's face as Charles offered his arm to Beatrice to lead her from the room, 'will you not, Arthur?

I know you are interested in such things,' and she took Arthur's arm herself so that Charles was obliged to extend the invitation with all the appearance of civility.

The Sandhams' library was magnificent, with a gallery around it and the books arranged, floor to ceiling, in perfect order. A round table stood in the centre, with some prints of engravings laid out upon it, and there was a great desk in the darker recesses at the far end of the room with more books upon it, and columns from which marble busts of great philosophers glowered down upon them. Beatrice was in raptures: what a delightful room, how well proportioned, and how wonderful to have so many books, all so new, and smart, and so handsomely bound! Eveline could not help thinking that she preferred her father's study at home, with its shabby chairs, and books in heaps here and there, and favourite volumes piled up at one's elbow; and also that Beatrice had never been particularly fond of reading, that she could recall.

They gathered round the table to admire the pictures, exclaiming over the palaces, and temples, and ruins.

'And photographs, Mr Sandham? Did you say there were photographs?' asked Eveline.

'Ah, yes, indeed' – he led the way over to the desk – 'the very latest examples of this new art! You will find it miraculous, I am sure, that you can see the sights of Paris just as they appear to the traveller.' With a flourish he untied a folder and spread before them a dozen photographs. There were stately buildings, graceful bridges, wide boulevards, and elegant parks, eliciting gasps of wonder from Eveline and Beatrice, and even a reluctant word or two of approbation from Arthur. There was a picture taken in a formal garden, with clipped hedges and gravel paths, where couples strolled between the flower beds, and a young woman held the hand of a small child; there was a street scene, where men and women sat at little tables outside a cafe, and a young man raised a glass to the unseen photographer. Eveline was entranced to see the people of Paris before her, going about their lives, so exotic, so glamorous, and yet real, and everyday, and human. She picked up each scene in turn, seeing how the scenes had been chosen, how the light fell upon the faces, how the shadows threw the buildings into sharp relief. The Professor came into her thoughts: how he would like to see these!

Beatrice, losing interest, began to move away. 'There are some watercolours of Rome and Florence around the gallery, if you would care to see those,' said Charles in a low voice to Beatrice. She readily assented, and they moved away to climb the spiral staircase, Beatrice's bell-like skirt rustling as she went. Arthur watched them irresolutely for a moment, his hands thrust deep into his pockets and something very like a scowl replacing his normally placid expression.

'I shall go back to the others,' he said to Eveline, 'I don't care for this art stuff much, and I might get a hand or two of cards.'

'Of course, Arthur,' said Eveline, 'I shall go up and see the watercolours myself now, and we will all be through here in a few minutes.'

She began to collect the photographs together, and as she arranged them she saw the edge of a second folder almost hidden beneath a large atlas, and eagerly took it out, hoping that there would be more views, of Vienna, perhaps, or Nice. Charles and Beatrice were still up on the gallery, at the other end of the room, apparently engrossed in the watercolours, and she opened the folder, sure that Charles would be happy for her to see more of the remarkable souvenirs of his travels.

There were more photographs, to be sure, but not of cities or gardens. These were of young women, reclining upon chaises longues, or seated upon satin chairs, or standing with their arms raised in balletic poses. Some wore jewels around their necks, or feather boas, or gauzy scarves, but apart from such decorations all were quite free of clothes. They looked at the camera with apparent unconcern, as composed as if they had been wearing stays and petticoats and gowns. She looked more closely; the photographs were finely done, with the light falling so that the women's skin looked soft and velvety, and their voluptuous curves were softly illuminated beneath the gossamer drapes suspended above them. Fascinated, she drew out more, and found another set of pictures, and in each of these two women, with pretty, rouged, dimpled faces, were embracing each other, none of them wearing anything but a pair of long gloves, perhaps, or a little lace skirt, or a velvet ribbon around her neck. The images were simultaneously beautiful and shocking to Eveline. She thought again of the books high on the shelves of her father's study, with the exquisitely coloured paintings of men and women so languorously and gracefully entwined. Those paintings, and these photographs, and the pictures of foreign lands that Charles had showed them, all seemed to be of a wider world of which she had no experience at all. 'You are a citizen of the world,' Aunt George had said, but Eveline felt all at once very ignorant, and provincial, and young. She sighed, and carefully replaced the photographs in their folder, and tied the ribbon neatly. Then she tucked the folder back under the atlas and ran up the gallery stairs to find Beatrice and Charles.

'Shall we join the others?' she suggested. 'The carriages will be waiting by now, I dare say.' She looked at Charles with new interest as they walked back to the drawing room, wondering if he had been present when those photographs were taken, even taken them himself, or merely bought them from some Parisian version of the Professor. She could hardly ask him, she supposed.

'You seem very thoughtful, Miss Stanhope,' said Charles, smiling at her. Beatrice was still by his side, her hand resting on his arm, her eyes downcast, but occasionally glancing towards him through her eyelashes.

'I was most struck with those views of Paris, Mr Sandham,' said Eveline. 'How marvellous they are! Beatrice, I think Arthur wishes to speak with you.'

She gave her sister a speaking look, and Beatrice detached herself from Charles's arm with some reluctance and moved to where her husband was standing, a chill expression on his face.

'There must be a great many painters and photographers in Paris,' she began. 'Did you visit studios and galleries? Did you meet many artists?'

Charles, pleased to have such an interested audience, and always happy to talk of his travels, launched into a long description of the elegant salons he had visited, and the quaint streets and eccentric painters; and although he did not mention any photographers, and there was no hint that his artistic interests lay anywhere other than fine views of monuments and gardens, she had at least succeeded in diverting him from Beatrice until it was time to leave; and Charles was so animated, and their conversation so lively, that Mrs Stanhope had high hopes that her youngest daughter had at last learnt to flirt, and that a match was perfectly possible. She was so well pleased with Eveline, in fact, that on the journey home she had softened to such a degree that she was in a fair way to being persuaded that Eveline's learning to swim with Jennie as her teacher was not so very much out of the question as it had seemed at the beginning of the evening.

Chapter Eight

Learning to Swim

Thus it was that the very next day Eveline (anxious to begin before her mother should change her mind) and Jennie walked down to the seafront to hire a bathing hut for the afternoon. In the gloom of the tiny cabin they struggled out of their bonnets, dresses, petticoats, stockings, boots, stays, and bodices, and struggled into the bathing dresses. Eveline, silently blessing her mother now for having ordered two, had persuaded Jennie to accept the dark blue as her own, while she wore the red – 'For I am sure it will fit you, Jennie, and I will feel less ridiculous if you are wearing a suit as well as me.'

They opened the door, which faced the sea, and Jennie stepped down into the water. It came up to her waist, making her skirts billow around her as she raised her hands to guide Eveline down the wooden steps.

The cold took Eveline's breath away. The water was glass-green, and waves broke white on the surface and tumbled towards the beach behind them. She felt the sand beneath her feet, gritty and firm, and then a sudden surge lifted her so that she lost her balance and the sea closed over her head. Then she surfaced, and Jennie was grasping her hands, and steadying her, and she began to cough, and then to laugh with a mixture of shock and delight.

'How will I start? How will I learn to support myself?' she asked, gasping as she tried to breathe.

'Here, I will hold you up, quite safe,' said Jennie, 'and you will feel the water support you . . . yes?' and Eveline relaxed against Jennie's arms, which were strong and steady; and she felt how the waves pushed against her body, buoying her up. That first day she managed to stay afloat for only a few moments before beginning to sink again, pushing and spluttering, with her feet flailing to find the seabed; but for a brief minute, at least, she was in a new element, with her arms moving so cleanly through the water, and the sun dancing in gold flakes all around her. They stayed in the sea until Eveline could bear the cold no longer, and they had to clamber up the steps into the bathing hut again, with their clothes waterlogged and dragging and clinging in chill heavy folds.

Dressing again was even harder than undressing had been, with their clothes sticking to their damp skin, and Eveline dropped her stays into her leather bag along with all the soaking garments because it was impossible for Jennie to lace them with her fingers numb with cold; and as they walked back through the streets, with their hair damp and pushed beneath their bonnets, and the taste of salt in their mouths, she felt supple, and light, and free.

So began a few delicious weeks for Eveline. In the afternoons, when she could be spared, and when Jennie was not wanted by Mrs Stanhope to mend or press clothes or fold linen, they walked to the sea to swim; and in the mornings, if they could, they spent an hour or two in the studio of the Professor of Photography.

The Professor was a kind and patient teacher. Eveline and Jennie soon learnt how to handle the glass plates with the utmost care, for the slightest speck of dust would be magnified and spoil the image. Their skin burnt as they warmed the negatives before a fire as hot as they could bear, and froze as they poured endless cans of icy water over each photograph. There were many frustrations and disappointments, as the varnish cracked the fragile collodion film, or the picture was too dark to make out; but gradually they became adept. The anticipation as an image appeared held them breathless; the dismay as they saw its failure, or the triumph as it gradually materialised before their eyes just as they had hoped. All Eveline's pin money was now spent (the Professor advising, and placing orders, and accepting the parcels as they arrived) on supplies, and the three of them talked constantly of their work. Should they try the ready-prepared paper for printing? Was preparing the paper themselves preferable? Would a lens with a longer focus lessen the distortion? Was the sepia tone finer than the yellowish print from the albumenised paper? And how could silver nitrate be so very expensive? Theodore Fry gradually began to treat the young women as though they were equals, and to their relief forgot to bow, or to fuss over their pretty hands and clothes being damaged by the chemicals.

They began to experiment with taking portraits of each other and of Mr Fry (for they had no other subjects) with exposures of varying times, and learnt how to adjust the lens to create a sharper or a softer focus. Eveline was particularly fascinated by the effects that could be achieved by changing the lighting. By removing some of the lamps that the Professor used, and drawing the blinds a little to make the light weaker, she found she could throw a face into partial shadow, so that the light and dark were in greater contrast; and although there were a hundred failures, pictures of indistinguishable dark smudges, or bleached ghosts, she did at last produce a few photographs that gave her a quiet feeling of triumph. Jennie was a natural model, and Eveline photographed her in a dozen different costumes and poses, but the one of which she was most proud showed Jennie turning away a little from the camera, her face half in shadow, and her hair falling around her. Eveline had dressed her in a white robe they had found in the Professor's dressing-up box, which he kept for the more dashing of his clients, and she had clasped her own string of pearls around Jennie's neck; Jennie looked regal, and haughty, and very beautiful. She had taken a portrait, too, of the Professor himself, wearing an old velvet smoking cap and a cloak, and a noble expression – 'You look as I imagine Leonardo da Vinci would have looked, Mr Fry,' she said, and although she had in fact no very clear idea at all what the great Leonardo had looked like, the Professor was delighted, and fixed the finished print above his desk in the shop. And Jennie had photographed Eveline, at her request, in her plainest dress, her dark hair loose and a little wild, with no jewels, turning towards the camera as though about to speak, the edges of the image blurring into dark shadows.

'I was taught, when I learnt my art,' said the Professor, as he studied these, 'that there is no place for smudges in photography, that all must be sharp, and clear; but I like these very much, very much indeed. They have something more than one usually sees; something speaks – it is the chiaroscuro, just as the great masters used, and if in painting, why not in photography?'

The complete absorption she experienced when working in the studio, and the physical exertion of learning to swim, were both new and delightful. Jennie's company was also a new pleasure, for she was the only female friend of her own age that Eveline had ever had, and an intelligent and enquiring one too. As the spring days passed, and summer approached, Eveline felt that life was at last unfolding and opening out, just a little, before her.

There was, however, a shadow from which she could not escape: the fate of the man whom she had seen lying beneath the wagon while his blood mixed with the rain and mud. That white face haunted her dreams, and came into her thoughts unbidden as she woke. There had been nothing she could have done, she told herself, it was all too late, and nothing to do with her; and yet she could not forget that scene. Even in her favourite retreat, on the branch of the great beech tree where the leaves now made a cool green private world, she could not escape: her pencil seemed to draw the dead man's face without her knowing what she did; she opened her book, and lines leapt from the page: *roots are wrapt about the bones*, the poet mourned, *O Priestess in the vaults of Death*.

How was it that she was so immersed in thoughts of a man she had never known, whose name, even, she did not know, while, as she recalled, she had not wept long for a beloved father? Had she been too young to grieve properly for Papa? She closed the book and leant her head against the familiar comfort of the tree; the leaves murmured around her, and the sun dazzled in golden patterns across her eyes. Beyond the high wall an occasional shout, or the rumble of a cart, rose to her ears; and then suddenly, there below, she saw the familiar figure of Mr Watson walking along the road, and without thinking she scrambled down from her tree, and through the little door in the outer wall of the garden that the servants used. She was just in time to call his name as he reached the corner of the road, and he turned, and came back towards her.

'My dear Miss Stanhope – Eveline! Are you quite well? What can I do for you?' and Eveline realised all the oddness of suddenly emerging, hatless and breathless and alone, onto the street.

'Quite well, Mr Watson, thank you. I saw you pass and I wished to ask you something, if I may?'

'Of course; will you walk with me? I am a little late for an appointment, but we can talk as we go.'

Eveline assented, and fell into step beside him. Even her mother, she thought, could not object to her walking with Mr Watson, so old a friend, and such a respectable gentleman.

'It is the man who died – who fell beneath the wagon,' she said without preamble. 'Did he have a family – a wife? Do they need help? It was such a very shocking thing, and I was there, you know, and saw him.'

'It was indeed, most shocking,' said Mr Watson gravely, 'but you will have to ask Thomas, for he is the one who hires the men, and knows about their circumstances. Since you ask me, I cannot think he would let hardship befall a family on account of an accident at work; he is scrupulous about such things.'

'Thomas?'

'Yes, Tom Armitage, you know. Your dear mama was kind enough to invite him to dine, at my request, you will recall; for he is a protégé of mine, and knows very few people here, so far from his home.'

'Mr Armitage – of course.'

'I am walking to the site office now, my dear, if you wish to accompany me. Tom will be there; you can ask him yourself about the poor young man who died. Your kind heart does you credit.'

He offered her his arm, and they walked together along the high wall that bounded the Stanhope gardens, down towards the seafront, along the little high street, and then turned towards the narrower lanes. The houses seemed to close in around them. In the part of the town where they, and the Sandhams, and Beatrice and Arthur lived, there were spacious, airy roads, and fine villas with gardens and views of the sea; here, the dwellings were cramped, and dark, and low.

'I am sorry to bring you this way; it is the quickest route, but I should perhaps have walked the longer way round,' said Mr Watson apologetically. 'Young ladies should not be seeing such places.'

'Young ladies should perhaps see such places a great deal more often than we do,' said Eveline. 'I am scarcely half a mile from where I have lived my whole life, and yet this is like another country to me. I am ashamed that I do not know it better.'

The office was next to the new railway station, which was now very nearly complete. Inside it was pleasantly cool after the heat of the day and smelt of sawdust and paper.

'I am due for a meeting with the town dignitaries, to make arrangements for the grand opening,' said Mr Watson, 'but wait here, if you will, and I will get Tom to come to you.'

She wandered around the room as she waited, looking at the drawings and plans pinned to the walls. Despite the ruin it was causing, there was something grand, she thought, in the scale of this enterprise: to join city to city, so that people could move about from place to place with such ease, and even such a little seaside town as theirs be linked, at last, with the greater world.

Thomas Armitage looked very formal and forbidding, here in his own world, but when he saw who his visitor was, he smiled at her.

'Miss Stanhope. How are you? Forgive me, I cannot be long – there is a consignment of rail fixings gone missing – but what can I do for you?'

'I wanted to ask you about the man – the man who died,' she said. 'I cannot stop thinking of him.'

His smile faded. 'It was a bad business, indeed. But these things happen. There is nothing you can do for him now – nothing that any of us can do.'

'No, indeed, but for his family, his children, perhaps? Will they be left destitute? The houses the working people live in, the streets I have just walked through, they are horrible places, and I cannot help imagining how things would be for a woman alone, living in such circumstances, with no money, and no help.'

'She will have a family to help her, I dare say.'

'So there is a wife – a widow? Children?'

'Yes, since you ask. It seems Elias had a wife and two children, hardly more than babies.'

'And you – you men, who run the railway, who have such power, can just shrug, and leave them to their fate, whatever that might be?' Her voice rose, fiery with indignation. 'The railway has killed a husband and father, and you do nothing? It is a monster – it spoils, and takes, and ruins lives. I hate the railway, and all the destruction it has caused, and is still causing.' She stared defiantly at him, her head held high, and colour rising into her cheeks.

He looked back at her, his arms folded, and his lip curling impatiently, and then seemed to make up his mind to something.

'Do you have half an hour, Miss Stanhope? There is a place you might be interested to see. We can walk there; it is just a short distance.'

'If you are going to take me to the railway track and extol the virtues of progress, Mr Armitage, then I do not wish to see it.'

They glared at each other for a moment: he frowning, she mutinous.

'No, that is not what I intend.' He moved towards the door, opened it, and waited for her.

Chapter Nine

A New Perspective

They walked in silence away from the railway tracks and the station building, along a newly made road, which climbed a little, leaving the dark warren of streets below them. Eveline tried to get her bearings; they were high above the river now, with a view over the valley.

'Is this not part of the Sandham estate?' she asked suddenly. 'Surely this land is Sir William's – he used to have deer, here, and there was a copse, I think – how is this now a road?'

'Sir William was very happy to sell a couple of acres to the railway company.'

'No, surely, that cannot be so. He was vehement in his dislike of the railway, he told me so many times; fearful for his shooting, and his view, and his pheasants.'

'Perhaps the price he got softened the blow. I imagine he could buy a good many pheasants with the sum he negotiated; and he will no doubt be looking forward to realising his investment in the railway bonds, in due course.'

Eveline was silent as she digested this information.

'Now,' he said, 'look ahead.'

A new street had appeared where before there had been grass and trees. All along the broad road was a row of terraced cottages, of yellowish brick, and each with its own neat front door. The little gardens in front were too new to be anything but raw earth, and at the end of the row men were still up ladders working on the roofs, and glazing windows; but all was very nearly complete.

'The railway company has built these, for the workers. Many of those who came to labour will not stay here, of course; but there will be jobs and houses for drivers, and guards, and maintenance men, and signalmen.' He sounded as though he were immensely proud of this. 'It will bring some security to many, and a better life, I trust.'

She walked up the path to one of the cottages, peering into the dim interior. The rooms were modest, but there was a fireplace, and shelves, and the walls were painted, and at the rear there was a scullery, and a bigger garden.

'And are they given to the workers, as gifts?'

'No, not as gifts. We cannot afford to be so generous. But they will have the house while they are employed by the company. Come, if you will.' He led her further along the street, towards where the men were working. 'Here, you see, look at the construction. I had the devil's own work to get the Railway Board to accept the idea at all, and then they held out for a rough-and-ready row of dwellings, poor and mean, built of the cheapest materials. But constant dripping wears away stone, you know, and at last I got my way, and worked with the architect on the designs myself, and these are good, sturdy houses. The roofs will not leak; the walls will not crack; they will stay dry and safe, and there is room enough for them to be proper homes for the men and their families.'

Eveline had never heard him sound so warm, or so eloquent. She looked again at the new houses, with their pleasing proportions, and their new glass windows gleaming in the sunshine, and then looked back at her companion.

'That is a step forward, indeed. There will be many families who will be grateful. But what of the men who cannot work? Who fall sick, or are injured by their work, or killed, like Elias? This will not help them.'

'We cannot help everyone, Eveline.' He looked abstracted, and sombre; she supposed he had not realised that he had once again used her name. 'But I thought you might like to see that some things will change for the better, even though there are many changes you do not care for.'

'Yes; and I thank you. I am glad to know it.' She wished, suddenly, to be alone, so that she could ponder this new knowledge and her own feelings. 'I should go, now, Mr Armitage; I did not mean to be away for so long.'

'I will walk with you back to your house, then, if I may.' He offered her his arm, and after a moment's hesitation she took it, and they began to move towards the town. A silence descended once more as they walked, and after a while Eveline said, 'You must think it strange that I am out walking with no hat, Mr Armitage. I saw Mr Watson, you see, walking past, and I left my house without stopping to think about such things.'

He glanced at her. The cloud of dark curls fell around her shoulders, blown a little by the breeze into soft tangles, and she was pushing the unruly strands away from her face.

'I do not care particularly for hats,' he said, and then suddenly he stopped, and turned towards her.

'Can I hope, Miss Stanhope – could your feelings change at all – towards the railway, that is – now you have seen another side of this great enterprise?'

Surprised at the note of urgency in his voice, she said, 'You have shown me another side of it, indeed, Mr Armitage. I think the housing scheme is a fine plan, and you are to be admired for your perseverance in carrying it through.'

He nodded, his expression very serious now; but he said nothing more, and they resumed their walk.

As they drew near to the house, she felt she should offer an olive branch.

'Will you come in, Mr Armitage? Can I offer you some refreshment?'

'No, I thank you. I should get back to the offices. The rail fixings—'

'Ah, the rail fixings,' she said, smiling. 'Of course.'

He stood for a moment, then said, 'Will you come to the opening of the railway? It is the sixteenth of June – will you be there? I should like it if you will. You will see the railway operating then, in all its strength, and glory – I know you have not welcomed its coming, Miss Stanhope, but I hope you will be open to seeing the good it will bring, as well as the bad.'

She hesitated; then, seeing his earnest look, said, 'Yes, I will be there.'

He smiled, at last. 'Thank you. You may even enjoy travelling on the railway, Miss Stanhope; you never know.'

She offered her hand, and he shook it; then he turned, and strode away, and was gone.

She went in through the gates, quite lost in thought; but before she reached the house her aunt, emerging from the shrubbery, hailed her in a loud whisper.

'Eveline, my dear – I thought you should know – your mama is looking for you, and has been this past hour. She thought you were with us, you see, in the garden; but there was something she wanted to tell you about having the Sandhams to tea, and when you were nowhere to be found she grew alarmed.'

'Oh, heavens! Is she very cross, Aunt George?'

'She is worried, and will be glad that you are safe; but yes, she may be a little cross,' said Aunt George.

Mrs Stanhope, it transpired, was more than a little cross when she had discovered from Eveline exactly where, and with whom, she had been.

'You have been walking – hatless, and looking like a hoyden – actually walking about town with a man we scarcely know! Is he, even, a gentleman? I extended that invitation to dine entirely at Mr Watson's entreaty, but that young man is not a proper acquaintance for you. Your reputation, Eveline, your reputation! Have you no idea at all what it means for a young woman to be thought fast? How are you to marry well, how are you to marry at all, if you behave in such a fashion?'

'Mama, I am sorry that I did not tell you where I was; but I am perfectly safe, as you see. And of course Mr Armitage is a gentleman, in every way that can possibly matter.'

'That is not the point at all, and you well know it! Here am I, moving heaven and earth to get Charles Sandham here so that you may have a chance of an excellent match, even though it means putting up with Augusta Sandham far more often than I could wish, and you are tramping about the streets with some great tall, stern, scowling young man who works for the railway! Well, I have myself to blame, I dare say, for letting you roam about with Jennie, swimming and goodness knows what else. And photography – photography! – spending hours in some shop in the high street, getting filthy marks all over your hands and face and clothes. What was I thinking?'

'I am always accompanied by Jennie, Mama, which makes it perfectly respectable.'

'No, it does not! And that is another thing. I employ Jennie to be a lady's maid, and she is never to be found when she is needed for anything; I swear I have not had my hair curled for a month.'

'That is not Jennie's fault, Mama,' said Eveline, by now beginning to feel alarmed, 'she is only doing as I ask, and if you wish her to be at home more, I can easily swim alone now; I would be quite safe.'

'Swim alone! Good heavens, that is the last thing you will be doing. I have neglected my duties as a mother, but now I see it, and I will do things differently. From now on you will behave as a lady should. There will be no swimming, or photographing, or going anywhere without me, or your aunt, or your sisters. You will dress suitably, too, and put your hair up, and not run about the garden in that old green frock, or disappear for hours on end.'

'No, Mama, no, I cannot be confined like that – please do not say so!'

'That is enough, Eveline,' said her mother, with dreadful finality. 'I wish you to go to your room now, and by the time you come down to dinner – properly dressed, mind, with your hair arranged – you will have reflected on your behaviour, and be in a more dutiful frame of mind.'

Eveline lay on her bed. For a while her indignation and outrage at her mother's unreasonableness were all she could feel. Her new-found freedom, so wonderful to taste, was to be snatched away for one small misdemeanour – not even that – how could a brief walk, a conversation, be a misdemeanour for an adult woman? How was she to get about the world, and see things, if she was not even able to walk about the streets of her own small town? At last she tried to overcome her fury. There was nothing to be gained by it, except the luxury of feeling herself to be very much put upon; and she began to think that the thing to do would be to make a plan. Her mother's anger might not last; she would relent, perhaps, a little. If she went along with her mother's wishes for a short time, she might gradually regain the freedom she now seemed to have lost entirely. That was it, then; she would behave beautifully, and Mama would forgive her, and she would be able to get back to the Professor, and the studio, and the sea, and Jennie's company. Perhaps she would ask Beatrice and Louisa to advise her, for they seemed to have managed to learn how to behave suitably, and to dress elegantly, and not to outrage their mother. And yet, she thought gloomily, for what? For a house and a husband, and a life of children, and nursemaids, and parties, and dresses. Well, for her it would be merely a means to an end; she would concentrate on being as her mother wished her to be, for a while at least, for there was clearly nothing to be gained by resisting. She sat up and rang the bell for Jennie.

'So you see,' she said, gazing dejectedly into the looking glass as Jennie pinned her hair into strange coils over her ears, 'I shall have to give up our swims, and our visits to Mr Fry, just for a while. But I am sure that it will not be long before Mama relents and I can resume. Will I forget how to swim, do you think?'

'Once you learn to swim, Miss Eveline, you never forget,' Jennie assured her.

'And how I shall miss our work with the photographs! We had made such progress. That last picture, when we used the longer lens – I was so pleased with that – and poor Mr Fry, what will he think when we do not arrive there tomorrow as usual? We were going to dress you as Vivien, with Mr Fry as Merlin; oh, it would have been wonderful!'

'It is my afternoon off, tomorrow, miss. I could go to see the Professor, to tell him what has occurred, and explain that you will be coming back as soon as you can. He will be sorry, but he will understand.'

'Oh yes, would you, Jennie? How kind. That would be the very thing. Tell him – oh, tell him everything, for there is no point in spinning some polite fiction about an indisposition, or some such nonsense. Explain that I am in trouble with Mama, and that I expect it will pass, and say how sorry I am, and how I long to start again. And remind him about those silver prints that we left to dry, last time – I have high hopes of those.'

The dinner that evening passed, if not comfortably, at least without further recriminations, and her mother did relent enough to say that Eveline's hair was very neatly done, for a change, and she was glad that her words had been taken to heart. The next day, however, brought a new source of outrage for poor Mrs Stanhope; for Jennie, returning from her afternoon off, politely handed in her notice.

'And where am I to find another maid, now, with the summer before us? We shall all look like ragamuffins. Louisa will have to bring Betsy, when she comes, and Betsy is a silly girl who has not the first idea about how I like my caps. This is all your doing, Eveline, this is just the sort of thing your careless behaviour causes.'

'How can it be my fault, Mama?' asked Eveline. 'I am much sorrier than you that Jennie is leaving us; I will miss her terribly.'

'Well, miss, you should have thought of that before giving her ideas above her station; for she has a new position, if you please, with Theodore Fry. She is to be his assistant, and work in his studio, and spend her days dabbling in those vile potions and so forth. I hope you are satisfied.'

Chapter Ten

Beatrice Gives Advice

Eveline's first emotion on hearing that Jennie was to work for the Professor was one of pure envy. To spend one's days actually creating photographs, with all the fascinating and absorbing processes and possibilities of the art; to be a person respected for one's abilities and rewarded for one's skills; to be regarded as a fellow worker by a professional man, and not as a young lady who must not soil her pretty hands with work or her pretty head with problems – these things had never seemed more desirable as now, when Jennie was to have them, and she, Eveline, had no hope of ever even aspiring to them. She tried to imagine telling her mother that she wished to work for a living, and almost laughed aloud at the idea. And then, there was the sense that somehow Jennie had betrayed her, by finding this new position; for if it had not been for Eveline, Jennie would never have thought of such a thing, or had the chance to learn the things that now equipped her for such a role. In that, at least, she found herself briefly in agreement with her mother. It was not until bedtime that she had a chance to see Jennie alone, and she was still shocked and a little resentful. However, she took a deep breath, and reminded herself that a generous spirit would be happy for her friend; and so as soon as Jennie came into her room that night to brush out her hair, Eveline went to her, and embraced her.

'Jennie – I shall miss you so much,' she said truthfully, 'but what a wonderful thing for you, to go to work for the Professor! How did it come about?'

'I went to call on Mr Fry, Miss Eveline, as we agreed,' said Jennie, 'and he was very sorry to hear we would not be coming in for a while, for he said that he enjoyed our visits, and we were most helpful to him. And then we got to talking about how busy he was becoming, which of course he is pleased about, for it means more customers and more money, and he said he had been thinking of taking on an assistant, but where was he to find some lad who understood all the delicate processes, or had an aptitude to learn quickly? And then I only said, need it be a lad, Mr Fry? Could it not be a girl, just as well, for you know, Miss Eveline, how often you have said that women are quite as quick and clever as men.'

'Yes, I have said that,' said Eveline wryly, 'many times, I know – do go on, Jennie.'

'Well, then he gave me a surprised look, as though I had said something remarkable, and started to laugh, and then said, I don't suppose you would come and work for me, Jennie? And at first I said no, I could not, because I could not leave you, or your mama, when you have been so good to me, but after a while I began to think that you would encourage me, miss, to be a woman who made her own way in the world. And,' she added, 'Mr Fry will pay me two shillings a week more than I get now, and I will not be working at all on Sundays, so I may see Ned more; really, it is a fine thing for me.'

'Oh yes – it is, Jennie, though we would pay you more, I am sure, if it is just that,' she said, a little awkwardly, for the question of Jennie's wages had never really crossed her mind.

'Then you would have to pay the other servants more, miss, for they would be sure to find out, and I do not think your mama would want to do that,' said Jennie. 'Mrs Groves has wanted a new kitchen maid for many months now, but the mistress says it cannot be, for it would be too expensive. And Mr Fry is to write me a letter to keep, also, saying that he will give me a month's notice and a reference if business declines, so that I will have a chance to look about for something new, and that is something too, for all servants can be turned off in a moment without a character, if they should not give satisfaction.'

'We would never do such a thing!' said Eveline, shocked. 'What a horrible idea, Jennie!'

'Thank you for saying so, miss; yet Miss Louisa's last maid, Hannah, was sent away with no notice, and hardly time to pack her bags, and has not found work since, so you see it may happen, even in such good families as yours.'

'I did not know! Hannah . . . yes, I recall her – pretty, and very young – she was Louisa's maid before Betsy. However did you know this, Jennie?'

'Servants' talk; for whenever Miss Louisa and her family visit, we all talk of our news, and what has happened, and there was a deal of talk about Hannah.'

'What talk? What was the reason for her leaving so suddenly? It must have been something grave. I cannot think Louisa would cast her off for some trivial mistake.'

'I cannot say, miss.' Jennie looked away, hesitating, and a shadow crossed her face. 'Perhaps she deserved it, after all. Now, your nightgown, and then I shall say goodnight.'

In the interests of furthering her plan to win her mother's approval, Eveline had decided to consult Beatrice about clothes.

'For the Sandhams are coming to tea,' she explained to her sister, 'and then there is the railway opening, and heaven knows what else, and apparently I look like a hoyden, so will you advise me, Beatrice? You always have such an air, and look so elegant, and although I know I will never be as pretty or graceful as you, still I had better try to be a little more as Mama wishes me to be, or I shall never hear the end of it.'

'You are pretty enough, Evie,' said Beatrice, 'at least, you are striking, and your eyes are very lovely; and tall girls are quite the fashion now, so you need not despair.'

'Oh, well, that is something,' said Eveline, laughing despite herself.

Beatrice threw herself into the project with gusto. Pattern books and magazines were sent for, and a visit to Madame Delphine arranged. Eveline submitted to having swathes of fabric held against her skin, to check for the most flattering shades, and to having Beatrice arrange satin tippets and lace collars around her neck, to see what would be most becoming. She sat patiently, trying to read while Beatrice pinned her hair up, and took it down, resisting only the idea of having her hair straightened with irons and then re-curled into ringlets. 'Ringlets? Really, Beatrice? My hair will never go into ringlets, I feel sure, and if it did I would look like one of Sir William's bloodhounds.'

'You may be right,' said Beatrice. 'Look here, then, at these hair fashions from Paris. Madame Delphine assures me they are quite the thing, and that the Empress Elizabeth of Austria wears her hair so, just caught at the back and then tumbling loose.'

Eveline rolled her eyes, but she acknowledged that Beatrice knew a great deal more than she about such matters and put her book down long enough for her sister to arrange her hair in a way which she declared to be a great deal more flattering than the previous efforts.

'And I have been thinking about dresses, so that we may be prepared for our excursion to Madame Delphine tomorrow,' said Beatrice. 'For afternoon parties, a white gown would be just the thing; very suitable for a young girl.'

'I am nineteen, Beatrice, practically an old maid in Mama's eyes.'

'Nonsense! You have plenty of time; I was not married

until I was nearly twenty; and if you heed my advice you will not be an old maid at all. Charles Sandham will have eyes for no one else, I declare.'

'I think Charles prefers to look at you, Beatrice, rather than anyone else.'

'Oh, as to that: he is a flirt, indeed, but there is nothing in it,' said Beatrice airily.

'I do think he likes you very much, Beatrice,' said Eveline seriously, 'and Arthur thought so too, I could see.'

'You know nothing of the matter, Eveline,' said Beatrice, a flush rising across her face. 'I cannot help it if someone admires me, and one cannot be shut away from other people. A little harmless flirting is just the way of the world; common politeness, really, nothing more. When you are married you will understand.'

'*If* I am married.'

'Silly girl! You will be married within a twelvemonth if you put your mind to it. The white gown, now, do concentrate.'

'No frills or bows, please, Beatrice; I should feel ridiculous.'

'I have already decided that plain styles will become you best, so you need have no fear on that score. A velvet ribbon trimming the neckline and the sleeves, perhaps in dark blue, and the skirt falling in soft folds, very simple. Louisa will be surprised when she sees you looking so grand.'

The visit to Madame Delphine was declared by Beatrice to be a wild success, for they had found a new delivery of muslins and silks simply waiting to be pounced upon. Mrs Stanhope accompanied them, for she was not yet ready to let Eveline out of her sight for more than an hour or so, even with Beatrice as a chaperone, and she herself was not immune to the charms of a morning spent perusing the latest fashions.

'Did you see, Mama, how well the purple costume looked on Evie?' asked Beatrice, as the carriage lumbered home with a dozen parcels piled beside them on the seats (for as well as the dresses they had ordered, there were hats and gloves and fans to be thought of). 'The matching hat, too, with the feathers, so à la mode! And of course, that delicious ruby-striped satin, such a flattering shade. I was very pleased, too, with the pale blue I found for myself. I do not think Arthur will be very cross, for it is an age since I had a new day dress, and I know he likes me in blue.'

'You looked very beautiful in the blue, indeed, my love,' said Mrs Stanhope. 'You are lucky, Eveline, to have such a kind sister to guide you.'

'Yes, thank you, Beatrice,' said Eveline hastily. 'I am grateful, truly.'

'If Madame gets the white dress to us in time, Eveline, you can wear it when the Sandhams come to us. Which reminds me that there is a great deal to be done before that, for I do not want Augusta Sandham to be looking down her long nose at us. If the weather is fine enough, we could perhaps take tea on the terrace, for the garden is looking very pretty at the moment, and if there is one thing Augusta envies me I know it is the garden. Adelaide, she said to me last summer, your garden is a picture. She would have had Barnabas off me if she could, for she is not above stealing servants, but he would not go, for he said that working with the two ladies was what he liked best; and in any case it is not Barnabas who has the eye for colour, but your aunt and Miss Angell. I could hardly tell her that, however, for if she knew that those two are virtually my gardeners, she would think us odder than she already does, and you may be sure that she would waste no time in telling everyone she knows. She has already told Jane Debourne that the governess dines with us, but luckily Jane has too much sense to care about a thing like that.'

'We could set the tea out under the weeping ash, Mama,' suggested Eveline. 'It is like a perfect umbrella just now, and the view of the borders is so pretty from there.'

'Under the tree! There is a thought. We could have the table carried out, and your grandmother's lace cloth, and a bowl of roses in the centre. Augusta will be green with envy. How very delightful it will be! Evie, that is an excellent idea, and you are a good girl.'

Jennie had agreed to stay on until Louisa arrived for her visit the following week, bringing Betsy, whose attentions Louisa had graciously said she would share while she was staying. Each evening as Jennie's departure approached felt a little more melancholy to Eveline, as she sat before the looking glass to have her hair brushed.

'Your mama will allow you to resume your visits to the Professor one day, will she not, Miss Eveline? And then we may work together as before.'

'Yes – at least, I hope so – but I do not know how long that may be, and you will have learnt all sorts of new things. You will have to teach me, I expect.'

They both pondered this strange reversal of the natural order of things.

'Of course, miss, but you are a quick learner, so that will not take long; and you have such an eye for the lighting, and the composition of the shots. That will not leave you.'

'Thank you, Jennie. That is kind. But oh, how I am missing it, already! And the swimming too, for I had begun to feel quite adept; that last time, I dived to the seabed, and swam out quite far, and it was glorious! I felt so strong, and so free. And now the focus of my life is tomorrow's tea party, and whether I should or should not wear a blue sash. Really, I could scream with vexation. But we may still be friends, may we not? And meet, perhaps, when we can?'

Jennie smiled shyly at her in the mirror.

'Of course – I would like that, very much, if you think it possible, Miss Eveline. But will your mama approve of such a friendship?'

'Yes – that is, it is not up to Mama whom I choose as my friends. Although she is being so dreadfully difficult at the moment. And, Jennie, when you are not my maid you must not call me *Miss* Eveline. I can just be Eveline.'

'Eveline.' Jennie tried the word. 'Eveline. Eveline. Eveline.'

They both started to laugh.

'Oh, I shall be very sorry to leave you, Miss – Eveline, I mean. I hope Betsy will take good care of you, and of your pretty new clothes. That reminds me: I have had your favourite dress cleaned, the green one.' She took the dress from the wardrobe. 'It is nearly as good as new, apart from a tiny mark on the sleeve, which I think must be from the time we spilt the collodion.'

Eveline looked at the dress. It was exactly the colour of old moss.

'Hold it up against yourself, Jennie. Yes, you see, it suits your colouring much better than mine. Now Beatrice has explained these things to me, I do see it. You must take it as a parting gift. We are much of a height, and I think it will fit you. I loved that dress! And it never showed any trace even if I had spent hours in my beech tree. But I think perhaps my tree-climbing days are over, at least for now.'

Chapter Eleven

Tea and Roses

Aunt George and Miss Angell had been very nearly as excited as Mrs Stanhope at the prospect of putting Lady Sandham's nose out of joint by exhibiting the glories of the Stanhope garden. For days they had dead-headed roses, and removed every weed from the herbaceous borders, and staked anything that might require it. Miss Angell had then had the happy thought that a particularly fine pair of stone urns, planted up with white delphiniums and silver thyme, might be moved to flank the steps that led down from the terrace, and Aunt George arranged for extra pots of lavender to cluster beneath the coppery gold roses which clothed the high grey stone wall at the end of the lawn. The morning of the tea party dawned fresh and clear, with a promise of heat to come, and chairs and a table were carried out to be arranged beneath the ash tree; while in the kitchen, tiny sandwiches of cucumber, and of foie gras, were assembled, with a mayonnaise of salmon, brown shrimps in butter, strawberry tartlets, a Madeira cake, and petit fours; and at the last minute Mrs Stanhope thought that as well as the tea, she would offer an iced claret and champagne cup. The table was laid with lace and silver, and the Spode felspar porcelain, which had been a wedding present to the Stanhopes, and a great bowl of the palest pink roses was set at the centre of the table.

'And now – heavens, it is two o'clock! Eveline, what are you doing, just idling about? Do go and get changed. Beatrice, make sure she looks respectable, please.'

Beatrice and Arthur had been included in the invitation – 'Then it will not look as though we have invited the Sandhams just so you may be with Charles, Evie,' said Mrs Stanhope, 'though you must be sure to take him for a little walk – around the rose garden, perhaps, after tea, so you may be alone.'

'I thought I was not allowed to walk alone with a young man.'

'Now you are just being obtuse. This is not at all the same. Now go, go!'

Eveline dressed in the new white frock, and Jennie arranged her hair while Beatrice gave instructions, so that the dark curls were piled up a little and then fell down her back in a long cascade.

'Perfect! And there is no need to tell Mama, for she thinks rouge a little fast, I know; but just the merest hint, here, and a little dab on your lips, and no one will know, except that you will have a little more colour. There! Now do admit, Evie, that you look very lovely.'

Charles Sandham certainly seemed to be taken with Eveline's looks. He glanced at her, looked away, and looked again, and then positively manoeuvred the seating arrangements so that he was placed, to his evident satisfaction, with Eveline on one side of him and Beatrice on the other.

'Your gardener has surpassed himself, Adelaide,' said Lady Sandham. 'This planting scheme is most artistic. I am very fond of that sort of thing, you know, and no one appreciates more than I how much beauty is to be found in nature.'

'Indeed, Augusta; though nature needs a little helping hand sometimes, does it not?'

'Oh, yes; although *we* have such an extensive park that we cannot tame it all, by any means.'

Mrs Stanhope felt generous enough to let the remark pass, for, as she reminded herself, the aim of the afternoon was that the Sandhams should feel that a match between their nephew and her daughter would be an advantageous one, when they saw with what taste and style the Stanhopes lived; and piquing Augusta's envy was merely a side effect, although of course highly agreeable.

'What are these roses?' asked Charles, idly pulling a fragrant bloom from the artfully natural arrangement that Mrs Stanhope herself had created as a centrepiece. 'You see how fortunate I am, surrounded by the loveliest roses of summer,' and he smiled at Beatrice and Eveline in turn.

'My sister-in-law will know – Georgiana, my love, what are these?'

'Maiden's Blush,' said Aunt George. 'Pleasingly appropriate, Mr Sandham, do you not think?'

'Oh, perfectly so. A Maiden's Blush is a most lovely thing.'

'Although I think that the French call this rose by another name, however – what is that, Maria, do you recall?'

'They call it *Cuisse de Nymphe*,' said Miss Angell.

'I say,' said Charles, 'do they really? That is even more lovely, is it not? Miss Eveline, may I offer you some more of this iced cup?'

'Eveline, my sweetest girl,' said her mother from the far end of the table, 'why do you not take Charles to show him the walled garden, since he is so fond of roses? He will like that, I am sure.'

'Indeed, I should like that very much,' said Charles, with alacrity. 'Would you, Miss Stanhope? May I offer you my arm?'

'Oh . . . thank you . . . Beatrice, will you not come too?'

'I was just about to ask Beatrice something important, Eveline,' said her mother. 'You need not wait.'

After the cool shade of the ash tree, it was very warm within the walls of the rose garden. There was a drowsy murmur from innumerable bees, and the distant clink of the teacups and the faint sounds of conversation from the others. Charles and Eveline walked slowly along the paths between the rose beds, making desultory conversation on the beauty of the flowers and the heat of the afternoon, until they reached a seat canopied with a wooden arch, which supported a cloud of tiny white honey-scented flowers.

'Shall we rest in the shade for a moment?' suggested Charles. 'The heat is so fatiguing, and this setting would frame you so perfectly. A maiden in a white dress, surrounded by white roses!'

It was pleasant in the arbour, and they sat for a while in the agreeable languor induced by the afternoon heat. Charles plucked a rose and twirled it around his fingers, breaking off a dead leaf, and then raising it to inhale its scent.

'There! A perfect rose.' He held it against Eveline's face. 'Such a picture!'

He let the rose trail softly down to her throat, and rest in the little hollow at the base of her neck. She felt her breath catch slightly in her throat at the sensation of the velvet petals touching her skin, and he drew the rose very gently downwards until it reached the low neckline of her dress.

'Have you ever had your photograph taken, Miss Stanhope?' he asked. 'I should like to have this scene captured for ever.'

'Indeed I have; and I have taken photographs myself, too, many of them. It is a most interesting art – a science, too. I would like to do more, much more, but Mama does not . . . does not altogether approve. She thinks it not a suitable pursuit for a young woman.'

'You have taken photographs! You understand the art of photography? You are a most intriguing person, Eveline.' He began to draw the rose gently to and fro across the curve of her breasts. 'Now, would I be able to have a photograph of you, one day, to keep, do you think?'

'I do not see why not,' she said. 'And there is something I should like to ask of you, Mr Sandham, so perhaps we could make a bargain?'

'That sounds intriguing. Is it too much to hope that you are longing for a photograph of me, too?'

'No, thank you – it is something more practical than that, and something I feel sure you would be glad to help with, when you hear what I have to say.'

He sighed, and took the rose away from her skin.

'Then do ask. And would you call me Charles, perhaps, and not Mr Sandham?'

'Charles, then. It is to do with the railway, and a man who was killed a few weeks ago working there. He was young; he has left a wife and children, and there is nothing that will compensate her for that loss, or help her and her children in the life of hardship that surely awaits them. You see how terrible this is; how unjust.'

'Oh, a sad story, indeed. I can make a gift of money, if you wish it, Eveline: be glad to, really. What do you think? Fifty pounds, perhaps?'

'Oh, no – that is, thank you for that thought, but I am talking of a much larger picture here. Charity is a noble thing, but it cannot be a substitute for fairness and justice. No, I feel we need to change the law of the land, Charles, so that there is proper provision for everyone. This poor woman is but one in thousands, I dare say, living in fear and poverty, and yet we are a country of immense wealth. How can this be right? How can it be fair?'

'No – well, yes, I see what you mean, and it does you

116

credit. You are a tender-hearted girl, I can see that. But I hardly see what I can do.'

'You are a man, Charles, and a well-connected one. You have influence; I expect you know people who can change things. And you are young – you could influence those in high places, even be a member of parliament yourself, and have real power, and use it for good – to make things better for people. Oh, the world is yours! You have every freedom, every privilege, where women have so little.'

'Parliament! No, no, I have no ambition in that direction. A little gift of money, now, that is what will really help this poor woman.'

'You had not thought of entering public life? Of having the chance to change the lives of people so much less fortunate than we?'

Charles began to look slightly hunted.

'No, I had not thought of that at all. The world seems pretty much to go on all right, you know. Lots of fellows are good at that sort of thing, but it is not my line. Let me give a bit of a sub to help out. That will be best.'

Eveline was silent for a moment. It seemed a feeble, pale scheme beside the ambitions she had dreamt of; but for now, she supposed, it was a start.

'Well, thank you. I suppose I could start a fund to help those in distress, and you would be my first supporter.'

'I would be honoured to be your first supporter,' said Charles gallantly, and with more than a little relief in his voice. 'And in return, a photograph of you – that was our bargain, was it not?'

'Certainly; I always honour a bargain. I will ask Jennie to bring a print back from Mr Fry's studio. Do you have a preference for the style of photograph? There are dozens, and in various poses and costumes.'

'Are there, indeed? How marvellous. Could I, perhaps, go to the studio with you, and choose my own?'

'Yes, why not?' She stood up, and turned to meet his eyes.

'I should tell you, though, Charles, that I am wearing clothes in all of them.' She smiled at him. 'Shall we go back to the tea party?'

Chapter Twelve

A Visit to the Offices of the Railway Company

That evening, when the guests had departed and the last crumbs had been cleared away, there was much discussion about the afternoon. Mrs Stanhope was in a state of high satisfaction.

'The garden looked superb, George! You two had excelled yourselves; if Augusta Sandham asked me once who had arranged the planting of the border, she asked me a dozen times, for now she clearly suspects Barnabas is not the artist at work. And those urns with all the pretty white and silver flowers as well, Maria; she was racked with envy, I could see. And the tea was excellent, though I had worried about the Madeira cake, which can be a little heavy; but I believe she drank so much of the iced cup she would hardly have noticed if it had been a rock cake. And, Eveline, my love!' She turned to her youngest daughter. 'You had a pleasant walk with dear Charles?'

'I did, thank you, Mama.'

'Well, Evie?' Beatrice was as impatient as her mother to find out the details. 'What did you talk of? Did he seem interested in you?'

'Oh, yes, we had a most interesting talk.'

'I mean, interested in you, wretched girl; in *you*?'

Eveline chose her words carefully.

'He has asked if I would walk with him, into town, one day soon.'

'That is splendid!' said Mrs Stanhope. 'Of course you must.'

'I knew that purple walking dress would be needed,' added Beatrice. 'Why do you not walk with him to our house, Evie, for a luncheon perhaps? It would be quite informal.'

'He is keen to visit Mr Fry's studio,' said Eveline. 'Photography is a special interest of his, you know.'

'Well,' began Mrs Stanhope doubtfully, 'I do not know that I want you going back to that place – and yet, if Charles wishes to see it—'

'He does, very much, Mama.'

'Then I suppose there would be no harm – but you must not be saying that you ever got involved in all that grubbing about with chemicals. He would think it most peculiar, and you may be sure Augusta would consider it very low.'

'Oh, I have told him that I have taken photographs, Mama, and he was very complimentary about that. He said he found it *very intriguing*.'

'He did? Well, well, young things today, I suppose, have different ideas of what is proper. If Charles Sandham does not mind it, then I am sure I do not; and Augusta is very old-fashioned in her views, I know. You may walk there with Charles, Evie, whenever he likes; but attend to what your sister says about the walking dress, and do not ever go without a hat.'

A note from the Sandhams, thanking Mrs Stanhope for her kind hospitality, arrived the next day, and there was a separate note from Charles, requesting the company of Miss Eveline Stanhope on a walk to visit the studios of the Professor of Photography. At the appointed time, Eveline dutifully dressed in the new walking costume, with the matching hat trimmed with purple feathers.

'I loathe this hat,' she said.

'I think it is the latest style, however,' said Jennie.

'Oh well, how can it matter, really? The good thing is, I am to visit Mr Fry, Jennie, but not, alas, to work, merely to accompany Charles Sandham while he chooses a photograph. Do you have any messages for the Professor? He will be looking forward to your starting work with him. It is not long now; only a few days, and you will have a new life.' She tried not to let any note of the envy she still felt creep into her voice.

'No messages, thank you, except that I will be there as we agreed next Monday morning at nine o'clock.'

'Of course. Jennie, you will be moving back to live with your mother, I suppose? Will you mind that very much?'

'Oh, no; I have my own room in my mother's house, for

you know she is married now to Mr Mason, and lives quite comfortably. And it will not be for ever. Ned and I hope to marry, before too long. My new wages will help us save for that.'

'Oh, that is good news! My congratulations, Jennie; I hope you will be very happy. Will you then live with Ned's family?'

'We want to have a house of our own, and we may be able to have one through the railway. And Ned's father has only one room to spare, and that is let. It is Mr Armitage, you know.'

'What is Mr Armitage?'

'It is he who rents the room from Ned's father. It is a fine big room, with a view of the sea from its windows. The cottage is very neat and respectable; Mr Armitage says he is very comfortable there, and he likes the sea being so close. He and Ned have become good friends, I think. Ned is teaching him to fish, and sail, for though Mr Armitage is the master, he is not proud.'

'I see! Well, I thought he seemed to know you, Jennie, when we encountered him in town.'

'Indeed, he is a very polite gentleman, and Mr Fox is glad to have him as a lodger. He could, I think, afford a grander lodging, but I think he may be saving money for his wedding.'

'For his wedding? Mr Armitage is to be married?'

'I think that must be the case, for when Ned told him of my new place with Mr Fry, and said that might mean we could marry soon, he said that he too was saving for a new life, or some such thing; so we reckon, Ned and I, that he must have a sweetheart in the north country, and he will go back and marry her when the railway is built.'

Eveline was silent for a while.

'Well, and why should he not?' she said brightly. 'I must be off soon for my walk. And, Jennie, I will be able to tell you later what Mr Sandham thinks of our photographic efforts, for he is something of a connoisseur.'

'Then I should like to know his views, for we have not had any judgements on our work, have we? Mr Fry has been our only critic, apart from each other. It will be good to have the view of a gentleman who has travelled and seen a good deal of art, and so forth.'

'I will let you know what he says; although Mr Sandham, I think, prefers photographs of ladies wearing far fewer clothes than we generally are.'

Jennie looked momentarily shocked, but then caught Eveline's eye in the mirror. At that moment Mrs Stanhope bustled into the bedroom.

'Evie, Charles is here! Do not be dawdling about. And whatever are you both laughing at?'

Theodore Fry was genuinely pleased to see his young protégée again.

'I am so sorry that your mama was not altogether in favour of your visits here; I would not have offended Mrs Stanhope for the world,' he said. 'And I miss your visits, and your work, Miss Stanhope, for you have a fresh view of what may be achieved with the camera.'

'Thank you, Mr Fry. I learnt a great deal from you, and I am determined that I will resume my photographic work before long.'

'And,' he added a little anxiously, 'I had offered Jennie the post here, before I thought that this would put you in difficulty.'

'I would not by any means stand in the way of a woman who wishes to find her own work, and make her own way,' Eveline assured him. 'Truly, I am glad for her.'

'And Mr Sandham! Dear sir, what can we do for you?'

It was explained that Mr Sandham wished to purchase a photograph of Eveline from those taken during her time working at the studio. Mr Fry did not seem to think this strange, and even if he had, the patronage of Charles Sandham was too valuable to endanger by even a hint of surprise.

'I will lay out the prints, and you may choose whichever you prefer, dear sir; they are indeed a very fine collection. I compliment you upon your taste.'

The picture Charles chose was one that she and Jennie had devised between them, when they were engaged in trying to produce images with dramatic contrasts between shadow and light. To that end, they had rigged up a black curtain, and Eveline had worn a dark dress, pushed slightly off one shoulder so that her skin showed very white, and her dark hair tumbled over the other shoulder in an unruly mass.

'This is the one I shall treasure always,' said Charles. 'Exquisite! Most artistic! And, if I may, perhaps I will take this also?'

It was a photograph of Eveline and Jennie together, flowered garlands in their hair, their arms around each other's waists.

'Oh, I remember this!' said Eveline. 'You took it, Mr Fry, when we had that new batch of paper, and we hung calico blinds to soften the light. We called it "*Snow White and Rose Red*", I think.' She did not add that she had found it horribly sentimental, as she and Jennie had both adopted rather mawkish expressions; still, the lighting was good.

The prints were paid for, and wrapped, and Charles and Eveline made ready to depart.

'I shall, no doubt, see you, this Monday week?' asked Mr Fry, as he bowed them out.

'Ah, the grand opening of the railway!' said Charles. 'My aunt and uncle are to be cutting ribbons or some such thing.'

'You will be there, Mr Fry?' asked Eveline.

'I have been honoured with the commission to take the photographs for the railway company,' said Mr Fry rather grandly. 'Mr Armitage himself came to the studio to ask me, and I shall be there to record the occasion for posterity.'

'Then it will be a veritable party,' said Charles, 'and we all get a ride on the thing afterwards, I gather.'

As they left the studio, Eveline suggested to Charles that they walk along the high street.

'But would you not rather walk by the seafront?' he asked. 'Or must I return you to your family so soon?'

'No,' said Eveline, 'I think we can take a little longer. But if you will walk with me, there is somewhere I should like to take you. Do you remember the conversation we had in the rose garden?'

'I remember every word, with extreme delight.'

'About the railway worker, the man who died?'

'Oh, that. Yes, Eveline, of course, I remember that too.' She could not tell if he was laughing at her or exasperated.

'I have been thinking a great deal about the idea of a fund to help widows and orphans. It would be a start – some immediate help, at least, and it would raise the idea with those who have power that something more lasting might be done. So a double benefit, you see.'

'Yes, I do see. A capital idea. But where are we going, now?'

'To the offices of the railway company. There is no time like the present, is there? We can discuss how such a fund might be set up, and how directed to those most in need.'

'It will of course be my pleasure to accompany you, but would your mama be happy for you to be walking in such streets as these, Eveline?' They had reached the part of town where, in fact, Mrs Stanhope had expressly forbidden her daughter to venture.

'This is more important than some absurd notion of Mama's. And there is no need for her to know exactly where we have walked, is there?'

At the railway company office, Eveline felt her courage slightly fail her, but she resolutely rang the bell, and asked if Mr Watson or Mr Armitage were in.

'Mr Watson is away from the office today, miss. I understand he has a meeting with the shareholders. But Mr Armitage is here, although I believe he may be preparing to go out before long.' As the clerk spoke, Thomas Armitage emerged from his office.

'Fred, have we heard yet from the Bristol works? The

rolling stock should be arriving later today, and—' He saw Eveline and Charles standing expectantly by the front door. 'Good grief, what is this? A social call?'

'How do you do, Mr Armitage?' said Eveline, a little reproachfully.

'Miss Stanhope.' He recollected himself, and shook hands with them both. 'Forgive me, but I am extremely busy. If you are wanting to look around the new station building, then I would be glad to show you, but it will have to be another time.'

'No, it is not a social visit; we have not come to waste your time,' said Eveline. 'Mr Sandham and I wish to establish a fund to help railway workers and their dependents. We would like to consult you, naturally, about how the money may be most usefully directed, and so forth. The poor man who was killed, for example. You said he left a widow and two children – how might we support them? And all the other unfortunates who have no doubt suffered – we wish to restore justice for them and their families.'

Thomas Armitage looked from Eveline to Charles, and back. His expression darkened.

'Oh, you do, do you?' He sounded deeply irritated. 'You are united in a mission of mercy, it seems. Well, very noble, I am sure, but perhaps you could write a letter, and we will give it some thought.'

'Absolutely,' said Charles. 'Very good plan, Armitage; we'll write in, won't we, Eveline? Now, we should get you back home, I think. Don't want to be in trouble, do we?'

Eveline looked from one to the other in disbelief.

'Cannot you both see how important this is?' she cried. 'We have only to look out of our windows to see how hard life is for so many people, and we have the power to make things better, at least in some small measure! What can be of greater matter than human life? Not rolling stock, whatever that may be, or getting home in time for luncheon.'

Charles looked uncomfortable.

'No, but Eveline, the chap's busy, and this scheme of yours needs some more thought, perhaps.'

'Really, Charles, I thought you were on my side!' said Eveline.

'Perhaps you would like to continue your lovers' quarrel outside,' said Mr Armitage, by now with a thunderously dark expression. 'Write me a letter, Miss Stanhope. I shall of course give it due consideration. And now, if you will excuse me, I have a railway to complete.'

Outside, Charles gave an elegant shrug. 'Well, I feel a bit as though we've been slung out on our ears!' he said. 'Still, the man was busy, you could see that.'

'Busy!' said Eveline, bitterly. 'Too busy to discuss the welfare of his workers! Oh, Charles, if you had seen what I have seen – the poor man crushed and lying dead in the road – I had thought Mr Armitage a feeling man, with a good heart, but it seems I was much mistaken. I cannot think why he should be so very angry, all of a sudden. A lovers' quarrel, indeed! How ridiculous!'

'I have seen terrible things, too,' Charles assured her. 'I had a valet – took him with me to Italy – fell from the roof of the carriage while stowing the cases. Dead in an instant. Hit his head as he fell, I think. A great shock, that was.'

'That was no doubt very dreadful too; but this is something more, something we can affect. No one can prevent every accident; but we can help, where poverty would make life insupportable. I shall not be deterred, however, by Mr Armitage's extraordinary behaviour. I shall write to him, and to Mr Watson, and to anyone else who may have influence, and I *will* make a difference.'

Chapter Thirteen

Mrs Groves has a Trying Day

Jennie was gone, and the house was in a fever of preparation for the visit of Louisa, Bevis, and their children.

'Louisa could quite easily come for the day, you know, Mama,' said Eveline. 'Why does she always make a grand visit, and stay? It makes so much work.'

'How can you say such a thing, Eveline? Your sister wishes to see her family as much as she can, naturally, and the dear little children like to visit me, I know.'

So Mrs Stanhope made lists, and discussed menus, and supervised the airing of the bedrooms, and worried about the draught through the old nursery windows. Aunt George and

Miss Angell picked strawberries and currants by the pound, and Eveline retreated to her bedroom to write letters to the directors of the railway company.

After half a dozen drafts, she was satisfied that she had composed a missive that was both eloquent and forceful. Her proposal was the establishment of a Benevolent Fund, intrinsic to the structure of the railway company, and supported by it in perpetuity; and its establishment begun through a scheme by which money would be donated by well-wishers from among the people of the town. She described the probable fate of the women and children left destitute by the death or incapacity of the husband and father whose work on the railway had caused the tragedy. The miserable hovels she had seen in the dark town streets, the white faces, the hollow eyes, all informed her prose; and yet she took care to balance her emotional appeal with a rational description of the enhanced reputation for the company, which would inevitably result from the public perception of enlightened generosity. This combination of heart and head, she felt, could hardly fail to succeed in stirring anyone with the slightest sensibility to action. She wrote eight copies of the letter in a perfect hand, and addressed one to Mr Watson, enclosing a further six copies with a covering note to ask him to give one to each of his fellow directors of the railway; the last, with a slight feeling of defiance mixed with apprehension, she addressed to Thomas Armitage. His face came into her mind as she wrote. How extraordinary his behaviour had been, when she had called on him with Charles! He had perhaps been very much preoccupied by his work, which might account for his

131

abrupt manner; but it had been more than abrupt – angry, furious almost. He had looked at her and at Charles in such a way, as though – well, as though seeing them together were the source of his anger. Surely it could not be that he was jealous – that he had behaved as he did because she was there with Charles – but no, that was quite absurd. Charles was nothing to her but a potentially useful ally, and Thomas must realise that, and in any case she was nothing to Mr Armitage; they were hardly more than acquaintances. It had been the unguarded temper of a man immersed in the business he felt so deeply about – a man who was not given to the superficial courtesies of polite society, and therefore did not trouble to hide his feelings. It was ridiculous to think that it could be anything else. She rose, ran downstairs, and having waylaid the scullery maid, sent her with the letters to walk to the offices of the railway company to deliver them.

Having seen Mary off the premises with the letters in her hand, Eveline felt a considerable sense of satisfaction. She had made a first step – as soon as a properly directed fund was established, she would ensure, somehow, that all their acquaintances contributed substantial sums, and the scheme would surely grow – funding might be found for an orphanage, for a school, a hospital, for extending proper housing. With a head full of such philanthropic schemes, she thought that she would read in the garden for the hour or so before Louisa was due, for after her arrival there would be very little chance of peace. Her plan, however, was thwarted, for she had only stepped onto the terrace, book in hand, when her mother called her.

'The tea will never be ready when Louisa arrives, Evie, for Groves is preparing the dinner and had left Mary to do the tea, and she says Mary has run off somewhere, and we will not have the apricot fritters that Henry likes so much if Mary does not help her. Have you seen her? She is not a bad girl, generally; I cannot think what has happened.'

'I have sent her to deliver some letters, Mama; she will be back within the hour, I should think.'

'To deliver letters! Whatever for? I hope this is not one of your wild schemes, Eveline; please tell me that you are not writing to Theodore Fry, or some other dubious person who will lead you astray.'

'I wrote to Mr Watson,' said Eveline, with the consciousness of telling at least the greater part of the truth, while she tried not to smile at the idea of Mr Fry's leading anyone astray.

'Why ever would you write to Mr Watson? He will be dining here tomorrow, so you might say anything you wished to him then. And now you have sent Mary off, and no doubt poor little Henry will not get his apricot fritters after all. Really, Eveline, you live in quite another world, I sometimes think.'

'I am sorry, Mama, but really, the letters were of far more importance than Henry's tea. But I will go and explain to Groves,' she added hastily, seeing that her mother was about to question her further.

In the kitchen, Mrs Groves – flushed and wild amid the clouds of steam from a boiling pudding and stirring a sauce with one hand while assembling beef olives with the other –

was not much mollified by Eveline's explanation regarding Mary's absence.

'That is all very well, Miss Eveline; but how am I to get the tea ready for Miss Louisa and the poor little ones? I am training Mary up, and she had got to be a dab hand at the fritters that the little boy likes so much.'

'I did not know that Mary could cook so well, Mrs Groves,' said Eveline with interest. 'That is excellent! She will one day find a better position, perhaps. But we should get another kitchen maid to help you, should we not?'

Mrs Groves regarded her with something very like exasperation.

'That would be just the thing, miss. I have said so to Mrs Stanhope a hundred times, I am sure, but she will not. If you can persuade her, I would be very happy. But that will not get today's tea on the table.'

'Then I shall help,' said Eveline. 'Show me what I can do.' She rolled up her sleeves and put on the apron that Mary had left hanging by the range.

'You, Miss Eveline? Will Mrs Stanhope not think that very odd?'

'She will not know – she is rushing about upstairs, for you know she likes to lay the table herself, folding napkins into fans and so forth. Please do let me help you.'

'Well, then, if you say so, miss; you could butter the bread, and cut the plum cake; and when you have done that, you could finish tying these beef olives, and I will see if the fritters may be rustled up after all.'

Dinner that evening was, after all, a scene of domestic

harmony. The guests had arrived, Henry had got his apricot fritters, and their nursemaid had taken the children away to bed. Beatrice and Arthur had arrived to dine with the family, and Louisa and Bevis regaled them all with a description of the journey, and how they had been held up because one of their horses had shied at the sight of the carrier's cart ahead of them, nearly sending them off the road, and it took Bevis a half-hour of soothing the horses down before they could continue.

'And it was dreadfully hot in the carriage, Mama, and crowded too because we brought Betsy; but you will be glad to have her here, I know, and as we are staying for two weeks, you will have time to look about for a new lady's maid, I suppose,' said Louisa. 'Evie, you look very well, with your hair like that; rather Bohemian, and probably the best thing to do with hair such as yours.'

'Her dress, too,' said Beatrice eagerly. 'Do you not think that ruby red suits her? I chose it myself. I have given her quite a new look, I think.'

'Yes, she does look better. Although rather brown, from running about outdoors, I suppose.'

'Who is she? The cat's mother?' said Eveline; but the others had turned to talk of the grand railway opening, and the arrangements for the day.

'We are to assemble at eleven o'clock on Monday, at the station,' explained Mrs Stanhope, 'as invited guests, of course, and then the Sandhams will make a speech, and declare it all open. Augusta will not mind that, you may be sure. And then I believe we will all be invited to ride on the railway, to Newport, and there will be a grand luncheon served there. I will be terrified, I am sure, to go aboard such a great machine.'

'The children are overexcited at the idea of a ride on a railway train,' said Bevis, yawning. 'Personally, I cannot see why there is so much fuss; it will be a short-lived thing. Horses will never be out of fashion. In a few years they will be tearing up the lines, you may be sure, and then these railway chaps will look pretty silly.'

'Do not let poor Mr Watson hear you say that; he is coming to dine with us tomorrow, and he is so full of the whole thing that it is quite endearing,' said Mrs Stanhope.

'Oh, of course, I shall pretend to be an enthusiast. He is a fine old fellow, and I would not dampen his spirits. What are we eating here, by the way?'

'I think it is beef olives,' said Mrs Stanhope, a little doubtfully, 'but they do look odd, I must say.'

'I have a piece of string in mine,' said Louisa. 'Really, Mama, you should speak to Groves about it.'

'Mrs Groves has had a trying day,' said her mother. 'Eveline will tell you why.'

Faces turned expectantly towards Eveline but she was saved by the entrance of the pudding, since it chanced to be a boiled blackcurrant pudding, which was Arthur's favourite, and Aunt George distracted them by recounting how she and Miss Angell had freed a blackbird that had been caught in the fruit cage while they were picking the currants. As soon as the last of the pudding had been devoured, Bevis and Arthur decided to take their port into the billiard room, and the ladies were left to themselves.

Eveline had promised to sketch her aunt's designs for the new rose garden, and they sat together at the tea table while Aunt George described the layout she had in mind.

'We will keep the arbour, and the roses along the south wall, for sure. It is the central beds that are looking tired now, and too formal for our tastes. Can you draw me a curving bed, here, so that the eye is drawn along to the arbour? Yes, that is it; with a path that follows it round, and the lavender will spill over the edges to soften the line.'

Eveline drew a plan, and then some views of how the finished garden would appear, and then a set of alternatives when Miss Angell added a tentative suggestion that a focal point in the centre, of a fountain or a statue, would lend it even more charm. She was so engrossed in the drawing and the discussion that she did not attend much to what her mother and sisters were saying. Her aunt and Miss Angell, however, were both wont to retire early, and when they had left she joined the conversation in time to hear one of Louisa's complaints about her servants.

'Betsy has a way with my hair, there is no denying' – here she paused to toy with one of her glossy ringlets – 'but she is a sly girl, and lazy. I found her actually asleep last week, in the middle of the day, on the sofa in my own room. She said she had sat down just to mend some silk stockings, and had not meant to sleep; but I gave her a warning, you may be sure.'

This reminded Eveline of something that she had meant to ask her sister.

'Louisa, what happened to your last maid, Hannah? Jennie said you had turned her off without a character. She seemed such a sweet girl when you brought her here; it must have been something very dreadful.'

Louisa flushed scarlet.

'You should not listen to servants' gossip. Jennie has no right to be telling you such things. And *she* has left you and Mama in the lurch, I hear, to go off and work with that silly photographer man in his shop. She must have been a very vulgar creature herself.'

'No, indeed! Jennie is a thoughtful and intelligent person. She has had the good fortune to find an interesting occupation and to be able to make a living by it. I envy her that.'

'Really, Eveline, whatever can you mean? Envy a servant?'

'Yes – for her freedom – for her independence. But you have not told me about Hannah.'

'Hannah was a wicked minx. She may have looked as mild and innocent as a milkmaid, but she was nothing of the sort.'

'Good heavens!' said Mrs Stanhope, interested. 'Do tell us, Louisa.'

'You may guess, I suppose,' said Louisa.

'Oh, dear me! An unwanted stranger, I suppose you mean. That is very shocking, my dear, and of course you had no choice but to turn her out. Was there a man in the case?'

'I would imagine there must have been,' said Eveline. 'But Louisa, who was the man in question? And what became of Hannah? Did you make some provision for her?'

'Provision for her! I? No, I did not, Eveline, and you should not even be talking of such things, and you would not if you had any sense of decorum at all,' and with that Louisa burst into tears and ran from the room.

'Now,' said Mrs Stanhope wearily, 'look what you have done. You know poor Louisa is very highly strung. I shall go and find her; I expect a little brandy and water will restore her.'

Beatrice and Eveline were left to look at each other in some dismay.

'I did not mean to upset her,' said Eveline, 'but she is being very dramatic, is she not? I merely asked—'

'Yes, Evie, I know what you asked; and I may say, you sound very worldly-wise for an unmarried girl. I am sure I did not know as much before I was married.'

'Did you not? Then marriage must have been something of a surprise, Beatrice. If you had looked in Papa's library, you would have found he had a whole shelf of books that would have explained things to you in some detail.'

'Oh! Eveline, you are outrageous! Did Papa really have such books?'

'Certainly; I have been reading them since I was fourteen, which is just as well, since Mama never explained such things to me; nor to you, it seems.'

'No, she did not.' Beatrice shook her head. 'And I wish she had done so, for it took me some time to . . . not to mind married life, you know.'

'Well, the books are still there, Beatrice. I can show you where. You might want to read them, and your married life might be more exciting, if it is not sufficiently so now.'

'*Eveline*! Enough; you are so . . . so naughty!' Beatrice was blushing and laughing together.

'I am not at all naughty; I have very little chance to be, after all,' Eveline assured her. 'My knowledge is all theoretical. But, Beatrice, I do think you might find the books interesting.'

'I cannot believe my little sister is giving me advice on such a matter. But, perhaps, I may take a look at the books, if you think I could do so without anyone's knowing.'

'You will have the study to yourself; no one goes in there now but me. The top shelf, behind Papa's old desk, is the place,' she added helpfully. 'You will need the library steps to reach it. But Beatrice, do you know why Louisa is so upset about Hannah?'

'Well, I should not tell you, really; but I believe she once caught Hannah flirting with Bevis. Perhaps it is that.'

'Flirting? Flirting in what way?'

'Well – kissing him, if you must know. That is what Louisa said: that Hannah had shamelessly flung herself at Bevis and kissed him. Louisa came in the room and saw it with her own eyes. So it is not surprising, if she was a girl with such a wanton nature, that she found herself in trouble because of some man.'

'She looked barely fifteen, Beatrice.'

'What has that to do with it? She might still have been a hussy.'

'It seems to me much more likely that Bevis kissed her, than that she kissed Bevis. Does Louisa think Bevis is the father of Hannah's child?'

'I do not know what she thinks. She only told me what I have just told you, about the kissing. But these things happen, you know, Evie; even if it is Bevis, it is not the end of the world.'

'I would imagine it was the end of the world for Hannah,' said Eveline.

Chapter Fourteen

Dinner en famille

The subject of Louisa's husband and Louisa's maid was, by tacit consent, not mentioned the next morning. Louisa's eyes were red at breakfast, but she kept up a steady flow of chatter regarding the new dress she had brought for the railway opening; and Bevis and Arthur had gone out early to ride, so there was no chance to observe Louisa and her husband together. Eveline's concern for her sister would in any case have outweighed her impulse to enquire more about the welfare of the unfortunate Hannah, at least immediately. But if she had been tempted to do so, her mother's frown was too clearly meaningful to be ignored. Monday and its attendant excitement was the safe subject, and the children's joy at the prospect of a ride on a railway was a welcome focus for all.

'The dinner this evening is really en famille,' said Mrs Stanhope, with some thankfulness, 'for dear Mr Watson is practically family, I think. I have asked Mrs Groves to prepare a gooseberry fool, which I know he likes, and if she makes her oyster soup, we may do just with a leg of mutton and a hashed chicken.'

'I am surprised Mr Watson can spare the time to dine with us, so near the great day,' said Eveline. 'He must have a great deal to occupy him just now.'

She had not yet received any reply from Mr Watson, nor from any of his colleagues, to her letters. It occurred to her that it might be as well to discuss her grand scheme privately with their old friend, rather than have it broached when her mother and sisters were present. To that end, she dressed early for dinner that evening – this was easy to effect, since Betsy was expected to dress Mrs Stanhope, and Louisa, and Eveline; so that Eveline's offer to get ready early ('Then I shall be out of the way,' she had said, 'and I can welcome Mr Watson if you are not quite ready') was well received. She was, therefore, downstairs before any of the others that evening; and since she knew from experience that Mr Watson was generally a punctual guest, she was confident that she would be able to speak to him privately. When she heard his carriage on the gravel drive, she slipped out of the dining room through the French doors, and sped round to the front of the house, where he was just raising his hand to ring the doorbell.

'Mr Watson!' She managed to prevent his actually reaching the bell rope. 'Would you care to . . . to see the rose garden, while it is still so warm?' she suggested. 'My aunt and Miss Angell are planning changes for the autumn, so you will see it before the new scheme is brought in, and then you will be able to remark on the improvements.'

'Of course, Eveline. That sounds delightful,' he said obligingly, offering her his arm. 'And we may talk about your letter, which I had the honour of receiving yesterday.'

She was relieved that he had, apparently, understood her purpose so readily.

'Yes; I asked Mary to take the letters to you, because I did not know the addresses of your fellow directors.'

'I will be happy to forward the letters, of course. And we can discuss the idea you propose at the next full meeting of the board. Just now, though, you will understand that we are all much preoccupied.'

'Yes, I suppose you must be. But, Mr Watson, may I count on your support? For you will, I know, want to do what is right, and your opinion will carry more weight, I am sure, than anyone's.'

'We have already done a great deal more than most employers, you know. The houses we have built along the ridge above the station, now; they are a great thing: neat, sturdy houses, with everything well thought out. They will do more than anything else could to improve the lot of the working man.'

'I believe you; the houses are a splendid scheme. It is those who are left when accidents happen that I am thinking of.'

'You have a kind heart, my dear. And we will discuss it, in the fullness of time; but we must get everything right and tight for Monday, first. Shall we go back to the house? Your dear mama will be thinking I have forgotten my dinner engagement.'

Eveline did not feel entirely encouraged by this response, and she managed to sit next to Mr Watson at the dining table, in case there should be a chance to continue the conversation discreetly. During the first courses, he was giving his attention entirely to her mother, in an effort to reassure her that the railway journey of ten minutes which was to be part of Monday's celebrations would not be alarming in any way, despite the proposed speed of fifty miles per hour.

'Our drivers are trained, steady men,' he assured her, 'and the locomotive is new – built to the highest standards – while the carriage you will ride in has been fitted out delightfully, with plush seats, and everything most comfortable.'

Mrs Stanhope was sufficiently comforted to at last turn her thoughts to the poor little children, and whether they would be very much frightened by the noise and the size of the great machines.

'They are beside themselves with excitement, frankly,' said Bevis, 'and the only thing which could make their day even more thrilling than a ride on a railway train would be to see someone fall under its wheels and have his head sliced off, which is what Henry has told the girls is very likely to happen.'

Under cover of the reproaches that met this sally, Eveline turned to Mr Watson, to ask when the next meeting of the railway board might be held, so that her proposals could be discussed.

'In a fortnight's time, I believe; by then we shall be able to see how the enterprise is going; there will be problems to smooth out, no doubt.'

'A fortnight! but Mr Watson, what of those in immediate need? What of Elias's family?'

'My dear Eveline, we must make sure we have a viable railway before we start to deal with the people who depend upon it; otherwise it would be putting the cart before the horse, would it not, although carts and horses will be a bygone soon, eh?' and he laughed so heartily at his own witticism that Mrs Stanhope's attention was, unluckily, caught.

'Is there a joke? Have I missed a joke?' And then, as she remembered the events of yesterday, 'Now, Eveline, have you been bothering poor Mr Watson, when he has so much on his mind? You were writing to him; whatever was that about?'

'Really nothing, Mama; merely an idea I wished him to consider.' She hoped that might be the end of it; but it was not.

'An idea? And what do you know about railways, silly girl, that you have ideas that an important man like Mr Watson would be interested in?'

Mr Watson stepped in.

'Eveline was suggesting that the company should form a charity, or a benevolent fund, something of that nature, to ensure provision for unfortunate workers and their dependents,' he explained. 'It does her credit; she is a kind-hearted girl.'

'I do not think I am particularly kind-hearted,' said Eveline. 'It is less about kindness, and more about justice.'

'You are such a do-gooder, Evie,' said Louisa.

'You make that sound like a bad thing to be, Louisa.'

'Oh, not at all; but a little boring, perhaps.'

'My dears, do not be quarrelling in front of our guest,' said Mrs Stanhope. 'Eveline, I do not know what you are up to from one moment to the next! I am sorry, Mr Watson, that she bothered you.'

'Not at all; there is much in what she says. Eveline, do not concern yourself with Elias's widow. She will not starve; Tom has given her enough to support her for a good while.'

'Who is Tom?' asked Mrs Stanhope.

'Thomas Armitage,' said Eveline and Mr Watson simultaneously.

'Oh! Your young friend, who was so silent and stern.'

'He is a fine chief engineer, very fine; worked on the Manchester and Leeds, you know, and railways are the future, he thinks.'

'Did Mr Armitage arrange for the company to make provision for her, then?' asked Eveline.

'No, he does not have that power; he made her a present of his own money, I believe.'

'Indeed! I did not know. He . . . he did not sound sympathetic at all when we went to the office to speak to him.'

'Heavens, Eveline, what do you mean? What office?' asked Mrs Stanhope.

'The railway office. Charles and I walked there to discuss the matter. You need not worry, Mama, Charles escorted me home, all right and proper, and I was wearing a hat.'

'You dragged Charles Sandham to the railway offices,

and inveigled him into your ridiculous plans?' asked Louisa in disbelief. 'Whatever can you have been thinking of? How extraordinary you are, Evie.'

Mrs Stanhope was as outraged as Louisa at this revelation of Eveline's activities. When their guest had departed, she fairly rounded on her youngest daughter.

'I do not think I should let you attend the railway opening on Monday, Eveline. There is no knowing what you may say or do.'

Eveline found herself in the position of pleading to be allowed to do something that she had resolved a few weeks earlier to resist at all costs.

'I will behave beautifully, Mama, really. And Charles is expecting us all to be there; he will think it strange if I am not.'

'Well, that is very true. But you are not to be odd, Eveline. The Sandhams will not associate themselves with anyone they do not think is respectable.'

'I am not sure I wish to associate myself with them, either, so there we are equal.'

'I shall assume that you are just talking nonsense, now,' said Mrs Stanhope with dignity.

'Not really, Mama. Charles is pleasant enough; but the Sandhams are quite dull, are they not?'

'What has that to do with anything? They are the first family in the neighbourhood. Upon my word, you are very high and mighty, miss.'

'Eveline thinks herself too good to do as normal people do,' said Louisa. 'You keep grumbling about not having any freedom, Evie, but you will find that as a married woman you have a great deal more freedom than you do as a spinster.'

'Your sister is right; a happily married woman, with a rich husband, is the most fortunate of creatures,' said Mrs Stanhope. '*Daughter am I in my mother's house, but mistress in mine own* – have you never heard that saying, Evie? When I married your papa, I was very glad to have my own house, and be in charge of everything. You will feel the same, I am sure.'

'You speak as though I had but to decide to marry, and the deed would be done. No one has asked me to marry them.'

'No, and they will not, unless you start behaving in a more ladylike fashion,' said Louisa.

Eveline bit her tongue, in case arguing with Louisa should provoke her mother even more, and went to bed. She was brushing her hair (having assured Betsy that she was quite capable of doing this for herself) when her mother came into the room, and sat on the chair by the window.

'Do try not to be so cross about everything, Evie,' she said. Eveline turned from the mirror to look at her mother.

'You look weary, Mama,' she said. 'I am sorry if I am causing you trouble; I do not mean to, really.'

'I know, my love. But truly, if you do not make a good marriage, what is to become of you?'

'Not every woman marries. Look at Aunt George.'

Her mother sighed.

'George is fortunate. We all love her, but it is because your papa always insisted that she should have a home with us that she is here; and then she begged that Miss Angell should stay on, too, as a companion, so that is another expense. Your father had no idea how much things cost, you know.'

'But I do not have to marry. Some women do work to earn their living, you know, Mama.'

'Work! And do you not think that I work? I have run this household since the day I came into it as a bride of eighteen; and since your father died, I have done everything. I have managed all the income, which is nothing like what I thought it was, and dealt with the servants, and kept the household accounts, and made every decision on my own. And we cannot afford half as many servants as we need, so I am the housekeeper as well as the mistress, and constantly trying to make sure we put our best face forward, so that our neighbours do not realise how tight things are. That is work, young lady, you may be sure.'

'Oh, Mama, I am sorry. I had no idea. How stupid of me!' She knelt on the floor to embrace her mother. 'Why have you never said this before? I will help, I promise you. And we can live more simply, perhaps; I do not need new clothes – I have enough now to last for years. And,' the thought struck her, 'when the railway is here, we will not need a carriage! That will be a saving, for sure.'

'You do not see it at all, Evie. If we do not keep a carriage, and you wear old clothes, we will fall from the circle of the best people. Can you imagine what Augusta would say if we did not keep a carriage? Goodness knows, it is hard enough now to keep up appearances.'

'Then let us not try. It would be more dignified to live simply.'

'No, it would not; it would be giving up. Once you are married, things will be easier, and I did not want to frighten you, my dear, just to explain how things are.'

'I have been very selfish, Mama, I can see. Do not worry. Let me think, and I will find a way to make things easier for you.'

Her mother kissed the top of her head and stood up.

'Do not think too hard, my love. We will manage, if you will but conduct yourself as you should.' She sighed. 'And when you think, Evie, you know trouble is apt to follow.'

Chapter Fifteen

The Opening of the Railway

It seemed as though the entire town had turned out to witness the opening of the railway. Every friend, every acquaintance of the Stanhopes was present, and there were servants, shopkeepers, fishermen, publicans, clergymen, street-sweepers, all surging towards the newly constructed station building, exclaiming at the sight of the neat ticket office, and the comfortable waiting room, and the handsome house for the stationmaster. There was Mr Watson, and with him his fellow directors, and Sir William, and Charles, all in morning dress and top hats, with flowers in their buttonholes as though it were a wedding, and Lady Sandham resplendent in fur and a jewelled toque despite the heat of the day. The invited guests – the Stanhope family among them – were standing on the station platform, which smelt of fresh paint and tar.

'A photograph, dear ladies and gentlemen, if I may!'

It was a familiar voice; Eveline turned to see Mr Fry beaming from behind his camera tripod.

'Now, if you would stand in a line, perhaps, with the railway track behind you; perfect! And now, please, do your very best to keep still, just for a minute; thank you, you are most patient; my assistant will tell you when you may breathe again,' and there, beside Mr Fry, was Jennie, in a smart blue dress, smiling and holding a pocket watch to check the exposure time. Eveline stayed motionless as the seconds ticked by, but as soon as the photograph was taken she went to Jennie, and took both her hands.

'How are you? Is it delightful to be working in the studio? Are you very busy?'

'Yes, it is delightful – and we are very busy, Mr Fry, are we not?'

'Indeed, I am glad to say we are, and honoured to be part of this great event.' He bowed in the general direction of the party.

'Well, I am so happy to see you both,' said Eveline, 'and I miss the work very much.' She lowered her voice, since her family were only yards away. 'I hope I may be able to visit the studio soon, but I do not know exactly when.'

'Whenever you can do so, you will be most welcome,' said Mr Fry, and Jennie added, 'Oh do, Eveline, do! We have a new camera coming, with a universal lens; you would wish to see that, I am sure!'

Just then there was a general murmur of anticipation, and an announcement from Mr Watson that everyone must stand well back from the track, for midday was approaching, and the appointed hour for the arrival of the train. The crowd fell silent, and those nearest the platform edge stepped away, a little nervously, and everyone gazed expectantly along the shining rails. For a moment there was a perfect hush, and then a faint rhythmic noise could be heard.

'Is that it? Is that the train?' voices asked; and then suddenly there was the wild, unearthly shriek of the whistle, so that everyone jumped and gasped with the shock, and the noise grew louder, and a huge feathered plume of steam rose into the sky as the engine came round the curve of the track and into view. There was wild cheering, and applause, and the train's whistle blew again in triumph as it thundered towards them; and then it began to slow, and drew to a halt alongside the platform exactly in front of the scarlet ribbon, which stretched across the tracks. The locomotive was painted sky-blue, lined out in white, black and red, with a shining brass dome and copper-capped chimney, and a banner had been hung across the front, which read SUCCESS TO THE RAILWAY. Four carriages ran behind, each in polished teak, with brass door handles, and FIRST CLASS picked out in gold paint on the doors of the frontmost carriage.

Eveline could see the driver of the engine giving a triumphant salute from his cab, and the fireman smiling broadly; and beside them stood Thomas Armitage, looking serious and proud. He shook both men warmly by the hand, and then stepped down from the train and strode over to

Mr Watson, to exchange nods and a few words; he looked strained, she thought, as though he had not slept. Then Lady Sandham stepped forward with an air of conscious dignity, and declared that the railway, a bringer of prosperity and advancement, was officially open, and cut the ribbon with a pair of gilt scissors handed to her with a flourish by a very gratified-looking Mr Watson.

Once the cheering had died away, it was announced that the train would depart for Newport in fifteen minutes' time, and that the first return ride was free for as many as could be accommodated. The first class carriage was reserved for the invited guests, and Mr Watson ushered Sir William and Lady Sandham into a compartment, and then, to Mrs Stanhope's immense satisfaction, he turned to her and invited her to join them.

'And Miss Georgiana, and Miss Angell, of course,' he said, courteously, handing them up into the carriage, and then turning. 'Charles? Eveline? Then that will be all the eight seats filled here. Louisa and Beatrice will want to be with their husbands and children, of course; do take the next compartment, my dears,' he called, and the others duly climbed aboard, with much squealing and excitement from the children, and only a slight difficulty in Louisa's wide crinoline needing to be pushed physically through the doorway by Bevis. The red plush seats, the antimacassars, the neat racks above the seats, were all the subject of much admiration, in which Mr Watson basked with satisfaction. He had had a hand in designing the interiors himself, it seemed; had chosen the very fabric for the seats, and had specified the leather trims to the armrests. Eveline, by the window, found herself rather charmed by the whole thing; and she was high up, far above the ground, so that she could see over the heads of the crowds still milling on the platform. People were boarding the other carriages, and calling to their friends, and waving to those who were watching, and Eveline saw Mr Fry and Jennie hauling the camera between them into the guard's van at the end. At last there was a shout of 'All aboard!' and a series of slamming doors, a whistle blew, and then the train gave a lurch, and moved.

Eveline never forgot that journey. The train began to roll forward, and then to move faster, as it left the station, and almost as soon as it had picked up speed, and rounded the curve of the line, they plunged into the darkness of a tunnel, and emerged in a flash into the sunlight again. The buildings fell away, and the view opened before her, and the sensation was so exhilarating that she felt as though she were flying over the fields and woods. She could see the river shining, looking so wide from up here, and there was a slender bridge across the line – the bridge built to let the fishermen have easy access to the river, she supposed. The trees blurred past her vision so that it took her breath away, and the noise of the wheels as they drummed out their beat on the rails, and vibrated through her, was intoxicating, and she laughed in sheer delight.

'You are enjoying this, Eveline?' said Charles, from the seat opposite her. 'I have travelled by train a good deal, of course, and I always like it.'

'It is wonderful – I have never travelled so fast – it is such a sensation!' She felt something like guilt, as she added, 'Of course, I think it is very terrible that the river path has gone, and so many trees felled, and it will never be so peaceful again.'

'Indeed; yet progress, you know, has to happen, I suppose,' he said vaguely.

She glanced towards Sir William, in the far corner of the carriage. His outrage concerning his own land seemed forgotten, as he nodded graciously at Mr Watson's description of how the tunnel had been made, through very unstable clay soil, and how it had required wooden shuttering to support the earth while the brickwork was laid.

'The tunnel, now, reduced interference with your own property, sir, I am glad to say,' added Mr Watson.

'Will your pheasants return, Sir William?' asked Eveline. 'You were worried about them, I think.'

'Oh, I dare say they may,' said Sir William comfortably. 'Shockingly stupid birds, pheasants; they will soon get used to a train whistle, I suppose,' and Eveline smiled a little to herself as she recalled Mr Armitage's view on Sir William's pragmatism.

Too soon, it seemed, they saw church spires, and houses, and the train was slowing to a shuddering halt.

'Well!' said Mrs Stanhope. 'We are all alive; I never thought I should survive such a thing, we went so fast! And my heart is pounding away.'

'You were immensely brave,' said Mr Watson, smiling, 'and I hope you will find it a little less alarming in the future.'

On the platform, they were reunited with their fellow passengers. The children were ecstatic; Daisy had screamed when they went into the tunnel, but only with excitement, she maintained, and Henry had leant out of the window and his hat had nearly blown away, and he had a huge black smut on his face, which he wore as a badge of honour. Bevis and Arthur were, despite themselves, admiring the locomotive, and the driver was explaining to them the advantage of coupled wheels over single driving wheels; while Louisa and Beatrice both wanted to know what Charles had thought of the journey, since he had the experience of having travelled on other railways, and was therefore an expert.

'The Great Western Railway, now,' he said, 'there is a fine railway – from Paddington, all the way to the West Country, it runs. Magnificent. Although I myself got off at Maidenhead for a spot of fishing. I think we are heading for that marquee, now. May I escort you?' And he offered Louisa and Beatrice an arm each, which they accepted with alacrity, and everyone made their way towards luncheon. The tables had been decorated with geraniums, and lilies, and ferns, and huge pyramids of apples; a string band played; and a feast of cold chicken and lemon cream was served, while outside a hog roast was under way. Eveline, seated next to her aunt, caught sight of Mr Armitage, who was in earnest conversation with the directors, and thought that he looked less anxious than before. There was a good deal of back-patting between the men.

'I think the day has been a success, this far, Aunt George,' she said. 'Did you enjoy the journey? I felt I should not, that I ought not, perhaps, and yet it was thrilling, beyond anything I had imagined.'

Her aunt agreed. 'Delightful. And they have thought of everything, you know; there's a waiting room for ladies on each station, with a water closet, which one pays for with a penny piece put into some ingenious mechanism, which opens the door! Remarkable; and in itself, a helpful thing for women, since one must be practical about such things.'

Many people had dispersed after the luncheon to take advantage of the journey to visit friends and family in Newport, and there was to be a further return trip later in the day, so there were fewer passengers waiting for the three o'clock journey back to their own little town than had travelled earlier. Charles, on account of his superior experience as a traveller, had assumed a leading role, which the others seemed happy to accord him.

'Now, shall we travel all together?' he said. 'Louisa, Beatrice, allow me,' and he handed them into the carriage, with the children scrambling after, and Bevis and Arthur following them. Charles was the last in, and he stood on the step, and turned to her.

'The children will squash in,' he said, 'come, Eveline, in here,' and he held out his hand to grasp hers; but something in his easy assumption that she would take it made her stand back, and say, 'You will be too crowded, with me; I shall travel in the next compartment,' and she walked quickly along the train, and stepped up through the next open door. She had gone beyond the first class carriage, now, and the compartment she entered was plainer, and simpler, with seats upholstered in a brown cloth, though still neat and pleasant. She had it to herself, and she sat by the window, and pushed down the sliding glass pane so that she might feel the breeze in her face, and glory in the rushing air. Then, just as the whistle blew, and the guard shouted, and the train began to move, Thomas Armitage leapt up into the carriage, and slammed the door shut behind him.

He fell into the seat opposite hers and grinned at her.

'Well, thank God, we seem to have got through just as planned!' He looked suddenly carefree, and the frowns and disdain of their last meeting seemed all forgotten. 'We had a crisis last week, you know, when one of the new carriages was being hauled up by horse, and then ran back down the gradient and very nearly smashed into the station house. Still, Ned and I managed to thrust a sleeper under the wheels just in time; but it was a very near thing! And today – I don't mind telling you, I have not slept for days now, there has been so much to do; but here we are, at last, and the line is open!' He seemed to recollect himself, and said, 'Miss Stanhope, forgive me. I should have asked if you have enjoyed the day. I know you have been distressed about the destruction of the woodland; I hope you managed to find some pleasure in the ride, nonetheless?'

'A great deal, believe me,' she assured him. 'I did not know how delightful it would be to travel so fast, with the sensation of simply flying through the countryside! And there is something so very splendid about the train itself, and its power and speed.'

'Is it not wonderful?' he said, eagerly. 'I knew you would think so – at least, I hoped – there is a freedom, you know, in being able to travel, and it will open the world up for so many people, who would otherwise never stray far from their own streets.'

'Yes, indeed. I feel that I was wrong to complain to you as bitterly as I did, about the loss of the woods. You must have thought me very narrow in my outlook; very provincial.'

'No,' he said earnestly, leaning forward, 'no, I think you a person of strong views, and admirable views at that. There is a loss, always, when change comes. I dare say I was not very sympathetic; you will forgive me, I hope.'

'Of course,' she said. There was a pause. Then, 'But, Mr Armitage, did you manage to have any luncheon?' she asked. 'You looked so busy and preoccupied; did you eat anything at all?'

He sat back and laughed. 'No, you are right, I did not eat a thing. But I managed to take this,' and he produced an apple from his pocket, and bit into it.

'There will be some splendid photographs of the day, I think,' she said. 'I was so pleased to see Mr Fry, and Jennie, there. Will the pictures be displayed, so we can all admire them?'

'Yes, certainly they will. And you, Miss Stanhope – Jennie told me that you were a photographer yourself, and a skilled one, she says.'

'She is too kind. But yes, I was learning. I liked it so much – it is an art and a science, you know, and there is so much one can do with the medium. I had barely begun, and there is so much to learn. I found it enthralling.'

'Why have you stopped, then? You sound truly passionate about this. You should pursue it.'

'I cannot; at least not just now. I am forbidden.'

'How is that?'

'Mama thinks it unsuitable, along with a great many other things. I must not swim, or walk alone. I am confined to the house, really, unless I am with someone respectable. I am afraid that my walk through town with you was the last straw.'

'Ah. I take it that I am not respectable?' He looked amused.

'No, I fear you are not.'

'And you – what, are you then a prisoner in your own home?'

'A prisoner! No, of course not. It is just that I have a duty to poor Mama.'

'Not to yourself, then, Miss Stanhope? Do we not all have a duty to live, to think, to create, as best we can?' There was silence between them; he seemed to be searching in her face for the answer to his question, but she hardly knew how to reply. He raised an eyebrow, and she felt herself flush a little under his gaze.

At last he leant back in his seat, finished the apple, and threw the core accurately out of the window. 'Will that grow into a tree, one day, do you think? Look, we are nearly back.'

They plunged once more into the tunnel, and then the train was slowing, and the station was in sight, with the bunting and laurels of the morning still decorating the fences alongside.

'You always call me *Miss Stanhope*, in such a formal way,' she said suddenly. 'You called me Eveline, once or twice. I preferred that.'

'Did I? How very forward of me. Well then, thank you. Eveline it shall be. And Thomas, please.' The train shuddered to a halt, and he opened the door and sprang out, and then, as if it were the most natural thing in the world, he reached up to take her by the waist, and swing her down onto the platform, and for a long moment they stood facing each other, with the smoke and steam from the engine swirling around them in a cloud, until she disengaged herself, and took a step away from him.

'Goodbye, Thomas,' she said, a little breathlessly. 'It has been a . . . a memorable day. I wish you every success – you, and the railway, of course.' She paused, and added casually, 'Now that the railway is finished here, you will be leaving us, I imagine?'

'Yes, but not quite yet. I shall be here for another couple of months, to iron out any difficulties with the line, and to oversee the construction of some sheds to house the rolling stock.'

'A couple of months! Then we may meet again.'

'Of course we will meet again – that is, you will be travelling back and forth on the railway constantly, I hope,' he said, smiling. 'You will not resist its charms, now, surely?'

She laughed. 'No, indeed. I do not think I can resist.'

'Goodbye, then, Eveline. Until your next railway journey.'

Chapter Sixteen

Household Economy

Fortunately for Eveline, Mrs Stanhope and her party had assumed that she had been travelling with the young people, and they in turn had assumed her to be with her mother; and in the general throng, it was not noticed that she had descended from quite another carriage.

The talk was all of the journey, and how extraordinary it had been to travel so quickly.

'Although it is very dirty, I think,' said Louisa. 'My new parasol is covered in black soot. And Eveline, you have a smut on your cheek, and your hair is all blown about,' but even Louisa was too cheerful, in the glow of the day, to pursue the subject of Eveline's appearance for long.

'Dear Mr Watson was so attentive!' said Mrs Stanhope. 'He made us so welcome; we felt quite as important as the Sandhams, and even they were unusually gracious to us. Augusta likes to be grand, and she did her little speech pretty well. Sir William would have her do it, she said, instead of him, for he does not care for the trouble of learning what he is to say. In any case, Augusta says he only thinks of his yacht, now, and says railways will be for the common herd; although if the dear queen travels by the railway I am sure I do not see why the rest of us should not.'

'His yacht, now,' said Bevis, 'Sandham mentioned that to me. Yachting is a fine sport, he says, and he means to invite us all for a day on Sir William's boat.'

'A day at sea! Well, I hope very much he does not expect me to go,' said Mrs Stanhope. 'I have been quite brave enough today, and have had enough dangerous adventures to last me, I think. I shall not be going anywhere near a yacht.'

'But I should very much like to,' said Louisa hastily, 'so if there is an invitation, do not leave me out. It seems to me you are all having a great deal more excitement here these days, what with the railway, and Charles becoming such a friend, and now yachting. We do not lead half such interesting lives, Bevis, do we?'

Eveline wondered how Bevis would answer, given the putative source of her sister's tears on that recent evening, for she thought that perhaps his own life was more exciting than he was willing to own; but he did not look abashed, and merely said that for his part he was content with his sport and his horses, but if there was to be yachting he was game for anything of that sort. Bevis and Louisa were to leave on the morrow, and after such an eventful evening everyone declared themselves ready to retire early; and so Eveline, not tired at all but very glad to escape and enjoy some solitude, was able at last to think seriously about her mother's disclosure of the difficulties they were facing. How could she not have realised that money was short? Mama looking tired and strained; Mrs Groves struggling in the kitchen; and all the while they were entertaining, and setting out lavish dinners for their friends and neighbours, and keeping a carriage, and ordering new dresses and hats as though there were no tomorrow. She would start, she thought, the very next day, by looking at the household accounts, and seeing where the money was going; and then, she would arrange a council of war.

That was decided, and she lay down to sleep, but sleep would not come. The railway journey was still assailing her senses; the noise, the locomotive, the fields rushing by; and then the journey back, with Thomas; the way he had lifted her so naturally down from the high railway carriage, the strong grasp of his hands around her waist; and then his challenge: *are you then a prisoner in your own home?* What an absurd idea – that her mother, however strict and unreasonable she could be, would actually keep her a prisoner. And yet, she thought, I am not free. Is it just respecting Mama's wishes that keeps me from the things I long to do? Or fear that I shall be an outcast from society, as Mama had threatened, if I do not conform? Or something else; cowardice, perhaps?

She got up and moved to the window. There were no stars to be seen, and only a faint glow from a moon half-hidden by the cloudy night. I would like to go out, now, and just walk about the garden, she thought; to breathe the night air, and feel the grass beneath my feet. Suddenly, it seemed imperative that she did so, now. She put an old cloak round her shoulders and fastened it so that it covered her white cotton nightgown and opened her bedroom door with the utmost caution. She padded down the wide stairs, and then hesitated, for the front door was huge, and heavy, and bolted. It seemed unlikely that she would be able to draw back the bolts and open it with no noise, and moreover her mother's room overlooked the front of the house, and there was a chance she might be seen. The drawing-room French doors, then, would be better, for they opened to the side of the house, and the key was left always in the lock. Absurd to think she was a prisoner! Thomas was quite wrong: she had merely to walk out, and there was no one at all to stop her. She stepped out onto the terrace, and down the steps to the lawn. The grass was cool and damp under her bare feet, and the white flowers that Miss Angell had so lovingly planted were pale as ghosts. Clouds scudded across the moon, and a faint breeze rustled the leaves of the plane tree. There was a hedgehog making its way across the lawn. She crossed to the archway, which led to the walled rose garden, and went to the velvety crimson roses, which were almost black in the faint light, and buried her face in the blooms to inhale their rich delicious scent. From the distance came the sound of the sea.

In the morning she might have thought that she had dreamt that night walk, had it not been for the hem of her cloak's still being soaked with dew. With no Jennie, now, to whisk away her clothes and return them magically clean and dry and pressed, she was at a slight loss to know what to do with it. In the end she hung it behind her bedroom door to dry and brushed away the leaves and grass that clung to it into the fireplace. It did not seem likely, however, that anyone would notice; her mother seemed increasingly distracted these days.

After the departure of Louisa and Bevis, and many hugs for the children, and promises of future railway rides, Eveline asked her mother for the household account books, and after overcoming a little resistance on her mother's part, she took them into her father's study to try to understand them. She emerged several times during the morning to seek clarification from her mother of a list of figures, or copies of bills, or letters from the bank. With almost no experience of understanding such things, it was a struggle; but she persevered, and gradually began to make sense of how the income from her father's investments was formed, and how much the servants' wages, and the running of the household, all took. She drew up a chart, with the figures in neat columns, and a list of queries. She double-checked all her sums, and wrote her concerns and ideas down for future reference. It was the end of the day before she emerged, with her head full of figures and her eyes tired from reading numbers.

Dinner that evening was a quiet affair, with only Eveline, Mrs Stanhope, Aunt George, and Miss Angell, to discuss the still-present excitement of the previous day and lament the departure of Louisa and her family. Once the dishes were cleared, and they were all in the drawing room, Eveline spoke.

'Mama, I think we need to discuss some serious matters. We are living above our income – not hugely, but if we continue to do so we will find ourselves in trouble. I have some questions, and some suggestions.'

'Eveline!' said Mrs Stanhope, 'this is not something we should discuss with George and Maria; they should not be troubled with such things. And I am very sure you should not be troubled, either; a young girl has more important things to think about and should not be burdened with cares of this sort. I shall find a way to manage, I am sure.'

'No, Mama, we are all involved. We are all grown women, and strong, and clever, and we all share this house, and together we should be responsible for it. Why should it fall upon your shoulders alone?'

'I am the mistress of the house, Eveline, and your father would have wanted me to maintain the household just as he liked it, with elegance and generosity. I have let you look at the accounts, because you are old enough, I suppose, and one day you will need to run a household of your own; but I do not want you to start having absurd ideas, and upsetting your aunt, and so forth.'

'But Eveline is right, Adelaide,' said Aunt George. 'Of course you are the mistress of the house, but you should not be trying to manage things without letting us help.'

'You do help, George,' said Mrs Stanhope, 'for if it were not for you and Maria, I should not have such a delightful garden, nor such good company.'

Miss Angell had been looking stricken.

'My dears,' she said at last, 'I am a burden to you. I am

not family, and I live here because you have been so very kind to me; but I must not continue to do so. I can find another position, you know; I am not too old, yet.'

'Don't be ridiculous,' said Aunt George. 'You are my family, Angell. If you are to leave, I will be leaving with you.'

'Neither of you will be leaving,' said Mrs Stanhope. 'That is quite out of the question. You belong here.'

'Indeed, Aunt, there is no need for anyone to leave,' said Eveline earnestly. 'If you will but listen to what I have been thinking of, you will see that a very little economy will turn things about.'

Mrs Stanhope sighed.

'Very well, Eveline. Let us hear what you have to say. But I warn you, I shall not agree to anything that means Augusta Sandham may condescend to me any more than she already does.'

So Eveline began to outline her findings. The investments were steady, but had not kept pace altogether with an increase in prices. Their way of life was not wildly extravagant, but it had gradually grown a little more grand over the past years: new furnishings for the dining room, keeping up a carriage, giving suppers, a thousand little luxuries, had all added up.

'I have just a few questions, Mama,' said Eveline. 'Firstly, we seem to have very large bills from the dressmaker; can we really have had so many clothes?'

'One must dress elegantly,' said her mother. 'It is a little weakness of mine, I own: I like to have pretty things to wear. But I can stop, certainly. At my time of life, I should not be so vain, I dare say.'

'You have every reason to be vain, Mama,' said Eveline. 'But I do not think all these bills are for your clothes, or for mine. Here, you see, a rose-pink satin gown, with matching shoes, and this one for a parasol, with a fan, and a purse, and half-boots; I think you may have been paying Beatrice's bills by mistake. She will be mortified when she discovers it.'

'Oh, do not be troubling poor Beatrice,' said Mrs Stanhope hastily, 'she has enough concerns without dressmakers' bills. I like to treat my daughters a little, and why should I not? I seem to remember you had several pretty new dresses not long ago, Evie. I did not hear you complain about those.'

'Oh, of course, and you were so kind; but, Mama, it is all so expensive, and it is not just one bill. See, they go back over the last two years, and there is all sorts of costly stuff – walking costumes, furs, French lace, velvet capes. Are they all Beatrice's?'

'Well, mostly,' said Mrs Stanhope, 'and perhaps a few little things for Louisa, too, as she would feel it so unfair if she knew I was treating Beatrice and not her.'

'But, Mama, we are speaking of hundreds of pounds! And both Beatrice and Louisa have money to spend on clothes.'

'I know, my love, but there again, Arthur gets a little cross with poor Beatrice if she but wants a new frock once in a while, which is very unkind, and she is so pretty, you know, it is not right that she should not be dressed to show off her looks.'

'Arthur unkind! I can hardly believe that.' A thought struck her. 'Is Arthur, perhaps, not as rich as we have thought? I do not know anything about their income.'

'No, and it would be very vulgar to ask. But she does not like him to know of her new clothes, always, that is all.'

'Does he not notice when she has new clothes?'

'No, he does not, and that is another thing against him,' said her mother.

'Adelaide, it does seem that you must stop spending so much on your married daughters,' said Aunt George. 'For their own sake, perhaps, as well as yours.'

Mrs Stanhope said nothing, but she looked mulish.

'Then there are other things we might do to save money,' said Eveline, seeing that it would be profitless to pursue the last topic for now. 'We have managed without Jennie for a while now; I think we are all able to dress ourselves and do our own hair. No lady's maid would be a handsome saving.'

'And we are all to look like perfect frights, I suppose,' said her mother.

'Maria and I have never needed a maid,' said Aunt George. 'We do not care so much. As long as we have our gardening clothes on, you know, we are happy.'

'That is all very well for you, but how am I to look at all presentable?' demanded Mrs Stanhope. 'And how is Eveline to get a husband if she looks like a ragamuffin?'

'Does Eveline want a husband?' enquired Aunt George. 'Not every woman does, you know.'

'I am not perfectly sure, yet,' said Eveline. 'I do not want a husband who only cares for how I look, that is certain. But Mama, I can curl your hair; I have watched Jennie do it many a time. My own hair is untameable, you know; Louisa is always saying there is no point in doing anything with it. And we can dress ourselves. We are not children. Shall we try, for a few months, to manage? If it is impossible,' she said coaxingly, 'then we will find a maid, after all.'

'Well, we can try,' said Mrs Stanhope doubtfully, 'but I will look shockingly plain, I know.'

'Then there is food, and wine,' said Eveline. 'We save on fruit, of course, because Aunt George and Miss Angell planted those currant bushes and raspberry canes a few years ago, and now we have those all summer long, and preserves for the winter. But we seem to use dozens of eggs, and the greengrocer's bill is still surprisingly large.'

'Chickens,' said Miss Angell, suddenly. 'Chickens, and a vegetable garden.'

'Yes,' said George, 'certainly the vegetables, Maria – but chickens? We would have to learn to raise them. How are we to do that?'

'My father was a farmer – a gentleman farmer,' said Miss Angell. 'I know a good deal about poultry. If we can but get a sturdy chicken house to keep out the foxes, then we may have as many eggs as we can eat. They will live on the scraps from the kitchen, and I will tend them; yes, and wring their necks when they are grown too old to lay.'

The others regarded her with some awe.

'Then chickens it is,' said Eveline, busy making notes. 'And we seem to have spent a lot on brandy, and Madeira, and port. Mostly for other people, I assume, when we entertain.'

'Your papa would not have wanted me to keep a parsimonious table,' said Mrs Stanhope piteously.

'I only recall Papa drinking claret,' said Eveline.

'Yes; he always said claret was not so much a wine as a medicine,' said her mother. 'He ordered dozens of cases at a time; he said he would never run short, if he could help it.'

'Did he? Then is there any left?' asked Eveline.

'Oh, the cellar is full of it,' said her mother. 'And a few cases of champagne, I think, but mostly claret. I could not bring myself to broach it, you know; it was so particularly his favourite.'

'I am sure Papa would prefer us to have the benefit of it,' said Eveline firmly. 'We will drink claret, from now on, and champagne now and then. Our guests will be very happy with that, and I am sure we will be too.'

'Mr Watson likes brandy,' said her mother.

'He likes claret too, I am sure.'

'And Bevis likes port. All the gentlemen like port.'

'Perhaps Bevis would give us a case of port next Christmas, then,' said Eveline. 'I shall suggest it to him. Now, the last thing, which is a great expense, is the carriage. John Coachman is elderly, and he has said many a time that he will be glad to go to live with his married daughter. The horses cost a great deal to stable and to feed. And the carriage itself is so old and creaky that I am sure it will fall to bits soon. We must do without a carriage.'

'Impossible!' said her mother. 'Are we to be marooned here, and never go anywhere?'

'We are within walking distance of all the shops that we need, and of our neighbours, and of the church.'

'But not of the dressmaker, or the smarter shops in Newport.'

'We have the railway now. We can be in Newport in less time than it takes John to get the poor horses into their harness.

If we wish, we can be in London, or in Leeds, I suppose.'

'The railway! Well, but to travel with all sorts of people, instead of in our own private vehicle. I can only imagine what the Sandhams would say if we did not have our carriage.'

'I have been thinking, Mama,' said Eveline, 'that if you were to hint to Lady Sandham that using the railway is the very latest thing to do, and that it is considered a little *old-fashioned* to keep a carriage when we have the good fortune to live so close to the railway line, she might see things differently.'

'That is true,' said George. 'Augusta Sandham is always anxious to be in the forefront of fashion, you know, Adelaide; she would gnash her teeth to think she was behind the times, and that we were much more *à la mode*.'

'Well,' said Mrs Stanhope, 'that is a thought, indeed. Augusta can never bear to be outdone, and she loves to be the first to have anything new. How I shall laugh when I mention that we have decided to live in such a modern way! She will turn green with envy, you may be sure, and she will be giving up her own carriage before the year is out, and pretending that she thought of it first.'

Chapter Seventeen

A Gift

'There is a parcel arrived for you, Evie,' called Mrs Stanhope. 'A great wooden crate, indeed; it must be a mistake, I think, unless you have been ordering brandy after all, and have not told me.'

Eveline emerged from the basement stairs, a little flushed, and wearing an apron tied over her dress. Her mother stared at her.

'I have just been helping Mrs Groves,' explained Eveline. 'She and Mary have so much to do, you know, Mama, and we cannot afford a new kitchen maid, so I am helping her for an hour or two each morning.'

'And what do you know of cooking, pray? I think you must be more hindrance than help to poor Groves, and in any case, have we come to this, that my daughter is working below stairs?' Mrs Stanhope looked genuinely distressed.

'Mama,' said Eveline gently, 'you are working as a housekeeper for us all; you said so yourself, I recall. You have been taking care of so much. I am just being practical, and I really do not mind. In fact, I am learning a good deal, and one never knows when it might be useful to have such skills.'

'I sincerely hope no one ever learns of this,' said her mother tragically. 'So what is in this box, miss? Some newfangled kitchen implement, in case you do actually go into service?'

'I have no idea at all,' said Eveline. 'I have not ordered anything.' She walked round the crate, which stood squarely in the entrance hall. 'But you are right, Mama, it is addressed to me. And look, there is a letter tied to the top.' She slid the letter from the string that bound it to the rough wooden crate, and opened it.

My dear Miss Stanhope,
I hope most earnestly that you will not regard it an impertinence on my part to offer you this small token of my esteem. When we had the pleasure of working together, I observed you to have a most particular talent for the art we both admire so much. I have recently taken delivery of a new camera, and I no longer have the space for this model in my modest premises. You would, therefore, be doing me a great service if you would accept it as a gift. If

*it enables you to continue your interest in photography, I
shall consider myself honoured to have played even a small
part in that process.*

Believe me your friend always,
Theodore Fry

Eveline felt tears spring to her eyes.

'It is a camera, Mama.' She read the letter out loud to her
mother. 'Dear Mr Fry! How very kind, how thoughtful! I am
sure he could have sold it, and yet he makes me a gift of it,
so generously.'

'That is all very well, Evie,' said her mother, 'but where are
we to put it? I am sure there is no room for it in any of the
reception rooms, be it ever so decorative.'

'Oh, no, it is not a decorative object, but a working
camera,' said Eveline. She had wrenched the lid from the crate
and was peering in. 'Don't worry, Mama. I shall not unpack
it here. The potting shed that Barnabas used to use, before
Aunt George had the new one built; that is where I shall put
it. There is a half-glazed roof, which should give me some
interesting lighting effects, I think. I am not sure how I shall
manage for a darkroom – the old ice house perhaps. Oh, bless
you, dear Professor! What a wonderful thing.'

'Evie, you are surely not planning actually to use this
thing?' asked her mother, in some alarm.

'Of course I shall use it; this is a good camera, and although
I should be very interested to try the new universal lens, still
I like the chance to alter the focus and experiment with the
effects one may obtain with this one. Jennie and I once took

some portraits that were deliberately out of focus, and we liked the softness of the impression.'

'You are becoming as eccentric as your aunt,' said Mrs Stanhope, 'and without the excuse of age. She and Miss Angell are even now measuring up a plot for chickens, and interrogating Barnabas about growing salads. I do not know where it will end.'

'It will end with our having delicious food to eat, and not having to worry about money quite so much,' said Eveline. 'And who knows, Mama, I may become sufficiently skilled at photography to earn a living by it, and then I will no longer be a drain on the family finances.'

'Earn a living by it! We are not so sunk into penury as to require that,' said Mrs Stanhope firmly. 'And if you will concentrate on being attentive to Charles Sandham, Evie, all our problems will cease, for I am sure he likes you, and he does not show signs of going back to London, so that is surely a sign of his interest.'

'He likes being in the country for the summer months, I expect, riding, and sailing, and so on. I do not think it is I who keep him here.'

'Well, we shall see; but I am sure you could charm him if you would, Evie.'

Eveline had a chance to exert her charms over Charles that very afternoon. Once she had written a letter of grateful thanks to Mr Fry, she had spent the rest of her morning clearing cobwebs and dust from the old potting shed, and moving her new camera in. Over luncheon, Aunt George and Miss Angell talked of nothing but chickens, George having once admired some Dorking fowl at a show, while Miss Angell – enjoying her unaccustomed role as the expert – pressed for Lincolnshire Buffs as the poultry of choice.

'I should like to see your plans for the chicken run,' said Eveline. 'Will you show me where you will keep them? I know nothing of poultry-keeping and would be glad to learn.'

'As long as they are hidden from sight, I do not care,' said Mrs Stanhope. 'I do not want visitors to see them.'

'They will be quite tucked away,' Aunt George assured her. 'Even you will hardly know they are there.'

Eveline was intrigued to know where the chickens were to live, and her aunt and Miss Angell led her to the walled garden.

'I know you have grand new designs for the roses,' said Eveline, 'you would not let the hens run in here, would you?'

'We have changed our plans,' said her aunt. 'This will not be a rose garden; we will have the henhouse over in this corner, and we will take all the roses out of the beds. They will have plenty of ground to scratch at, and the walls will keep them hidden from view; we knew your mama would want that.'

'But your roses!' said Eveline. 'You had such plans; you were to send for new varieties, and create such lovely vistas. Surely you will be sad to give that up?'

'Oh, we will still have the mixed borders along the lawns, with space for new varieties if we wish,' said her aunt, 'and we will keep the climbing roses around the walls; they need not go. And chickens! It is a new adventure, and Maria knows a good deal about keeping poultry, it seems, though none of us had the least idea.' She looked admiringly at her friend, who blushed and looked extremely pleased.

'Then I think it will be a wonderful scheme,' said Eveline, smiling.

'Thank you, my dear; and we are most grateful to you, for telling us how things are. Poor Adelaide! We have been both blind and selfish; but we will be able to help now.'

'No more blind or selfish than I, Aunt,' said Eveline. 'But we will make a little world of industry, far more noble than just living for pleasure, will we not?'

'We will. And, Eveline, I think you have a visitor.'

Eveline turned to see Charles Sandham enter the walled garden.

'Forgive me, ladies!' he called. 'Mrs Stanhope was kind enough to tell me I might find you here; she said I did not need to stand upon ceremony.' He bowed elegantly to them all. 'Perhaps we might walk a little, Miss Stanhope, if you are not too busy?'

'Oh, certainly,' said Eveline, 'although I have a good deal to do. Still, I could spare half an hour. I have a camera,' she explained, 'newly delivered, and I am anxious to try it out.'

'A camera of your own! You are a most surprising lady, Eveline.' He bowed to Aunt George and Miss Angell, and offered Eveline his arm.

'Who, and what, will you photograph?' he asked, as they walked out of the walled garden and beneath the trees. 'Your pretty maid, Jennie, perhaps?'

'Jennie is a photographer herself, now. She is working for the Professor of Photography as his assistant.'

'I see. And now you have bought yourself a camera!'

'No, it was a gift. A gift from a kind friend.'

'I wish I had thought of it myself. I should have liked to give you such an inspired present. The man who did think of it is a true gallant.'

'Yes, he is,' said Eveline.

'I shall challenge him to a duel.'

Eveline laughed. 'You had better not. It was Mr Fry. He would not care to fight you, I think.'

'That old rogue! What does he mean by giving you gifts?'

'It is a camera he no longer needs, that is all.'

'Well, I will not call him out, this time. But he had better be careful. If I find him sending you flowers, I shall certainly fight him.'

'I am very sure he will not send me flowers. And now, if you will forgive me, I am impatient to see how my camera will work in its new home.'

'Of course; I see I must not detain you. But I did come with a purpose, Eveline. My uncle is very proud of his new yacht, and I have persuaded him to let me bring a party of friends aboard to admire it. I came to ask if you would be among the party.'

'You are most kind, but I do not think I am suited to yachting, Charles. I have watched them often enough from the shore, and it does not look like the sort of thing I should enjoy, at all.'

'We would not be going out on the high seas, merely a very short sail along the coast, to the next bay, and back; an hour or two altogether, that is all, and then you will be ashore again, and we will have a picnic luncheon, perhaps.'

Eveline cast about for a way to refuse without giving offence.

'I do not think Mama would care for my going aboard a yacht,' she said at last. 'She is very strict, you know, about such things.'

'Oh, I have already asked Mrs Stanhope,' he said airily, 'and she is very happy for you to go, Eveline; she would not come herself, but she assured me she would be delighted if you would agree to do so.'

Eveline gave in, reluctantly.

'Then of course, I shall,' she said.

'Excellent! You will like it, I know, once you are aboard. I hope to arrange it for next week, if the weather is kind to us. Will your sisters like to be of the party, as well, do you think?'

'Louisa is gone back home now, but Beatrice may like to; I do not know.'

'I shall ask her, then. I may call on her, perhaps, before I walk home. You will both find it delightful, I am sure. It is marvellous to be out on the ocean; we Englishmen have salt water in our veins, I do believe.'

'Have you done a great deal of sailing, then?'

'A little, in Italy; but I should like to do more, and my uncle is quite mad for it, you know.'

'You are not planning to return to London, then, any time soon?' asked Eveline, vaguely imagining business interests, or property, which must be requiring attention.

'No; there is nothing to draw me to London, and a great deal to keep me here,' he said, with another gallant bow, and took his leave.

Eveline walked back to the rose garden, where the two ladies were now measuring plots and writing busily in notebooks. Her aunt looked up at her approach.

'That young man likes you, Eveline,' she said. 'I hope you are not giving him encouragement if you do not feel the same.'

'Really, Aunt. I am in trouble with Mama if I do not flirt, and in trouble with you if I do.'

'Be serious, Evie. He looks at you in a very decided way.'

'He looks at most young women in a very decided way, Aunt.'

'Well, I do not know about that. You will make your own mind up, I dare say; you always have.'

'You have taught me to do so.' She smiled, and embraced her aunt and then her old governess. 'Thank you for all you are doing; I am sure you must feel the loss of your scheme for the new rose garden very much. But I am sure Mama already looks less careworn, despite her protests.'

Eveline spent a happy afternoon with her new camera. A trip to the attic yielded a couple of chairs, and some dark velvet curtains, and an unexpected treasure in the form of a chest of old clothes, which she thought might form accessories when she took portraits: lengths of muslin; shawls (a little moth-eaten) in fine wool, embroidered with flowers and birds; a top hat with a veil attached; a bunch of ostrich plumes. By the end of the day, she had rigged a curtain across the wall of the old potting shed as a backcloth, and devised a way of hanging another so that she could adjust the amount of light that entered the little cabin. All she needed, now, were subjects.

* * *

Eveline now spent the first part of every morning in the kitchen. Mrs Groves and Mary had accepted her presence initially as no more than the inconvenient and eccentric whim of an employer, but now they instructed her, and reprimanded her, and laughed with her, as though she were the newest servant with everything to learn. 'Which I am,' she reminded them. 'This fire will not draw, Mary; what am I doing wrong?'

She swept the floor, and scrubbed the table, and peeled potatoes. She shelled peas, and strung beans, and sieved currants. She learnt to fillet a fish, to make jam, to knead dough and set a loaf to prove. She churned butter, and strained the curds to make cheese, and salted beans down for the winter.

'You are a fast learner, miss,' said Mrs Groves. 'We shall make a cook of you yet.'

'I hope so,' said Eveline. 'I had no idea what goes into preparing just one meal. We are hopelessly spoilt, above stairs. I shall make sure my family know how much work it has taken when they toy with a dish and then send it away because it is not to their fancy, or grumble that it is mutton again when they had a taste for beef.'

'You will take their appetite away, and then I shall be turned off,' said Mrs Groves. 'Or they will all learn to cook, and I shall have no work. I think you had better let things be, miss; your lady mother is doubtful enough about your helping here without causing any more trouble.'

In fact, Mrs Stanhope was trying very hard not to think about the fact that her youngest daughter was not only working below stairs but gave every indication of enjoying her new tasks. There had grown a tacit agreement between

Eveline and her mother not to discuss the arrangement, and it was never mentioned to anyone outside the household. Beatrice, to be sure, commented on her sister's hands – how rough and reddened they had become, and darkened with stains from the nasty chemicals she used to make photographs, and if only Eveline would use the rose-salve, and dip her fingers in lemon juice every day, she might have hands as white and delicate as Beatrice's own – but apart from this, Eveline seemed to be escaping detection. She rose a great deal earlier than she had been used to, and was sometimes the first in the kitchen, so that she would light the fire and have water boiling for tea and for washing by the time Mrs Groves and Mary were ready. The black beetles, which scattered as soon as she entered, still made her flinch, and the war against the coal dust and grease was never-ending; but the satisfaction she felt was immense.

The daily menus had always been decided by Mrs Stanhope, and Mrs Groves would climb the stairs every day after breakfast to receive her orders, and suggest dishes that might be suitable, and make tentative hints on the economical use of the cold meat left over from the day before. Now and then, however, Mrs Stanhope would descend to the kitchen herself, and she did so one morning when Eveline was mincing some lamb, and adding onions and herbs with a look of fierce concentration.

'It has been an age since we had poor Mr Watson to dine,' said Mrs Stanhope. 'The dear man lives quite alone, you know, and I do not think that housekeeper of his feeds him properly. I saw him in the street and asked him for a little supper tonight. I know we are being economical, Evie, but we must not desert our old friends.'

'Of course he must come,' said Eveline. 'We will have lamb patties, and a hot raspberry pudding.'

'Will that be elegant enough, do you think, for him?' asked her mother. 'He is used to half a dozen courses, I dare say, when he dines out.'

'It will be delicious,' Eveline assured her. 'I have learnt a good deal since the beef olives, Mama.'

'Well, to be sure, my love, we are eating very well, these days. Though your poor hands! What did Bea say about the salve?'

'I have given the salve to Mary, who works all the time, and has painful chilblains. I am just dabbling.'

'One day,' said her mother, 'you will look back, when you are a grand lady, and wonder that this should ever have been.'

'I am not sure I wish to be a grand lady; grand ladies do not seem to be free to do the things I would like to do.'

'Oh, Evie, you will change your mind, I know. Dear Charles! But I must not say more. If he should happen to call, he may stay to dine, too. Are you sure the patties will look well enough?'

'They will taste good, you may be sure, and we can trick them out with parsley so they look perfectly respectable.'

'Well, then, let there be enough, just in case we do have an extra visitor . . . *what is that*?' She let out a small scream. 'Evie, there is a creature over there!'

'Oh, do not worry, Mama; that is Autolycus. He is a hedgehog,' she explained.

'I can see he is a hedgehog! But whatever is he – I mean *it* – doing in my kitchen?'

'He eats the black beetles. We give him bread and milk, and he comes in and out through the scullery, and we have had far fewer beetles since we brought him in, have we not, Mrs Groves?'

'To be sure, miss, we have. It was a grand idea of yours, though I had my doubts to start with.'

'A hedgehog!' said Mrs Stanhope, faintly. 'I do not know what the world is coming to. I am going to get a couple of bottles of claret from the cellar, for this evening, and I think I shall take a glass now, just to make sure it is good enough for Mr Watson, and to restore my shattered nerves.'

Chapter Eighteen

Eveline Addresses a Meeting

It was fortunate that Eveline had made so many lamb patties, for there were more guests that evening than had been anticipated. Arthur had been prevailed upon by Charles to take a look at the yacht, now anchored in the harbour, and the two men called in to say that the sailing excursion planned for next week would certainly go ahead, if the weather was clement. Mrs Stanhope met with very little resistance when she begged Charles to stay for dinner.

'But you will be wishing to get back to Beatrice and the children, Arthur,' said Mrs Stanhope, as the dinner hour approached.

'Oh, Bea will have a headache, and not mind my staying out,' said Arthur. 'She has taken to going to bed early; she will be glad of a little peace, I imagine.'

'A headache! My poor dear Beatrice. She has not mentioned anything to me. Have you fetched the doctor?'

'She says it is merely tiredness, from Kitty's being so lively; and she does not look unwell.'

'I shall certainly go to see her in the morning,' said Mrs Stanhope. 'But do dine with us, Arthur; you are always welcome, you know.'

So Arthur stayed, and he and Charles had a great deal to say about the yacht, and how it would fare if raced. Arthur had more than a common interest in such things, for his fortune came from a family business of sailmakers. His grandfather had become wealthy, and his father ambitious, so that Arthur had been sent to university, and had become a gentleman. Still he looked in most days to see the men and women who worked in the sail lofts and offices, and Eveline saw how his expression changed when he spoke of the latest designs and advances in sails and in sailing boats, and she thought that although he played the part of a man of leisure he might still have preferred to be a man of business.

The lively discussion between Charles and Arthur gave her the opportunity to press Mr Watson for news of the railway company, and her letters.

'The Board is to meet tomorrow, as it happens,' said Mr Watson. 'I shall raise your concerns at the end of the meeting, Eveline; they have all had your letter – they will be expecting it.'

'And do you think they will be minded to help?' asked Eveline. 'Now that the railway is running, and the grand opening was such a triumph, they will be feeling benevolent, I hope.'

'Oh, they are a good set of fellows,' said Mr Watson, rather vaguely, 'I dare say they will give it their best attention; but you must not be disappointed, my dear, if nothing comes of it.'

'Will you send me word, when you know what they have decided?'

'Certainly. It will not be till late, however, for we do not meet until three o'clock, and there is a good deal of business to discuss.'

And with that Eveline had to be content. The meal passed well enough, and the lamb patties were declared delicious by everyone; although Mrs Stanhope had expressly forbidden Eveline to acknowledge her part in their creation, so that she was obliged to take only a secret satisfaction in her culinary triumph. As all the gentlemen took their leave, Charles reminded her of the yachting party.

'For you promised, did you not, Miss Stanhope? You will like it, once you try it, I am certain.'

'Of course she will like it!' said her mother. 'I am sure I should have, when I was young: sunshine, and sea air, and young men!'

'I may have all those things without putting to sea,' said Eveline. 'But I have promised,' she added hastily, seeing her mother and Charles and Arthur all regarding her reproachfully, 'and of course I will be there.'

* * *

Mrs Stanhope herself had a headache the next day, which she put down to the last bottle of claret's having been corked, and to her concern for Beatrice. Eveline, therefore, after her morning stint in the kitchen, offered to call on her sister to enquire after her health.

'Very well,' said her mother, weakening, 'as long as you walk straight there, Eveline, and wear the purple costume with the hat. And take poor Beatrice some of that jam you made, so that she may have blackcurrant tea; it will do her nothing but good.'

Beatrice was in the morning room, looking at fashion magazines, and drinking coffee, when Eveline arrived.

'Arthur is being foolish,' she said, 'it is nothing; I get a little headache from time to time, but he has no business telling everyone about it.'

'You do look perfectly well,' said Eveline. 'Prettier than ever, in fact.'

'Do you think so? It may be this lace collar, perhaps. It is new; I went into Newport on the railway – only fancy! – and saw this, and bought it on a whim. It was not expensive, really.'

'It is pretty. But I meant that your eyes look bright, and your cheeks rosy. I do not think there can be much wrong with you, Bea.'

'No, I keep telling you! There is nothing wrong. I am quite well, and I will be of the party going onto the yacht next week, you may be sure.'

'I am glad of that, for I do not think I shall enjoy it much. Your company will be a consolation, at least.'

'Oh, Evie, you are a funny girl. I suppose you would rather be at home with your chemicals and bits of glass.'

'I would, actually.'

'You are not very grateful. Charles has invited you and me most particularly. He was very flattering when he called to ask me; said that if I did not come, he would delay the whole excursion until I would say yes, for without me the sun would not shine, or some such nonsense.'

'Did he? And did Arthur mind his being so very pressing?'

'Oh, Arthur was down at the sail loft, as he always is, when Charles called.'

'Bea, are you quite sure you are not on dangerous ground? Charles can be very charming. You would not make Arthur unhappy on his account, would you?'

Beatrice flushed.

'That is absurd. I cannot help it if Charles admires me. I have explained this to you before, Evie: a little harmless flirtation is quite acceptable for married women, if one is discreet.'

'When you told me that Louisa's maid had been flirting with Bevis, you did not sound as though you thought that was acceptable.'

'That is entirely different.'

'I do not see why.'

The sound of the front door, and Arthur's return, interrupted this discussion; and the call for fresh coffee, and an account of Arthur's morning, which had involved the delayed delivery of some cotton duck sailcloth from India, which might prove lighter than the linen they had used until now, gave both sisters the chance to regain their tempers.

'I will tell Mama you are well, Bea,' said Eveline, as she prepared to leave. 'She will be relieved.'

'Yes, do; and tell her not to be making such a fuss.'

'I will walk a little way with you, Eveline,' said Arthur, 'since I may just go back to the loft for ten minutes to see if that cloth has arrived after all. Will you come with me, Bea?'

'No; I shall go to the nursery and see if Kitty has done her lessons, for I have not seen the poor child all day. We married women have duties, you know, and I cannot be walking about the town just as I choose, unlike the rest of you.'

She was not to be moved; so Arthur and Eveline set off along the road.

'Do you think she is well, Eveline?' asked Arthur. 'She has not been herself this past few months, it seems to me. She looks well enough, and yet she will go to bed early, and she seems cross with me for no reason I can find; yet she is cheerful enough with other people.'

'Have you asked her, Arthur? Have you talked about why she is cross?'

'No, I suppose I have not. Not too good at that sort of thing, you know. We did have a bit of a set-to, a while back, about money. We haven't quite as much as Bea would like, I fear. It's possible she has not forgiven me for that.'

'I don't wish to intrude,' said Eveline. 'Do not tell me anything you would prefer to keep private.'

'To tell the truth, I am glad to talk about it. Can't discuss this sort of thing with the chaps, you know; Bevis and

Sandham and Armitage, all very good fellows, but one can't discuss one's wife with them.'

'Well, you can talk to me, Arthur,' said Eveline. 'I will not disclose anything you say to anyone else, I promise.'

'The thing is,' he said, 'Bea should have married someone a good deal richer and smarter than I, Evie. She likes clothes, and jewels, and fellows who are a bit more men of the world. I am a disappointment to her.' Eveline glanced at his face and saw the set line of his mouth and the blank look in his eyes.

'I do not know what to say, Arthur. I am sorry you are unhappy. If you listen to her – ask her how she is feeling – perhaps that may help? I do not know; I am no expert in these matters. But I have had people talk to me, and at me, a great deal, being the youngest child, you know; it is more unusual for someone to listen. I do know that much.'

Arthur sighed.

'Well, thank you for hearing me, at least; and I will try to talk to her.'

'Listen, first,' Eveline reminded him.

'Eh?'

'Listen. As opposed to talk.'

'Ah! Got it. I'll give it a try,' he said, sounding a little more hopeful. 'Shall I walk you back to your house, before I drop back into the loft?'

'No, thank you,' said Eveline. 'What is the time, Arthur? Is it nearing three o'clock?'

He consulted his pocket watch. 'Half past two.'

'Excellent. Thank you. I am going this way.'

'That will not take you home; that is the new road towards the railway station and the railway office, is it not?'

'Yes; I am going there. I am going to call on Mr Watson.'

When Eveline was shown into his office, Mr Watson was startled, if courteous.

'My dear, Eveline – what a charming surprise – but, alas, the meeting of the board will be starting very soon. Can my clerk get you a glass of something to refresh you?'

'No, thank you. I am here because I thought it might be helpful for the directors to hear from me in person about the ideas I am proposing. It would not take long; but I am fearful that if it is left to the end of the meeting, the gentlemen will have run out of time, or energy, to consider it, so if I may speak first, I would be very grateful.'

'That is a little irregular, I fear. The item is not on the agenda for the meeting; it would have come up under *any other business*, you know.'

'I understand that, Mr Watson, but I imagine that the chairman of a meeting has the discretion to add something to an agenda, does he not?'

'Only if it is of pressing importance, my dear.'

'This is of pressing importance. It concerns the people who work for you. What could be more important than that?'

'The finances,' began Mr Watson, 'they must be secure, you know . . .' He quailed a little under Eveline's stare. 'We can discuss this, perhaps, another time – it is three o'clock, now, and the meeting must start.' He gathered up some papers from the desk and made for the door.

'Then I shall wait,' said Eveline. She walked into the lobby and took a seat on one of the hard chairs that stood around the wall. 'Is the meeting in that room? I shall be here. Please let me know when I may speak.'

Half a dozen dark-suited men had by this time entered the lobby and were trooping into the board room.

'What's this, Watson?' asked one of them jovially. 'Inviting the ladies for another trip on the railway, are we? How very charming,' and he bowed to Eveline.

'No . . . well,' said the harassed Mr Watson, 'that is, this is Miss Stanhope, Jones. She wrote that letter, you know, about establishing a benevolent fund. She wished to speak to the board today, but I have explained that, alas, it would be most irregular.'

'I should say it would,' agreed Mr Jones, who was stout, and red-faced, with luxuriant mutton-chop whiskers.

Eveline picked up a newspaper that lay on the table beside her.

'I do not mind how long I have to wait,' she said.

'Your dear lady mother will be concerned, will she not, if you are late?' said Mr Watson feebly.

'She will, I imagine, be furious,' said Eveline, 'but I am sure she will forgive you, if you explain that you had to keep me waiting for several hours because of an *agenda*.'

A slight look of panic now crossed Mr Watson's face.

'Now, then, Eveline,' he said, 'this really won't do, you know. We are men of business. We have important things to discuss.'

'As do I,' said Eveline, more calmly than she felt.

Mr Jones looked from one to the other. 'Tell you what,' he said, 'why don't you let the lady speak first, Watson? Won't take long, I imagine, Miss Stanhope? Five minutes; we won't mind that, will we, old man?'

Mr Watson sighed.

'Very well,' he said. 'Five minutes, now, Eveline, that is all.'

She jumped up. 'Thank you. I am most grateful.'

Her mouth was dry, and her hands a little shaky, but she held up her head, and walked into the room. Mr Watson introduced her, and Mr Jones gave her an encouraging smile, and she drew a deep breath and began to speak. She thanked them most heartily for their time and attention, and reminded them of the letter she had sent.

'I do not ask you to do this as an act of charity,' she said. 'You are all, I am sure, men of good principle, who would support the poor and the unfortunate by gifts, and donations, and so forth' – here most of them, though not all, nodded – 'and that is a noble thing to do. But should the railway one day be run by people less principled than you, there will be no safeguards for those who work for it. If you were to establish a benevolent fund, as an inseparable part of the company, how progressive, how enlightened that would be! How you would be admired by your fellow citizens now, and by generations to come!'

One or two of the men looked engaged by this argument; most looked dubious.

'I was against the railway when it was first proposed,' she said, 'as were many people in the town. I saw it as a monster, ugly, savage, brutal, tearing up houses and land as it came.'

Eyebrows were raised at this.

'But I have come to see it differently. It will transform our lives, and make changes possible for thousands of people. And so you, gentlemen, are in the vanguard of progress; you are the guardians of the future. You *are* the future. You will be far more influential in the years to come than the men who have held power in the past – the landowners, the aristocrats. That is why I am asking this of you: because you are the masters now.'

There was silence; it was impossible to know how her words were being received.

'My time is up, I can see,' she said. 'Thank you again, gentlemen, for listening.'

She walked out of the room, and almost into the arms of Thomas Armitage.

'Good God, Eveline!' he said. 'What are you doing here? Have you been addressing the board?'

'I have, actually,' she said. 'I was ridiculously dramatic. They are probably saying even now that I am a hysterical woman, and laughing heartily.'

'I imagine they are more likely to be in shock,' he said. 'This is about your letter, I suppose?'

'Yes. I thought they might take more notice if I spoke to them in person; but it was a stupid idea, I think. They did not look impressed, on the whole.'

'I am about to join the meeting. I will speak up for you,' he said.

'Thank you! Oh, thank you, Thomas – if you would – but only if you think it is right to do so. I would not wish you to support something you did not think was right.'

'I know it is right,' he said. He took her hand, and she thought for a moment he might raise it to his lips; but he dropped it again, and turned, and went into the room.

Chapter Nineteen

An Evening Walk

That evening, her mind still full of the railway board, and her hopes and fears for the benevolent fund, Eveline was too tense even to think of sleep. With no maid waiting now to undress her or brush her hair, she did not need to resort to subterfuge; everyone in the household was wont to retire very early these days. She went to her bedroom when the other ladies did so, remained in her clothes, read until the house was quiet, and then put on a hat, as a faint nod to convention, and went downstairs and out into the night. Walking in the garden in the darkness had become one of her pleasures, but tonight even the garden, with its high walls, felt confining. She pushed open the gate to the street, and stepped outside. A few minutes in the outside world would harm no one, surely. The road was deserted; she walked quickly down towards the sea and stopped to take deep breaths of the sharp salty air. The moon was just rising.

Two figures were coming towards her, walking close together. As they drew near, the shapes materialised out of the darkness, and she saw a face she recognised. It was Jennie, arm in arm with a young man.

'Good evening,' she said, laughing at the unlikeliness of the encounter. 'How are you, Jennie? This, I take it, is Ned?' and she shook hands with them both. Ned was stocky and bearded, with a broad smile, and his handshake was firm and strong.

'Miss Eveline – Eveline, I mean,' said Jennie. 'Are you out alone? Are you lost?'

'Lost, ten minutes from my own home?' said Eveline. 'No, of course not. I am walking, as you are – taking the air, I suppose.'

'We often walk out late,' said Jennie. 'We are both working, you know, until late some evenings, and some days this is our only time to be together,' and she smiled at Ned, who drew her closer to him, and nodded proudly.

'Will you come with us, a little way?' asked Ned. 'I am walking Jennie back to her mother's house, just now.'

'Oh no, I would not intrude upon your time together,' said Eveline quickly.

'Do, please,' said Jennie, 'we said we would stay friends, you know, and I should so like to hear all that is happening at the house; is your mama getting her caps starched the way she likes them?'

'Not entirely,' said Eveline. 'I will walk with you, then, as you are kind enough to ask me, just for a short while, and I can tell you all that is happening. The caps are the least of our worries.' Ned offered her his other arm, and they all three fell into step like old friends, past the bathing huts lined up along the shore, and on towards the high street, where the shops were now all shuttered, but the taverns were lighted and a great deal of merry noise rose from the open doors.

'Shall we stop for a glass of ale?' asked Ned. 'It is Friday; I have my wages; it would be my pleasure to treat you both. My friends will be mightily impressed that I have two women, now,' and he grinned at them both.

'I do not know what you are thinking of, Ned,' said Jennie. 'Miss Eveline cannot go into a tavern; that would not be a fit place for her.'

'You are usually happy to take a glass of ale with me,' said Ned plaintively.

'Of course I am, but Eveline is from a good family; she and her kind do not go to such places.'

'Plenty of gentlemen go to the inn, and drink with us, too.'

'Gentlemen, perhaps, but not ladies.'

'Please do not argue,' said Eveline. 'As a matter of fact, I should like very much to go into a tavern. I have never entered one.'

'I do not think your family would like it at all,' said Jennie.

'They will not know,' said Eveline. 'No one of my

acquaintance will be in there, I imagine, so I will be quite unknown.'

Jennie looked dubious, but Ned was already heading through the door into the smoky room. A few heads turned, and Eveline felt herself the subject of scrutiny; but the noise of laughter, and shouted conversations, and the clink of glasses, soon resumed. Ned found them a table, and three glasses of ale were brought.

'Your good health!' they said, and clinked glasses, and drank. The ale was very dark and bitter, but Eveline thought she might get to like it, with practice, and she took another mouthful. She looked around her: the groups of people were mostly men, but there were a few women, some perhaps respectable, others clearly not. A great shout of laughter came from an adjoining table, where four men were playing cards and smoking, and Eveline turned to watch them, enjoying the convivial atmosphere. One of the men looked up, and winked at her, and nudged his neighbour, and the second man turned to look at her. He was in the process of raising his glass to his lips, and when he saw her face, he very nearly choked; it was Thomas Armitage.

'*Eveline*?' He sounded as though he could not believe his eyes. 'What in God's name are you doing here?'

'Drinking with friends, like you,' she said. 'You know Ned and Jennie, of course.'

'This is no place for you,' he said. 'What were you thinking, Ned, to bring her here?'

'Do not reproach Ned,' she said. 'Jennie did not wish me to come in, at all, but I insisted.'

'I can imagine you did. Still, you had better let me take you home. I do not imagine your mother would be at all happy if she knew of this escapade.'

'Do not be reading me a lecture, Thomas,' she said. 'It is hardly your place to do so.'

'Are we to finish this game, Tom?' demanded the man who had winked at Eveline. 'Or are you going to introduce us to your friends?'

'Please do finish your game,' said Eveline, 'I would not interrupt it for the world. And I have not quite finished my drink, which I am enjoying very much, I must say.'

He shrugged. 'Very well. But then I will escort you home.'

'As you wish,' she said. 'I am perfectly capable of walking alone, however.'

He raised his eyebrows. 'I know you are,' he said grimly. 'Nevertheless.'

'Then I accept your *so* gallant offer,' she said.

He tried to repress a smile, and failed. 'Well, then, let me get you all another glass, since you are here. And take that damned hat off, Eveline; you look like a tart, and some lad will try his luck with you before too long.'

She removed the hat. 'It is a horrible hat, I know,' she said with dignity, 'but it is very fashionable.'

He turned back to the table, and the card game resumed, and Eveline regaled Jennie and Ned with an account of her new photographic studio ('The old potting shed, in truth,' she said, 'but I feel Mr Fry would prefer me to call it a studio') and how she had persuaded Barnabas to be photographed as Sir Lancelot; and Jennie told them all about her day with Mr

Fry, and their customers; and the time passed with a great deal of laughter and merriment, until Thomas stood up, and came over to her side.

'Come on, then,' he said. 'Ned, are you taking Jennie home? Then I will see you back at the cottage, no doubt, later.'

'I am taking you out of your way, perhaps?' said Eveline, with an attempt to be formal.

'No, you are not, as it happens, for I lodge at Ned's cottage, and it is beyond your house, out along the seashore.'

She took his arm, and they went back along the streets of Cowes, leaving the gas lamps and the sound of cheer behind them as they approached the shore. Absurdly, she could not think of anything to say as they walked, and Thomas too was silent. By now the moon was high in the sky, brilliant and clear, and making a silver path across the water, as they turned away from the sea to walk up the steep street that led to the Stanhopes' house.

'I had better go in through the side gate,' said Eveline, 'the gate in the wall; that way no one will see me.'

At the gate she turned.

'Thank you,' she said, 'I hope I have not spoilt your evening.'

He said nothing, but made no move to go. She held out her hand, and he took a step backwards, as though to avoid her touch; and then, abruptly, stepped toward her, and pushed her back against the wall, and his mouth came down on hers, and kissed her hard. For how long they stood in the darkness, she did not know – a few minutes only, perhaps much longer? – before he let her go, and said, his voice sounding almost rough, 'Go in, now; you had better go,' and she stumbled blindly back through the door into the garden, and ran silently across the lawn, and back up to her room, where she lay down, fully dressed, upon the bed. She could taste his kisses; something had happened to her breathing, and there was a strange turmoil inside her. Sleep did not come until the moon had set and the trembling she felt had finally ceased.

Chapter Twenty

An Unexpected Arrival

She could not concentrate, at all. Mrs Groves had asked several times if she were quite well, for she had taken an hour to shell a pan of broad beans, and then had put all the pods into a pan and very nearly thrown away the beans; and her aunt, bringing in the eggs, which were still warm from the nest, had found her staring out of the window in an apparent trance.

'You look pale, Evie. Perhaps you are working too hard, with the kitchen tasks every morning, and then locked away with the camera in the afternoons? You are short of fresh air, perhaps.'

'I am perfectly well, Aunt,' said Eveline; although she did, in truth, feel a little fragile. 'But some fresh air would do me good, I am sure. I will find a quiet spot outdoors, and read, this afternoon.' Solitude was what she needed, she thought; solitude, and some time to think, clearly, about her situation. Later, therefore, she took her book as an alibi, in case anyone asked her where she was going, and climbed unseen into the beech tree, and gave herself up to reflection.

The first thing was that, according to Jennie and Ned, Thomas Armitage had a sweetheart, a fiancée in all probability, in his own north-country home. She should not, must not, be encouraging the attentions of an engaged man, and should certainly not be drinking in taverns with him, or kissing him in the dark. A memory of the previous night swam into her mind, of his mouth against her throat; and for a moment she gave herself up to the delicious sensation, half-sweet, half-fearful, of remembering that, and feeling little ripples of delight surge through her, and the blood rise to her cheeks. She leant her burning face against the cool smooth bark of her tree. She would put him out of her mind; in all likelihood he would be gone in a few weeks, and she would never see him again.

Then there was Charles; she had not paused to think too deeply about Charles Sandham, despite – or perhaps because of – her mother's constantly reiterated hopes for him as a suitor and prospective husband. Had she, though, encouraged him while unsure of her own feelings? Her aunt and her mother had both said, with different motives perhaps, that she was flirting with him; and he did seem eager for her company, sometimes. And it was certainly both agreeable and convenient to have a pleasant man to escort one about now and then, and pay one attention. Yet it seemed to her that he looked at Louisa with very much the same level of flattering interest that he showed her, and at Beatrice with something more. She did not know, at all, what his real feelings were towards her; perhaps still less did she know her own towards him. She wondered how it would be if he did offer for her, and she accepted his proposal. Her mother would be delirious with happiness, no doubt, and it would be a comfortable, even luxurious, life to be married to Charles: carriages, clothes, a house; travel to London and Paris and Rome; and even freedom to pursue her photography, perhaps. The prospect was not without appeal.

'I will not encourage Charles. I will be polite, and observe him, in a detached way, that is all; and I will know, then, if he is serious in liking me, or merely amusing himself,' she thought, and then she closed her eyes, and tried very hard not to think about Thomas, or his kisses, or his voice in the velvet darkness, until she knew that only determined activity would stop her being so absurd, and she climbed down, and went to see how yesterday's prints of Mary dressed as the Lady of Shalott looked in the cold light of day.

She could not fail to be absorbed, as always, by her camera, and the process of conjuring images from light. Having examined the pictures of Mary, and feeling rather pleased with the results – there was a softness and delicacy about the face, and the folds of the old shawls, which she had arranged to simulate a flowing medieval gown, looked as though one could reach into the picture and touch them – she saw her aunt, carrying a bucket of scraps for the hens, passing the doorway to the cabin, which Eveline now thought of as her studio, and called to her.

'Dearest Aunt! Do you have a little time to spare for me?'

'If you mean, dear girl, will I submit to being photographed in some ridiculous fancy dress, then the answer is most emphatically no.'

'I do not always photograph my subjects in costume. Indeed, I would rather take your likeness as you are now.'

Her aunt regarded her with distrust.

'Barnabas is still shaken by being cast as Sir Lancelot, you know. I am not going down the same road.'

'No, I promise. Just as you are. It will not take long.'

'Oh, if you must. I suppose you want me to go and tidy my hair, and wash my hands? You had much better ask your mama to sit; she always looks just so.'

'I do not want to take Mama's likeness, just now; I want to take yours. Here, put down the chickens' food, and sit on the chair by the table – that is it – and I am going to move the blind, so that we angle the light somewhat, and then I shall adjust the lens . . . so . . . and if you will simply look towards me, and keep still, this will be exactly as I want.'

'Am I to smile?'

'No, be grave; think of the coming of autumn, and the leaves falling, for I know that always makes you melancholy. Rest your chin in your hands, perhaps.'

The minutes passed; the image was taken.

'Thank you, dear Aunt. I will take the plate out, now; you

are free. The photograph will be ready later. I shall tell you how successful I have been. You are very patient with me.'

Then came the long process of fixing, and washing, and drying. When the image was developed, it was everything Eveline had hoped it might be. George's face, rather long, handsome, and sombre, was exposed in every detail: the fine lines that cross-hatched her cheeks, and the furrows across her forehead; the greying hair escaping in long wisps and falling around her face; her strong mottled hands, the nails black with earth, framing that determined chin; and above all her eyes, intelligent and shrewd, clouded with thought, gazing directly into the camera. She would like to show this to Mr Fry, and to Jennie, for their opinion; it was different from the photographs she had taken up to now; there was no softness, no romantic blurring, but instead a harshness, a truthfulness, that interested her. She would write a note, to invite them to call; Mama would no doubt have some objection, but she would overcome that. No sooner had she got back to the house, however, and settled to write her invitation, than there was a commotion outside, and the sound of carriage wheels on the gravel, and voices in the hallway. It sounded very much like Louisa's voice, and yet her sister was not expected. She finished her note, and then went to find out what was happening.

Louisa and the children were there, and Mrs Stanhope was clucking, and exclaiming around them. Louisa's eyes were red, and the children uncharacteristically subdued.

'Eveline! Do not be just standing there; go and get your aunt and Miss Angell to mind the poor little ones,' said her mother. 'And before you do, get a glass of something for your sister – she has had a shock.'

'What is it?' exclaimed Eveline. 'Is someone hurt? Is it Bevis? Is it an accident?'

'Bevis is gone!' said Louisa, and burst into fresh tears.

'Gone! Not dead – oh, Louisa!'

'No, he is not dead,' said her mother. 'Dead would be one thing, but this is worse. He has disappeared, and Louisa does not know where he is, or what is to become of her.'

Eveline quickly fetched the claret jug, in the absence of brandy, for once rather regretting their frugal regime.

'Here, Louisa, drink this – and Mama, you have some too.'

Both drank, and Eveline thought she might as well pour a glass for herself.

'I will take Henry and Daisy out into the garden, where they may run about. You would like to see the new chickens, would you not, my dears?'

'Oh do, Eveline, please.' Louisa drained her glass and poured a second.

'But what happened to Bevis? Do you think he may be hurt – perhaps fallen from his horse? Should we be sending out search parties?'

'It is not a fall from a horse,' said her mother. 'A fall from grace, perhaps.'

'I came home,' said Louisa, between sobs and hiccups, 'from a morning visit to friends, and there was a note upon the mantlepiece, if you please!'

'What was in it? What did it say?'

'Here – you may read it,' said Louisa, fishing it from her purse. Eveline read the note.

Louisa, I have gone away for a short time. You will find I have left enough money for your needs. I may be gone a month, or less. Take care of the children, and do not try to find me.

'That is all!' said Louisa, beginning to cry again.

'It is a business matter, perhaps?' said Eveline. 'He does not like to trouble you with details, and has gone to do whatever it is he must do, and he has left money, you see, so he must have thought about it in advance.'

'Business? What business could it be? We have the estate, and the tenants, and the home farm. He is not a *tradesman*.'

'Might he have friends who are in trouble, and he has visited them, with no time to explain?'

'How could that be? What friends that I did not know of?'

'Friends from before his marriage, perhaps. There must be an explanation, Louisa.'

'That will do, Eveline,' said her mother. 'Do take the little ones, now; they should not be hearing all this.'

Eveline offered a hand each to Henry and Daisy, and took them into the garden, where she managed to amuse them for a while by letting them feed the poultry, and telling the children what the names of the hens were.

'And we have a hedgehog, now, who lives in the kitchen,' said Eveline, 'you may see him later, perhaps.'

Having found her aunt and Miss Angell, she relinquished

214

the children into their care, telling them only that Louisa had arrived unexpectedly, and was a little indisposed.

'I will tell you more, later,' she promised, and sped back to the house. Louisa had gone upstairs to lie down, and Mrs Stanhope was issuing orders for beef tea.

'What is going on, do you think, Mama?' Eveline asked. 'Surely it is nothing very terrible; he has gone off for some hunting, or shooting, and has been unthinking in the way he has done it, perhaps. You know Bevis; he is charming, but he can be selfish and careless.'

'You do not know the rest,' said Mrs Stanhope darkly. 'Poor Louisa could not say in front of the babes, but Betsy has told her something – I hardly like to say it to you, my sweet innocent child.'

'I am not a child, Mama, nor entirely innocent. You had much better tell me.'

Mrs Stanhope took another sip of wine and sighed.

'Well then, it seems that Bevis had a letter, last week, franked in London, and Betsy says to Louisa that she thinks it was from that little hussy whom Louisa had to dismiss – you remember how upset she was then—'

'Hannah; yes, I remember.'

'And Betsy says that Hannah had mentioned to her, when she found she was in trouble, that there was no one she could turn to, but a cousin living in London; so Louisa thinks Bevis has gone up to find the designing minx, and she will never see him again.'

'There are thousands of people in London who might have written to him. It is not very likely that Bevis would go after a girl whom he had not seemed to care about much before.'

'Then I do not know what he is about, I am sure. All I know is that he has made your sister very unhappy, and her good name will be ruined.'

'Why should Louisa's name be ruined? It is Bevis who has behaved badly, not Louisa.'

'The world will not care about that; nothing is more pitiable than a deserted wife. She will not be able to hold her head up again in polite society.'

'Then we must make sure polite society does not know,' said Eveline firmly. 'Although I cannot see why it is so very important.'

'You may not see, Evie, but Louisa does, and I do, and so will everyone of our acquaintance.'

'Yes, I know that, Mama. Well, then, we will say that Louisa and the children are come on an extended visit to us, because Bevis has been called away unexpectedly, to . . . to an aged uncle, in Scotland, perhaps. What could be more respectable? The uncle is likely to die – Bevis is his nearest relative – we do not know how long he will be at his uncle's bedside, so Louisa stays with her mother. No one will raise an eyebrow.'

'Do you think so, Evie? But we will be found out. People will know he has never mentioned an uncle in Scotland before.'

'The thing is not to explain too much,' said Eveline. 'Mention it once, if anyone asks, and then talk about something more thrilling – the railway, or the queen, or the price of coffee. Anything. It will all be well, Mama, you will see.'

'But we cannot sustain that fiction for ever! What if he does not return?'

'Then we shall have to kill him off – fictionally, of course. But it will not come to that, I am sure. He said in the note he has gone away for a short time; he clearly intends to return. And if he does not, we will find him.'

'Find him! Yes, we must find him, Evie, but however are we to do so?'

'I do not know, yet, Mama; but I shall think of a way. Here, let us finish this claret, and then I will go and see if Louisa will take a little tea.'

Chapter Twenty-One

The Yachting Party

Louisa was red-eyed, and pale, the following morning, and Mrs Stanhope took one look at her face and ordered her straight back to bed.

'I will take her some breakfast,' said Eveline. 'Perhaps things will not seem so bad once she has eaten,' and she climbed the stairs with a tray, and went to her sister's room.

'Look, Louisa, hot rolls, and marmalade,' she said, coaxingly. 'And a little coffee; won't you try?'

Louisa consented to sit up and sip the coffee, although she did not think she could eat anything.

'I am a forsaken woman,' she said. 'What could be

sadder? And Henry and Daisy – what am I to tell them?'

'Do not worry about the children. Aunt George and the Angell have them safe, and they are much diverted by the hens and by Autolycus.'

'By whom?'

'Never mind – it is a long story, Lou. Now, can you think of anything that might give us an idea of where Bevis has gone? There may be a very rational explanation, you know, and do not forget that he did say in his note that he intends to return.'

Louisa sighed, and spread some marmalade on a roll, and bit into it.

'I am convinced he has gone off to find that wretched Hannah. Oh, that I had not taken her on! That will teach me to employ a pretty girl. At least no one can say that of Betsy, I suppose. Which reminds me, Eveline, I had better send for Betsy to come here; if I am to be a tragic figure then at least let me look like a romantic heroine and not like a scarecrow.'

'You could never look like a scarecrow, Louisa. But yes, send for Betsy, by all means; she may have more clues for us, perhaps, about where Bevis can be.'

Eveline had almost forgotten, in the drama of Louisa's arrival, that she had invited Mr Fry and Jennie to call on her to see her latest photographs. They arrived, however, that afternoon, coming in through the side gate, and found her in the garden, under the weeping ash tree, reading to Henry and Daisy.

'Forgive our informal entrance,' said Mr Fry, 'we did not call at the front door, for Jennie had an inkling you would be out of doors.'

'I thought I should still use the servants' entrance,' said Jennie, 'it seemed easier.'

'You are not a servant now, Jennie. The front door, next time.'

'And I have brought your hat back, Eveline,' said Jennie, producing the purple-feathered straw from her basket. 'It is a little crushed; I think someone may have sat on it, but it will be as good as new with a little care.'

'My hat!' said Eveline. 'Wherever did I leave it?'

'In the tavern,' said Jennie. 'Do you remember – Thomas said—'

'Oh yes,' said Eveline quickly, 'of course, I remember what Mr Armitage said.' Her face felt hot. Mr Fry was looking at her with interest, but either good manners or sheer bafflement seemed to prevent his asking any questions. 'Do come and see my latest photographs. There are one or two I am quite pleased with; and then we shall have some tea. Henry, Daisy; will you take the books back to the house now, and see if there are any scraps for the chickens?'

The Professor was very much taken with Eveline's pictures. The likeness of Aunt George, in particular, he returned to again and again.

'This has a quality of directness and truth, Eveline, that is remarkable,' he said. 'I wonder, have you thought you might exhibit it? It is quite as worthy of being seen as many I have seen displayed on the walls of grand displays.'

'Exhibit it? Really? No, I had not thought. But how could that be? We are so out of the way here, so far from all such things.'

'The Photographic Society of London holds an

exhibition every year. I do not see why you should not submit something for consideration.'

'You are too kind, Mr Fry. But I would not know how to start – how to contact the society – and it is no doubt only for professionals, in any case.'

'Not at all. It is open to all with a genuine interest, amateur and professional. In fact,' he said modestly, 'I myself had a photograph exhibited there in '56. A view of some fishermen, down by the Thames. It met with some very pleasing approbation from one or two distinguished practitioners of our art, I am happy to say.'

'That is remarkable!' said Eveline. 'My warmest congratulations; I am very honoured to have been fortunate enough to have your guidance in learning to take photographs.'

He looked immensely pleased, and bowed to her, his face a picture of pride, while he made modest noises of self-deprecation.

'But what brought you here, Mr Fry?' she asked. 'If you had stayed in London, you might be famous, by now; what made you come to Cowes, so far away from great things such as that?'

'London has a photographer in every street, now,' he said, 'there is much competition; and I like the sea air, you know. And then Cowes is becoming such a smart place, with our dear queen at Osborne, and the regattas, and so on. It seemed to me I had a chance to make my living here in far more agreeable surroundings than in the city, and so it has proved.'

'Is Cowes becoming smart? I had not realised,' said Eveline. 'But do you really think I could submit something for an exhibition in London? That would be so exciting – just to be considered – but how is it done?'

'I have the details,' said Mr Fry. 'You may send a photograph in, and the members consider it; nothing lost, you know, if is not accepted.'

'I should like to, then, very much, if you think it not too presumptuous. And will you also be submitting something, Mr Fry?'

'I? No, I do not think so; I am a mere hack, now, taking portraits for money. Not that I mind that, at all – it is what I like to do, and the business is thriving more than I ever dared hope.'

'We took some fine pictures of the railway,' said Jennie. 'I wonder if we might send up one of those?'

'Ah, yes, that is a possibility,' he said. 'There were some unusual ones, were there not? All that steam, and smoke, and speed. Well, we will see. Did you mention tea, Eveline?'

Louisa had stayed in bed for the greater part of the day, but by the evening she was up, and dressed, and asking Eveline to do her hair.

'I cannot think how you manage without a lady's maid,' she said. 'Why have you not got a new one? Mama is being very lazy about it; I shall speak to her.'

'We have decided not to have a lady's maid at all,' said Eveline. 'Do not tease Mama about it; the truth is, Lou, we have to watch our expenditure. We were exceeding it, a little, and we are making some economies.'

'I have always thought economy a very *ugly* word,' said Louisa.

'I dare say you have,' said Eveline. 'There! You look as lovely as ever. Will you come down and join us for dinner?'

'I suppose I must. Although why I am dressing to have dinner with you and Mama, and Aunt George, and the Angell, I do not know. It hardly seems worth the effort.'

'But you must be glad we do not have any guests, when you are so unhappy, and feeling so wretched.'

'A guest might have done me good – distracted me from my sorrows. You seem to have Charles, and Mr Watson, and goodness knows who else, to dine every five minutes when I am not here, according to Beatrice.'

'If you think you will be able to face it, there is a yachting party proposed for next week. Perhaps that will lift your spirits.'

'A yachting party! That does sound like something that might do me good. I recall Charles mentioning something once – I wonder why he did not invite me?'

'Only because you were not here when he arranged it, I am sure. You had gone back home. I expect he did not think you would be able to come back so soon.'

'Yes, that will be it. Still, I think he might have written. And now, I suppose, I am excluded! I can hardly invite myself.'

'I am very sure Charles would be delighted if you can come. Why do not I write him a note, saying you are here, after all?'

'Yes, do, Eveline; I am sure he would want me to be there, for all Beatrice is forever claiming that Charles only has eyes for her.'

'I thought you and Beatrice were intending him for me. I am sure Mama is,' said Eveline wryly.

'Oh, of course; that is different. You should marry him, to be sure, if you can get him; a little light-hearted flirtation on my part, or Bea's, is neither here nor there.'

Eveline wondered at her sisters' views, but any further discussion on the propriety or otherwise of married people's flirtations might have led back to the distressing subject of Bevis, so she held her tongue; and in any case, she reflected, she herself could not now claim that her own behaviour in that direction was entirely proper. Thomas Armitage's kisses would keep coming back into her mind, despite her stern lectures to herself on the utter folly of such thoughts.

Charles was, naturally, most happy that Louisa could be a member of the yachting party; but the weather had turned, and the proposed day came and went in a flurry of cold rain and stormy skies. Louisa remained in bed every day there was no prospect of going out, merely dressing for the evening meal; but the end of the week approached, and the sun reappeared, and the excursion was fixed for the morrow.

'Is it proper, to be doing such a thing, on a Sunday?' wondered Mrs Stanhope, but it was agreed that if they went to church first thing, they might be there at the quayside by late morning, with no impropriety. Eveline, Louisa, Beatrice and Arthur, were to go aboard with Charles and Sir William, while the older family members, and the youngest, were to come down to the shore later, bringing a picnic luncheon. The children were outraged that they were not to go onto the boat, and were only mollified by the promise of a trip in the future – when everyone was sure such a thing would be safe – and some coconut candy.

The sailing yacht was a great gleaming thing, all polished wood and brass, and Sir William wore a blue blazer, white trousers and a peaked hat, and looked as smart as any admiral.

'I think I might get a hat like that,' said Charles. 'What do you think, Arthur? Would we look as dashing as my uncle if we had the rig?'

'You will have to become a member of the club to have the right to wear it,' said Sir William, 'and they don't let just anyone in, Nevvy.'

'And what do the ladies wear, Sir William?' asked Beatrice. 'Something equally fetching, I hope?'

'Ladies! No, we do not have lady members; this is a gentleman's sport, you know.'

'I do not think that is right,' said Louisa crossly. 'It is always the same: we are shut out of anything delightful.'

'You may drink tea on the lawn,' Sir William assured her. 'I shall invite you in August. You will like that, I am sure.'

The yacht did not seem so very large once they were aboard. Sir William conferred hastily with his skipper (for he was very new to the sport himself), and the skipper gave orders to the deckhands, and the ropes were cast off, and they began to move away from the shore. Eveline wondered if it were quite safe, for the boat rocked alarmingly, and the sails swung back and forth in a most dangerous manner. Soon, however, they were sailing more steadily; there was just enough breeze to take them forwards. In the distance, a vast ship moved majestically along, looming from the slight heat haze that had formed over the water.

'That is a liner, leaving Southampton, and on its way to some distant place – America, perhaps,' said Charles. 'That is a thought, is it not?'

'Indeed, it is!' said Eveline. 'I should like to travel on a liner. I think it might be more to my taste than yachting.'

'Oh, you are become very grand, Eveline,' said Louisa. 'More to your taste, indeed!'

'Less chance of being drowned, is all I meant.'

'You will not drown today, I assure you; we are barely a hundred yards from the shore. You could very likely swim if we run aground,' said Charles.

They rounded the headland and idled a little way along the coast. The wind had died away almost completely, and it was stiflingly hot. The skipper spoke to Sir William, and it was decided to turn the boat about, and head back, for with so little breeze they were virtually becalmed, and soon the tide would be against them. There was much *heaving on the sheets*, and cries to *beware the boom*, and still they did not seem to be moving either forwards or backwards. Sir William stood grandly at the wheel, but took no further part in the handling of the yacht, and Charles had disposed himself on the cushioned seats, with Louisa and Beatrice either side of him, while he regaled them with stories of sailing in Italy. Eveline thought longingly of the shore, and the picnic; at least they were not far away. Arthur seemed as disengaged as she, for despite his professional interest in the sails, he was no sailor, and he was leaning over the side of the boat with a greenish pallor over his face.

'Are you quite well, Arthur?' she asked.

'No, I am feeling dashed odd,' he said. 'I do not really care for boats, never have; I would far sooner be on shore looking at them, than on them,' and he clutched the rail a little tighter.

'I am not very keen, myself,' she said. 'At least we can say we have tried it, I suppose.'

There was a shout from the water below them, and Eveline raised her hand to shade her eyes so that she could see where the voice had come from.

'Here!' called someone. She squinted into the sun: there were heads bobbing in the water, sleek and wet, and one of the swimmers raised an arm to wave.

'By Jove!' said Arthur weakly. 'Is that Armitage? And two others: a woman, look – she is calling to you, Eveline.'

Chapter Twenty-Two

A Picnic, and Some News

It was Jennie, and Ned, and Thomas, all now lazily treading water, and smiling up at those on board.

'Coming in?' shouted Thomas, cheerfully. 'It's pretty good, today. You are a swimmer, Arthur, come and join us!' He swam a few strokes, with a strong, slow grace, until he was just below the prow of the yacht.

Arthur visibly brightened. 'I may well do so,' he said, 'for I am tired of this rocking about and going nowhere, and it is so dashed hot. I should feel a great deal better for a dip.'

Beatrice had turned to see what was happening.

'Who are you talking to, Arthur?' she called. 'What is going on?'

'Friends,' said Arthur, 'and I am just going to cool off. You need not wait for me, though. I had rather swim than sail.'

'We are here as Charles's guests,' said Beatrice, 'what are you thinking of? Please, Arthur, do not make a spectacle of yourself.'

'Sandham will not mind, I know,' said Arthur, struggling to remove his boots. 'I shall swim back to shore, and join you all later; I can walk back, you know.'

'No, Arthur,' said Beatrice. 'Whatever are you doing? Do not get in the water; it is absurd. I forbid you to get in, I absolutely forbid you!' But Arthur, having removed his boots and his jacket, and wearing only trousers and a shirt, executed a graceful dive from the side of the yacht, and reappeared moments later, looking much refreshed, and swam over towards the others.

'What has happened? Is it man overboard?' called Sir William, who was at the ship's wheel, very conscious of his role as the man in charge.

'No,' said Eveline, 'do not worry; Arthur is swimming off the yacht, that is all.'

Beatrice was looking exasperated. 'I am so sorry, Charles,' she said. 'He is behaving most oddly. Do not wait for him; he will have to get back as best he may.'

'You do not need to apologise to me, Beatrice,' said Charles. 'The man is free to do whatever he wishes. But the tide will turn; we cannot wait for him.'

'Eveline! Will you join us too?' shouted Arthur.

'No!' said Louisa and Beatrice together. 'Eveline, do not even think of doing so,' added Beatrice warningly.

Eveline looked longingly at the bathers. The sea was a pale milky blue, and the sunlight touched each ripple with gold. Jennie's hair was spread out around her like a mermaid's; Ned and Arthur were racing each other, with a good deal of shouting and splashing; and Thomas, floating on his back, raised an arm towards Eveline, and waved, and then took a gulp of air, and turned, and dived. How cool, how delicious the water would be on the skin, she thought; how glorious to feel the waves lift one up, and slide like silk over one's naked shoulders.

'Goodness me!' said Louisa, who had come to the front of the boat, and was looking over the side with interest. 'I am not perfectly sure those people are wearing bathing costumes, or indeed anything at all. Is that possible? In any case, Eveline, you must not swim; it would be so unladylike, and would very probably be the death of Mama if you were to do such a thing, and what would everyone think?'

Eveline gave the scene a last, regretful look, and then turned away. 'No, of course I shan't,' she said. 'Are we moving, at last? I do not care for yachting, very much. I have had enough.'

The picnic was spread on the shore, and the sailors were welcomed back to the feast as though they had made a lengthy sea voyage. Mrs Stanhope's initial conviction on seeing the party reduced by one member was that Arthur had certainly drowned; but that fear having been allayed, she was happy enough to preside over the party. Sir William sat beside her, and complimented her on the stuffed eggs, and Charles paid flattering attention to all her daughters; although of the three, strangely, it was Eveline whom anyone might have suspected of being out of sorts, rather than Beatrice or Louisa, who were masking their respective delicate health and broken heart very valiantly.

It was not until the last crumbs were being shaken from the picnic rug, and the children were releasing back into the sea the bucket of crabs that they had caught under Miss Angell's fond tuition, that Arthur strolled into view. Beatrice, laughing heartily at some sally from Charles, affected not to notice his return at all, and Louisa merely raised her eyebrows at his damp hair and less than usually dapper appearance.

'Arthur, you are safe! Thank goodness,' said Mrs Stanhope. 'I was so alarmed for you, and I could not quite believe that you were not in some terrible danger. But whatever are you wearing?'

'Armitage lent me some clothes, and these boots; he's a bit taller than I, and the boots are certainly too big, but it was very decent of him,' said Arthur. 'I had a splendid time, and I mean to swim every day, now; I had forgotten how much I used to like it.'

Beatrice sighed. 'I do not think it is a gentleman's sport, Arthur,' she said. 'Yachting most certainly is, however; you would do much better to learn to sail, like Charles. Just think of the people we would mix with! The grandest of the grand.'

'I prefer to mix with the people I like,' said Arthur stubbornly.

'And what about me, Arthur?' she demanded. 'It is all very well for you to be so high-handed, but you do not care for such things, and I do. Am I never to have the chance to go to really smart balls, and dinners, and parties?'

'I will invite you all to anything smart, if I can,' said Charles graciously. 'There are sure to be some splendid events here during the rest of the summer, and if I can secure invitations, I will certainly make sure you are all included.'

Louisa and Beatrice were full of gratitude and praise for this promised largesse.

'How pleasant it is to have such kind friends!' said Mrs Stanhope.

'Any occasion would be graced by your daughters, ma'am,' said Charles, adding as an afterthought, 'and, of course, by your sons-in-law.'

Arthur did not look very pleased by the prospect of gracing any occasions as Charles Sandham's guest; but he said nothing more. Eveline walked by his side as they left the shore, and tucked her hand into his arm.

'I am glad you swam,' she said. 'I envied you, so much!'

'You should have jumped in too, then, Evie,' he said, with a smile. 'Why did you not?'

'Oh, I should never have heard the last of it,' she said, 'and then, these stupid clothes; we have to go about in layers of stuff, you know, Arthur, even in the summer, and I would have been in trouble from Bea and Louisa beyond anything you can imagine, if I had swum in my petticoat.'

'I suppose so,' he said. 'Very hard, really, being a woman; I can see that.'

232

They walked in silence for a while.

'Did you ever get a chance to find out why Beatrice does not seem herself?' asked Eveline at last, in a low voice.

'Not yet,' said Arthur, 'I need to find the right moment, you know, and now I suppose I have blotted my copybook after today, and it will be even harder to get her to talk.'

The excitement of the day seemed to have left many of the party in lower spirits than before. Arthur and Beatrice returned to their own house, each speaking pointedly to Kitty rather than to each other; Louisa retreated to her bed for the remainder of the afternoon; and Eveline went to her studio to examine the latest photographs, a set of pictures of Daisy wearing wreaths of summer flowers, which she found were bleached and cracked and good for nothing. The discovery made her feel, absurdly, like bursting into tears. Dinner was a subdued affair, and it was generally agreed that the heat of the day had been insufferable, and had resulted in a universal headache, and that there was no remedy for it but an early night.

As so often, the morning seemed less dispiriting than the night before, and Eveline reminded herself, as she fed Autolycus, and hulled strawberries, and chatted with Mrs Groves and Mary, that she had very little to feel mournful about. Mary was in high spirits, for the next day she was to visit her family in Newport, and having saved the return fare was able to travel to them on the railway for one-and-tuppence, and be back in time for supper. It would be the first railway journey she had ever taken.

'I am not so much ahead of you, Mary,' said Eveline, 'for it is only a few weeks since I made my first journey.'

'And were you very frightened, miss?' asked Mary. 'They say it does go terribly fast.'

'It is delightful,' Eveline assured her, 'thrilling, and breathtaking, but I do not think you will be frightened.'

'I am sure I will not know what to do,' said Mary. 'How do I get my ticket, I wonder? And then will we be thrown about like chickens on the carrier's cart, when the train dashes forward?'

'Perhaps you would like me to accompany you?' said Eveline. 'I can amuse myself, while you see your family, and we can travel home together.'

'I cannot put you to that trouble, miss,' said Mary.

'I should like to,' Eveline assured her. 'How old are you, Mary?'

'Fourteen, miss.'

'I should not have been as brave as you at fourteen, Mary. Let us go together, and then next time you will be perfectly confident.'

'Is it right, though, for us to travel together?' said Mary doubtfully. 'Me being a servant, miss, and you being a lady.'

Eveline laughed. 'My sisters keep telling me I am not very ladylike at all, Mary. I do not really think it matters very much. You and I will have a perfectly nice journey together.'

'You'll be in different bits of the train, though,' said Mrs Groves. 'One in first class, one in second. That's how it is, I hear.'

'I have travelled in both,' said Eveline, 'and do you know, I rather liked the second class carriages. We'll both travel in the same carriage tomorrow, Mary.'

Having made this promise, Eveline's concern now was how she might persuade her mother not to stand in her way. She had been very much stung by the suggestion that she was a prisoner, and she was determined not to be weak-spirited or subservient; and yet she did not wish to defy her mother's express instructions that she was not to go about unaccompanied. She was mulling over this conundrum, when a morning caller was announced. Mr Watson had, it seemed, just been passing, and had only dropped in to enquire after the health of all the household. He had heard (he did not say from whom) that there had been a yachting party, and wanted to assure himself that no chills had been caught, or worse.

'I did not go aboard,' Mrs Stanhope assured him. 'Just the young people, you know, and I thought that with Sir William in charge they could not be in very much danger.'

'Sir William is an expert sailor, then?' asked Mr Watson.

'Oh, indeed,' said Mrs Stanhope, 'most expert; you could see that, from the way he stood so grandly on the deck, as though he owned it.'

'He does own it, Mama,' said Eveline.

'Yes, I know that; but what I mean is, he looked as though it were a very natural thing for him to be at sea, and in charge of such a great big boat.'

'I think the skipper, and the deckhands, and the engineer,

and the steward, knew quite a lot more than Sir William did,' said Eveline.

'Travelling by sea is all very well,' said Mr Watson, 'but when will you ladies be travelling on my railway again, is what I would like to know? Very much safer, and faster, you know, than any amount of yachts.'

Eveline saw an opportunity.

'I am planning a little trip tomorrow, as it happens,' she said gaily. 'I am very much looking forward to it, Mr Watson; just there and back, you know, and our little kitchen maid is making her first journey alone, so I shall be able to keep an eye on her.'

'That is splendid!' said Mr Watson. 'And your lady mother; will she join you?' and he turned to Mrs Stanhope with such a beaming smile of hope, that she could only smile back, and say that alas, poor Louisa was staying with them, and was a little low, and needed her mama.

'Another time, then, Mrs Stanhope? You will promise me?'

'Oh, I will, to be sure; but Eveline, I do not think it is right for you to be travelling alone.'

'I shall be with Mary, Mama.'

'Mary is a scarcely more than a child, and you know, Evie, that we have spoken about this sort of thing before.'

'Miss Stanhope need have no concerns,' said Mr Watson. 'Many of the very best people are travelling by railway, these days, and I will be at the station myself, tomorrow, and I can see her onto the train, all right and tight.'

There was nothing for Mrs Stanhope to do, but to accede with as good a grace as she could muster.

'Thank you, Mama,' said Eveline, very much cheered by the prospect of a day out. 'And Mr Watson, I may see you tomorrow, then. I think our train leaves at a quarter past ten.'

'That is it; the ten-fifteen!'

He gathered his hat, and walking cane, and made his farewells. 'Oh! Eveline,' he said, turning back, 'I had almost forgotten: the board did make a decision about your request. They did not decide immediately, you see, but asked for some information as to what other companies had done in that line. We were waiting for a letter from Camden Town, explaining about a fund that a group of railway clerks had established. It relies very heavily on public support, of course; but the upshot is, we think we will establish a fund of that nature here, to relieve distress among orphans and widows. Can't be having those Londoners ahead of us in such matters, eh?'

'Oh,' said Eveline, 'oh, Mr Watson! That is the most wonderful news!' and she stepped forward impulsively and kissed him.

'Well, well,' he said, pleased, 'it is the right thing, you know, and Tom spoke up for it, and made us see sense.'

'You are all very much to be admired,' said Eveline, 'and please tell me what else I may do to help? Shall I write letters to ask for subscriptions, do you think?'

'I cannot have you writing to our friends to ask for money, Eveline,' said her mother, shocked.

'I think most people will want to help; and if they do not, they certainly should.'

'How would it be,' said Mr Watson diplomatically, 'if Eveline were to draft something for us, and the letter can go out from me? She has a way with words, you know, and that would be most helpful; but I can sign the letters, of course.'

Both Eveline and her mother were very happy with this solution; and Mrs Stanhope even went so far as to say that she thought Augusta Sandham should most certainly be the first to be asked for a substantial sum to support the new fund.

Chapter Twenty-Three

Eveline Makes a Plan

Eveline and Mary were in excellent time for the ten-fifteen train.

'This used to be Hog Lane,' said Mary knowledgeably, as they climbed the little hill up towards the station, 'where my uncle had a piggery.'

'Did your uncle lose his livelihood, then, when the railway came?' enquired Eveline.

'He gave up the pigs,' said Mary, 'and he was sad to do so, for he loved them pigs. My aunt was very glad, for she had put up with the smell for so long; but now he has work at the coal yard for the railway, and she is just as cross about the black clothes she has to wash.'

They bought their tickets at the office, and Mr Watson appeared to greet them, and show them into the waiting room. Everything was delightful to Mary, and Eveline felt as though she were now, after her one previous journey, an experienced traveller, and enjoyed Mary's expressions of wonder at seeing the cushioned benches, and the framed prints, and the fireplace to keep passengers warm in the winter months. A bell rang to announce the arrival of the train, and they went out onto the platform to see the great plume of steam, and the magnificent sight of the locomotive rounding the curve of the track, and thundering towards them. They boarded a second class carriage and found seats by the window; the whistle blew, and they were off. Once again, there was the excitement of the tunnel, and then the prospect of the river opening before them, and the fields and trees whisking past them as they gazed.

The journey was over all too soon, and Mary made for her family's house, and Eveline walked down to the quay to watch the boats, and then wandered among the shops for a while. It was strange, but delicious, to be free to walk about the streets by herself; it felt like a holiday – 'far more so than yesterday's ridiculous trip on the yacht,' she said to herself. She went first to the apothecary's shop, and bought a tiny bottle of scent for her mother, and a pot of rouge for Louisa, and soaps perfumed with sandalwood and rose for her aunt and Miss Angell; and then to the bookseller's, where she found a copy of *Idylls of the King*, wondered if it would be an extravagance to buy it for herself, decided it would, and then guiltily purchased it anyway; and then went into the old teahouse on the corner where she ordered a pot of China tea and a plate of buttered muffins, and sat and watched the world go by through the bow windows until it was time to walk back to the station to meet Mary again for the journey home.

It was a quiet journey home, Mary very nearly asleep after the excitement of her day, and Eveline reflective. It had been altogether delightful to have no one but oneself to please, she thought, and to escape from her usual environs, even to another small town; and yet she felt a little wistful, although she hardly knew why. Perhaps it was the memory of her previous journey along this route, with Thomas opposite her. *Are you then a prisoner?* he had asked. What absurdity! And here she was, after all, travelling independently, and going about the town, and even dining alone. She closed her eyes, and a memory of his throwing his apple core out of the window came back to her. Perhaps she might see him at the station; he would see, then, that she was an independent spirit, and a modern woman, and have to eat his words; but there was no one on the platform as the train drew in but the stationmaster, and half a dozen men in sober grey jackets, clerks, perhaps, heading for home. Well, it was a contradiction, in any case, she thought, for an independent spirit to be wishing to see another person, particularly an engaged one; and she would put the whole thing out of her head, and concentrate on her photographs, and on her family, than which nothing could be more important.

Louisa did not come down to dinner at all that evening. She said that she had caught the sun from the day before, and it had made her feel rather feverish, and she did not want anything to eat. Eveline carried her up a glass of wine and sat on her bed.

'You do look pale, Louisa,' she said.

'Well, that is something,' said Louisa, 'if I look pale, then I have not gone quite brown from being out of doors on the yacht.'

'Look, I brought you a little present from town,' said Eveline, 'a pot of rouge. The apothecary said it was from Paris, and the very latest thing; just enough to give you a hint of a blush, nothing more.'

Louisa sat up and consented to look at the rouge, and to take some sips of wine.

'Thank you, Evie,' she said forlornly. 'I only wish—' but she could not say any more, for tears had begun to spill down her cheeks.

'Oh, Lou,' said Eveline, 'do not cry; it will be all right, in the end, I am sure,' but Louisa was now sobbing with real distress, and Eveline put her arms around her and rocked her to and fro until the crying resolved itself into gasps and hiccups.

'Oh, Evie,' said Louisa, trying to speak steadily, and not altogether succeeding, 'he has been gone over a week now, and there has been no word. Perhaps he is not coming back at all.'

'Might he have sent word to your home?' suggested Eveline. 'We can send over to enquire, in the morning; there may be a letter waiting for you.'

'I left instructions with my housekeeper that anything that arrived must be forwarded straight here,' said Louisa. 'I look for something every day, and nothing comes. The thing is, Evie—' she stopped.

'Yes? What is it, Lou?'

'The thing is, I love him.' She looked bleak. 'I have always loved him, since we first met, and I have always known that I loved him more than he loved me, but I thought that he would grow to love me more as time went on; and then he dotes on Henry and Daisy, really, though he pretends to be a little careless about them. I thought I would be the happiest creature in the world, to be married to Bevis. And now, instead, I am the most miserable,' and she burst into a fresh paroxysm of tears.

'Louisa, we will find him. There will be an explanation. I am sure he loves you too.'

'I do not see how you can say that,' she said, between sobs. 'And how can we find him? Who is to look for him?'

'I am thinking,' said Eveline. 'Something may be done; I promise you, I will make a plan.'

By the time she was back downstairs, Aunt George and Miss Angell had retired, and her mother was sitting in the drawing room alone, looking very nearly as melancholy as Louisa.

'Look, Mama, a tiny gift for you,' said Eveline, and gave her the little box printed with flowers and tied with a purple ribbon.

'Oh! Violet scent. Evie, you are too kind,' said her mother. 'I have always loved this, you know; your papa used to buy it for me,' and she looked for a moment as though she, too, might cry.

'I know you like it, Mama, and have not bought any for a while; I hope it does not upset you,' said Eveline.

'No, no, I have only the sweetest of memories,' said her mother. 'The very first time he gave me this was on our wedding day, you know; I carried a bunch of violets, and he gave me a pearl necklace, and a bottle of this perfume. I thought I should die of happiness, Evie.' She dabbed a little of the scent on her wrist. 'He used to call me Adèle, you know. Do you remember? No one else ever did, and I have never liked Adelaide as a name.'

'Adèle is very pretty,' said Eveline softly. 'It becomes you, Mama.'

'But if only he were here,' said Mrs Stanhope tragically, 'he would know what to do about poor Louisa. He would go up to London, and find Bevis, and make him come home. And now who is to do that?'

'I have been thinking, Mama, about that very thing. I do have an idea.'

Mrs Stanhope regarded her hopefully.

'Do you, Evie? Are you thinking perhaps that Arthur would try?'

'I do not think Arthur should go, for Beatrice needs him at home, just now. She is, I think, feeling a little lonely, or unsettled, or something – I am not quite sure – I think Arthur's place is at her side.'

She did not add: *for if Arthur were away for a while, Beatrice might very well fall into the arms of another man.*

'Then who is to do it? For we cannot ask anyone outside the family, no, not even Mr Watson, or Charles, be they ever so dear to us; this is such a shameful, shocking thing, that we must keep it quite to ourselves, for poor Louisa's sake.'

'I agree,' said Eveline, 'we will not ask anyone outside the family.'

'Then—oh, no, Evie, no, please do not suggest that you would go to London. Tell me that you are not thinking of that.'

'I think it is the only thing, Mama. I have a plan, though, that will make it all perfectly respectable.'

'I very much doubt that,' said her mother wearily.

'Do just hear me, though, Mama. I am planning to submit some prints to the Photographic Society, in London. What could be more suitable than travelling there, and taking the prints in person, and then staying for a few days while I hunt for Bevis?'

'Alone? No, impossible.'

'Here is the clever part,' said Eveline. 'Mr Fry may be sending some prints in, too. If he were to travel up with me – we can say he is an uncle, or a godfather, or something, if you wish – then that would be perfectly acceptable, would it not?'

'Theodore Fry! But he is not family. We cannot let him know what is happening. Oh, no, Evie, this will never work.'

'I will only tell him that I am travelling up to the society. He knows I would wish to do that – why should he think anything else?'

'But where would you stay?' cried Mrs Stanhope. 'You would need to be there for days, perhaps. And then, the expense!'

'I thought, with your permission, I would use a little of the money you said you had set aside for my wedding, Mama. To provide for that event is still, after all, not an immediate necessity; it may never be so. As to where I stay: there must be respectable hotels, even in London,' said Eveline. 'I will invent some reason – oh, buying photographic equipment, or visiting a friend; who is to know? Poor Louisa is distraught, Mama, and who else is to help if I do not? If Papa were here, he would do so; but he is not, and I am perfectly capable of trying, at least, to find Bevis, without coming to any harm.'

Mrs Stanhope raised her wrist and sniffed the violet scent. 'I am not at all sure, my love. And how will you begin to look for Bevis, in any case? You might search the streets of London for a year, and never find him.'

'Well,' said Eveline, 'I do have an idea. I have spoken to Betsy, and I asked if she could think of anything that might give us an idea of where Hannah had written from. If he is not with Hannah, then I cannot think where he may be; she seems our only hope. Betsy insisted she did not know at all, but when I pressed her to remember anything at all, even the slightest hint, she said that Hannah had once mentioned that her cousin lived in a lighthouse.'

'That does not sound very likely; are there lighthouses in London, do you think?'

'I have been looking at Papa's old map of London, to try to find such a thing, and I cannot. But there is a place called Limehouse, and when I asked Betsy if she could have been mistaken, and that Limehouse could have been what Hannah said, she thought it possible. So, if that is the only clue we have, I shall start there; just asking, you know, in shops, and so forth, if anyone has seen him.'

'How will they know? There must be a thousand young men

walking about who would answer to a description of Bevis; medium height, brown hair; it is not enough, Evie, surely.'

'Aha!' said Eveline in triumph. 'Here, you see, is where I have a trump card. A few weeks ago I persuaded Bevis to let me take some photographs of him. We have the one from Mr Fry, too, but that is rather small; the ones I took are much larger, and there are several, from various angles. Admittedly, he was dressed as Macbeth, but his face is perfectly clear, and if you ignore the tartan cloak it is a very good likeness.'

Mrs Stanhope sighed. 'I do not know, Evie; it seems a terrible thing for you to have to do. And yet I do not know what is to become of poor Louisa if you do not. Shall we not just wait, to see if Bevis returns?'

'We may have to, Mama, if I cannot find him. It is a little unlikely, I admit, but worth trying, I do believe. Louisa is so unhappy, and at least I would be doing something to help.'

Chapter Twenty-Four

Mrs Stanhope's Secret

Mr Theodore Fry, Professor of Photography, needed very little persuasion to think that an excursion to London in Eveline's company was a splendid idea. They would write to the Photographic Society in advance, to arrange a morning visit, and it would be a fine chance to see the latest advances in the art; and to take their own offerings in person would be far preferable to entrusting them to a carrier or the penny post.

'I shall take the chance to visit my brother's family,' said Mr Fry. 'They are in London, and I have not seen my nephews and nieces for a year, now; it will be very pleasant to see how they have grown, and they will be wild to hear about the island, which they think very savage and remote.'

'Perhaps they will come and visit you, one day?' suggested Eveline.

'They will need some persuasion to venture to such a far-off place; but if I can reassure them that there are no cannibals, or fire-breathing dragons, they may do so. And you, Eveline, where will you stay? You have some friends in London, no doubt, who will be glad to welcome you?'

Eveline replied vaguely to this kind enquiry, and changed the subject to which of their photographs they thought worthy of consideration by the august society. In fact, she had very little idea of where she might stay, and was at a loss to know whom she might consult. Louisa – who was so cheered by Eveline's plan that Mrs Stanhope had almost ceased to protest about it – said that she and Bevis had once stayed at Claridge's, in Brook Street, but that it was certainly a rather expensive place.

'That is out of the question, then,' said Eveline. 'I need somewhere that does not cost us a fortune. Mama, do we not owe the Sandhams a morning visit? Charles must know London better than most; perhaps he will know of somewhere. I need not say why I am interested.'

'We seem to be weaving an extremely tangled web,' said Mrs Stanhope, but she consented to go with Eveline to call on Lady Sandham, and Louisa said that she would go too, so as to keep up the appearance of there being nothing amiss, and she certainly looked a little less pale than before. The Sandhams were at home, and happy to receive them; Charles greeted them all with effusive compliments, and Sir William was very glad to relive with them the glories of their day at sea.

'What news of your husband, Louisa?' asked Lady Sandham. 'An uncle, I understand, in poor health; Bevis must be very fond of him, to stay away from you for so long.'

'Extremely fond,' said Louisa, dully.

Mrs Stanhope rose to the occasion. 'Bevis is his only relative. He would not stay away from Louisa if he did not know it to be his duty. Moreover,' she said, warming to her task, 'there may very well be a legacy, you know, of a Scottish castle, with – with a grouse moor, and deer, and all sorts of things.'

Eveline and Louisa looked at her in horror.

'Then that is certainly worth staying away for,' said Sir William heartily. 'I hope he will invite us up for the shooting when he is a laird, eh, Charles?'

'It must certainly be something very important to keep him away from such a pretty wife,' said Charles.

Louisa smiled weakly. 'Too kind,' she murmured, and looked imploringly at Eveline.

Eveline sprang to her feet. 'Charles,' she said, 'did you not promise to show me some more of your pictures from your travels? I don't believe Louisa ever saw the views of Paris, either, and I know she would like to.'

'My pleasure, of course,' said Charles. Once in the library, Eveline and Louisa admired the engravings and prints, and Charles had the grace to blush very slightly when Eveline asked if he did not have any photographs of the ladies of Paris.

'For we are naturally both very interested in the Paris fashions,' she said innocently.

Charles bit his lip. 'I would certainly have brought pictures of ladies in fine clothes, had I known they would meet with such an appreciative audience,' he said.

Eveline thought she had better stop teasing him.

'Do you prefer Paris to London, Charles?' she asked. 'I have never been to either city; Louisa thinks London very fine, though.'

'Both splendid, in their way,' said Charles, 'though I would not live outside England, you know; good to see other lands, but I don't care too much for foreign places, on the whole.'

'I wonder where people stay, when they visit London?' said Eveline. 'If I should, one day, go there, for example?'

'Oh, there are a thousand hotels,' said Charles. 'I lodged in the Tavistock for quite a time, myself; one of the best smoking rooms in London, the Tavistock.'

'Would a lady be able to stay there?'

'Not a place for ladies, really – at least, not for ladies like you. Are you thinking of making a trip up to town, then, Eveline?'

'Oh, no,' said Eveline hastily, 'of course not; it is idle curiosity, that is all, but in the future, you know, I might.'

'If you ever do, I gather the new railway hotels are said to be well-conducted establishments. Built near all the big stations, for travellers; pretty decent places, I imagine. But I feel sure that, when you do venture to the great city, it will not be to stay in a railway hotel. You will be protected by some fortunate companion, or, dare I say, by some even more fortunate man who has the honour to be your husband, and then you will be staying in the finest establishments.'

'Possibly,' said Eveline. 'Thank you, Charles, that is most helpful.' She gave Louisa a meaningful look.

'Oh! Yes,' said Louisa, obligingly. 'We had better return to Mama, had we not, Evie? We have stayed for far too long already, I am sure.'

Mrs Stanhope was only too ready to make her farewells.

'I fear I am becoming nothing short of an accomplished liar,' she said as they walked home. 'Augusta would not let the subject drop, you know, and I was obliged to invent a whole Scottish family who had met a terrible end, to account for Bevis's being the sole heir.'

'Heavens, Mama!' said Louisa. 'What did you say had become of them?'

'I am afraid I drowned them in a loch,' said Mrs Stanhope. 'It was a boating accident, you see. It seemed simplest; but then Sir William wanted to know what sort of boat it was, and what the weather conditions were, and was there an experienced sailor with them – you know what he is like – and then how many acres of grouse moor the estate had, and if it were near Balmoral. I declare I am quite astonished at my own powers of invention.'

'Oh, Mama,' said Eveline, 'you are a marvel, indeed. Perhaps you had better write down what you said, so that we can all learn it by heart, in case we are obliged to bring the story out again.'

Mr Fry had received a most courteous letter from the Photographic Society, cordially inviting him and Miss

Stanhope to visit; and the date for the journey to London was therefore speedily fixed. The Bradshaw timetable was consulted, and maps pored over, and Eveline's bag packed. But the day before she was due to travel, Mrs Stanhope again began to grow fearful that the idea was bound to end in the loss of Eveline's reputation, or her honour, or even her life; and it was very hard to say which of those alarmed her the most.

'People travel every day, Mama, without coming to harm,' said Eveline. 'I shall find whichever of the railway hotels is nearest to the Waterloo Bridge station, and I am sure it will not be in a dangerous part of town, you know.'

'But my love, you will be going into some dreadful places if you are to hunt for Bevis; Limehouse, you said, and the very word seems alarming. You will be a young woman all alone – you, who have led such a sheltered life, here in our little safe world.'

'Then it is time I ventured out into the wider world, surely?' Eveline looked at her mother with a mixture of affection and exasperation. 'Why have we been so confined, Mama? We could have travelled, a little, when I was growing up – at least to London, or some other city – but I have not ever left the Island. I have hardly left Cowes, or not above a dozen times.'

'Your dear papa was not one to get about very much,' said Mrs Stanhope. 'He cared for his books, and his walks, but not a great deal for travelling, or parties, or anything of that sort. And when he was taken from us, so suddenly, I could not find the spirits to do very much more than keep our day-to-day life running.'

'Of course, Mama. I do not blame you for that.'

'And now I am letting you travel to London, and go about that wicked city all alone. Oh, I am a very poor mother! Heaven forbid any of our acquaintance should discover what you are doing.'

'It is not so very terrible, Mama. After all, if I were a man – if I were a son, rather than a daughter – no one would think it at all odd.'

Mrs Stanhope rose from her chair, and walked to the window, and gazed out at the garden and the distant sea for a few minutes. Something about her mother's stillness, quite unlike her usual flutterings and fidgetings, kept Eveline silent. When at last Mrs Stanhope turned, and came back to sit by Eveline, her eyes were swimming in tears.

'There was a little boy, Evie,' she said. 'I had a son. He was born just a year after Beatrice. So little! Too little to survive. He would have been John, after your father, if he had lived.'

Eveline felt the tears start to her own eyes.

'Oh, Mama, I did not know. Why have you never told me this? Why have my sisters never told me?'

'Louisa and Beatrice were still almost babies themselves. They did not know what had happened; we did not speak of it, afterwards. One does not, you know. It was too painful.'

'You have kept this secret, all these years, Mama; how you must have suffered!'

'I have three daughters, and now I have grandchildren. I count my blessings, Evie. But I still think about my little boy, every day. I wish that I had something to remember him by, but I have nothing save my memories of that day: his birth, and how the midwife put him in my arms, but he did not cry, and I knew that I was the mother of a son, but it was all too late, and he had gone.'

Eveline held her mother's hand tightly. 'Is he buried in the churchyard?' she asked, as gently as she could.

'He could not be; he was not christened, because he died too soon; so the midwife took him away. I do not know where. I could not bear to ask.'

'I am so sorry, Mama. A brother! I should have liked a brother, I think. What can I do to help? Shall we, perhaps, plant a rose in the churchyard, in his memory; somewhere we could go to remember him?'

'I would like that, Evie. A white rose; yes, next to your father's grave, so that I can think of them together.'

'Then we will; and perhaps you will tell Louisa, and Beatrice, so that we may all think of him, and you will not feel quite so alone?'

'Yes, if you think it would not distress them too much. But I have not been altogether alone with my memories; your aunt was there when he was born, and she was very good to me. She let me talk about him, you know, for all the sad days and weeks that followed, when your papa could not endure it, and went out all day for long walks by himself. Men suffer, you know, differently to women. I do not know how I would have managed without George. She helped me beyond anything I can describe.'

'I am glad, then, that you had her there.'

'She is a wonderful woman. There again, you see, I have been very blessed, to have her company, and her friendship, all these years.'

'Thank you for telling me all this, Mama. It is right that I know. And I will do my best to do what a son might have done; I will see if I can find Bevis, and bring the family back together; or at least discover the truth. Will you have confidence in me?'

'Oh, Evie, you are a good girl, really; of course I have confidence in you. I know you are brave, and strong, and will do your best for us all. But you must take great care and you must try to be sensible; one week, that is the very longest time you must stay away. After that, come back, Bevis or no Bevis. Write to me as soon as you are arrived; and promise me that you will behave with propriety, and that you will remember to wear a hat.'

Chapter Twenty-Five

Eveline in London

Mrs Stanhope was a little comforted by the letter she received just two days after Eveline's departure.

My dear mama,
I am safely arrived in London, and have a room at the
Charing Cross Hotel in the Strand. I had only to walk over
the bridge from the railway station to find it, and the hotel
is most reasonable, though it appears very grand – built in
the Italian style, with great columns at the entrance, and
in the courtyard is a reproduction of the Eleanor cross, so
I am feeling very spoilt. It seems entirely respectable; there

are other ladies staying here alone, and there is a delightful
coffee room, an exceedingly fine apartment, set aside for
the use of ladies only; so you see you must have no fears for
me at all.

This is a brief note, because dear Mr Fry is to call on me
this morning, and we will go to the Photographic Society
together. Tomorrow I shall start my enquiries for Bevis. I
shall be perfectly sensible about it.

With my fondest love to you, and to Louisa —
Eveline
PS I will not forget about the hat.

'Well!' she said to Louisa. 'Perhaps your sister really is being sensible, at last. The qualities that have made her so headstrong and bold are now finding an outlet, I suppose; and if only she comes home safely, I shall never cease to be grateful.'

'As long as she comes home with news of Bevis,' said Louisa. 'The children are starting to be difficult now, always bothering me about where their father is, and when he is coming home, and what can I say?'

'Why do you not take them to the beach, today, my love? They always like that; we can get Beatrice and Kitty, too, and the sea air will do us all good. And we will just have to put our faith in Evie, and hope that our nerves can stand the test.'

Eveline, walking with Mr Fry through the streets of London on their way to meet the secretary of the Photographic

Society, with their most precious prints carefully wrapped and carried with breathless care, was conscious of a sense of exhilaration at the sheer vibrancy of the great city. So very many people – so many thousands, all busy, and purposeful. The noise of the streets, the shouts and the cries and the rattle of the hansom cabs, were all an assault on the senses that made her feel newly alive. There had been a moment of deep misgiving, when she had wondered what she was thinking of, to be here, with the intent of offering her own photographs to such an expert audience – I shall be found out, she thought, they will see through me, see that I am an amateur, a provincial girl, and I shall be sent away in disgrace – but Mr Fry's unfailing confidence and reassurances had restored her spirits.

'What is the worst that can happen, after all?' he said. 'They may not care for our photographs – what then? We will go away, and keep trying, and we shall no doubt have learnt something. That will have been worth the journey, in itself.'

'But you are already an exhibited artist, Mr Fry,' said Eveline. 'I am a novice.'

'You have the advantage of time before you, Eveline; yes, and a real artistic sensibility, I firmly believe. Here we are, I think; yes – shall we go in?'

The secretary of the society welcomed them into a room of such splendour it took Eveline's breath away: high friezes, of classical scenes, adorning every wall; an ornate ceiling high above them; glittering chandeliers. He was a tall, thin man, stooped, and kindly, and courteous.

'We do not have our own premises, yet,' he said. 'Photography is very new to the world; but we hope one day we will do so. For now, we are fortunate to have the kind patronage of the Society of Arts; they let us hold our meetings here.'

'It is wonderful – wonderful!' said Eveline. 'And so good of you to see us.'

'My pleasure, entirely,' said Mr Diamond. 'We are always interested to see new examples of our art. Will you take some coffee, Miss Stanhope? Mr Fry?'

The prints were unwrapped, and laid before Mr Diamond. They had brought three each, having agreed after much debate that more would seem pretentious; Mr Fry's were one portrait of Jennie, and two pictures taken on the day of the opening of the railway; Eveline's, a likeness of Daisy asleep, a study of the cedar tree in the early morning light, and her portrait of Aunt George. He studied them for a while, without saying anything; Eveline and Mr Fry sipped their coffee, and looked at each other, and held their breath.

'I do not have the power to decide on the merit or otherwise of work submitted, you understand,' he said at last. 'The committee sets aside time to assess new work, and select items for the next exhibition. That will not be for some time, I am afraid.'

'Shall we take the pictures away, then?' asked Eveline. She felt rather crushed.

'If you are happy to leave them with me, I will take good care of them,' said Mr Diamond. 'You must have a receipt, of course; but they will be safe. I have your address, sir, I believe; we can return them eventually.'

'Do you think there is any chance the committee will consider them?'

'Certainly I do,' he said. 'I would not give you false encouragement; but these are good – very good, I should say. I will be pleased to put these before my colleagues. And now, perhaps I may offer you some luncheon? The Crown and Anchor do a fine mutton chop; unless a tavern is a little rough and ready for you, Miss Stanhope?'

'Oh no,' she assured him, 'I like taverns very much.'

'Do you, indeed?' he said. 'Well, that is excellent. I shall look forward to hearing about how you came to photography so young.'

'It is all due to Mr Fry,' she explained. 'He is my mentor; he has taught me a great deal, and then he was kind enough to give me a camera of my own.'

'That is very much to your credit, sir.'

Mr Fry looked modest. 'Eveline was a very apt pupil. She will outshine me, very soon; and that is a great source of satisfaction to me.'

'You are too kind, Mr Fry,' said Eveline, glowing. 'May I order us a bottle of wine, to complement that mutton chop, do you think?'

The luncheon stretched out into the afternoon, with a great deal of talk, and good-humoured arguments about photographic techniques, and a second bottle of wine was brought to accompany the excellent marmalade tart, which followed the mutton. Eveline heard from their companion that there were several ladies who were keenly interested in photography, and were members of the society, and to her great satisfaction he seemed not to think there was anything extraordinary in that, or that this was in any way an exclusively masculine preserve. By the time Mr Fry and Eveline said goodbye to Mr Diamond, they felt as though he were an old friend, and he promised to let them know the committee's verdict as soon as it was humanly possible.

'Even if they reject us, I shall look back on this day with the greatest of pleasure,' said Eveline, and she bade an affectionate farewell to Mr Fry, and walked back to her hotel feeling very content with the world, and ready for whatever the morrow might bring.

She did feel less sanguine the next day, as she looked out of her window down to the street, five storeys below. A drizzling rain was falling on the stream of people and horses and carriages that surged along, turning the road into a quagmire; everyone hurried, collars turned up against the wet, everything was grey and drab. Here she was, quite alone, among tens of thousands of strangers, and with hardly an idea where to start on what now seemed a wildly over-optimistic plan. Nevertheless, after a hot breakfast, and a half-hour spent studying her father's old map of London, she felt braver; and she stepped out onto the Strand with her head held high, and hailed a hansom cab, and asked for Limehouse.

'Down by the docks, miss?' asked the driver. 'Sure you know where you're goin', do yer?'

'Certainly,' said Eveline. 'The West India Docks, if you

262

please,' for she had divided the map of the area into six, one for each of the days she could spend there, and meant to search each section methodically. The driver shrugged, and the horse lowered its head, and started to trot through the relentless rain. Inside the cab she was sheltered from the worst of the weather, and watched with interest as the streets grew smaller, and meaner, and darker, as they went further east. The buildings leant towards each other, shutting out the light, and tiny passages ran crazily in every direction. It was slow progress, for there was barely room in some places for two hansoms to pass each other, and there was much cursing and shouting as the cab slowed, and jolted, and inched round some obstruction; but at last, the driver leant down and said that this was Limehouse, and took his fare; and on receipt of a tip, showed her where the hansoms generally gathered so that she would know how to make her return journey, and then it rattled away, and Eveline was alone.

She put up her umbrella, took a deep breath, and went towards a boy selling newspapers.

'Might you have seen this man?' she asked, showing the photograph of Bevis that seemed to her to be the best likeness. No, he had not; so she moved on to a dingy printer's shop, and then to a stall that sold fruit, and then into a coffee shop. Some people were kind, some indifferent; some impatient. She was met with head-shakings, or shrugs, or helpful suggestions, or vulgar speculation, and occasionally invitations to discuss the matter further in a tavern; but there was nothing that seemed positive, no dawning light of recognition. The hours passed; she hardly stopped to rest, but walked, and walked, and asked, and asked, until she had been down every tiny alleyway, every narrow cutting, every dirty side street, in the section of her map that she had determined to cover today. By the time she was back in the hotel, soaked with the rain, cold, and exhausted, she was despondent, and lonely, and wondering if she might just abandon the whole thing and return home as soon as she could; but a pot of tea and a slice of currant cake, and then a hot bath in the huge tiled bathroom along the corridor from her bedroom, did a little to restore her optimism; and by the time she had dined on rump steak and a glass of claret, she felt her determination return. She would go back the next day, and the next, until she had asked every shopkeeper and stallholder in Limehouse if they had seen Bevis. If he was there, she would find him.

The second day of her search yielded a gleam of hope, from a woman who was selling flowers from a basket over her arm. The woman stared at the photograph for some moments, and then said she might have seen the fellow walking by the river, and she remembered him because he had bought a dozen bunches of violets from her on a day when she had sold almost nothing before, and had been wondering if she would be able to eat that evening. She showed Eveline the stretch of river where she thought it had been, down by the Wapping Wall, and when Eveline had thanked her, and given her a few shillings in gratitude, she stood on the banks of the Thames and watched the shining grey river. Gulls swooped over the water, and small craft rowed or sailed close to the shores, while bigger vessels headed downstream towards the sea. The late afternoon sun glinted on the water, reminding her for a moment of her home. The houses here were mean, and small, dwarfed by the tall warehouses, and there were no hotels – she had vaguely thought Bevis might be living in a grand hotel, but if he were, it was not in Limehouse.

By the evening of the fifth day, Eveline was almost disheartened. If she had no further information by the next day, she would give up; she would have to return home, she knew, mindful of her promise to her mother not to be away any longer than a week. She was on her way back to the street where she would find the hansom cabs lined up, when she saw a man ahead of her walking out of a tavern. The set of his shoulders looked familiar; she started forward, and was very nearly placing her hand on his arm, when he turned, and it was a stranger. Her disappointment was intense; for a wild moment she had been sure it was Bevis. She sighed, and then, on impulse, because she was thirsty, and weary, she walked into the tavern the man had just quitted.

It was a very different place from the Crown and Anchor where she had dined so pleasantly with Mr Diamond, and from the Union Inn where she had drunk with Thomas and Jennie and Ned. So dark and smoky that she could hardly see; so rank with beer, and sweat, and tobacco; so crowded, and noisy, and such a warren of little rooms. Yet it was warm, after the chill of the streets, and there was a cheerfulness and life that raised her spirits. She was wearing the purple-feathered hat, which Beatrice would have said made her look like a lady of quality, and Thomas would have said made her look like a tart; she did not particularly wish to look like either in this place, so she took the hat off, and shook her hair loose. She managed to get to the long wooden bar, and order a glass of ale. A few men looked at her, and she met their eyes, and smiled; but she raised an eyebrow if they got too close, and did not feel particularly threatened; there was an advantage in not being a tiny, frail-looking thing, all blushes and swoons, she thought, with some satisfaction. She squeezed her way through the crowd towards the rear of the tavern, where there was a small, dim, firelit room with just half a dozen people sitting with their drinks. There was one chair free, and she subsided gratefully into it, for her feet were sore from the stones and cobbles she had walked over for days, and her back ached. She took a gulp of ale, and leant over to the small, grimy window next to her, rubbing a little space on the dusty pane with her glove, so that she could look out. On the river, lights gleamed; fishing boats, perhaps, and barges, and great tea clippers, heading away to the ocean. She closed her eyes for a moment. I am quite free, she thought; no one knows where I am, no one in the world, at this moment. No one will reproach me, or tell me it is time to go home, or that I must put on my hat. She smiled at the thought, and drank the rest of her beer, savouring the moment and the strangeness of her situation, and reflecting that solitude, whether sought or unsought, was to be found most profoundly in the midst of a crowd; and then she began to think of her hotel, and a hot bath, and a good supper. As she stood up to leave, she moved the chair she had been sitting on, and caught the arm of the man at the next table, who had been drinking alone. He turned, as she began to apologise; and then the words died on her lips.

It was Bevis.

Chapter Twenty-Six

Bevis's Story

He sank back into his chair.

'Eveline – in God's name, how came you to be here, in this place?' He passed a hand over his eyes; he looked older by years, and very tired. 'I suppose they sent you to look for me?'

Eveline too sat down again.

'No one sent me, Bevis,' she said. 'I decided to come and see if I could find you myself, because Louisa is so unhappy, and my mother is distraught, and the children are missing you. But it was my idea, entirely.'

'And how on earth did you—oh, never mind. Well, you have tracked me down. You need not have gone to so much trouble; I would have come back, in any case, within a week or two. But what was your mother thinking of, to let you come to London and wander the streets of Limehouse? And walk alone into a tavern like this?'

'I don't think you are in any position to start lecturing me about decorum, Bevis,' she said tartly.

'No, I suppose you are right.' His mouth twisted in a rueful smile. 'Now you are here, shall we have another drink? I did not know you liked ale; is that what you want?'

New glasses were brought, and Eveline took a sip, and looked at her brother-in-law.

'Can you tell me about whatever has happened, Bevis?' she asked. She had thought, if she found him, that she would be furious, but now she saw him, so pale and strained, she spoke more gently than she had thought possible. 'You do not have to, but I must know what to say to Louisa when I return.'

'Oh, I might as well tell you,' said Bevis. 'It will come out, sooner or later, I suppose, and you seem very worldly, all of a sudden.'

'Hardly,' said Eveline, 'I wish I were; but I do not think I am likely to be shocked, if that is what you are thinking.'

Speaking in a low voice, he began to tell her what had happened. He had no excuses, none: he loved his wife and children, and Louisa's new maid had been just a very young woman, alone in the world. Hannah was pretty, and sweet-natured, and sad, because her sweetheart had been killed a few weeks before she had been hired, while working on the railway tunnel. Bevis had got into the way

269

of being kind to her, and paying her compliments, and she had come to him one day, red-eyed and distraught. She feared she would be turned off; could Bevis help her? And it transpired that she thought she was with child. She and her young man were to have been married within the month, and it had seemed no great sin, but they had anticipated their wedding vows, and now he was dead, and she was not a respectable young wife but a disgraced woman. He had put his arm around her, and dried her tears, and promised to intercede with Louisa to keep her on, if her fears proved to be true.

'So there is a child, but not yours?' asked Eveline. 'Then why have you been so secretive, Bevis? Where was the need?'

'There is more, Eveline.' He rubbed his eyes; they were red from lack of sleep. 'She was wrong, it seemed; she was not with child, and all was well again. She was so relieved, and she went about her duties singing, and smiling, and carefree, and then one day when Louisa was away somewhere, shopping or visiting or whatever it was, Hannah came to me with a gift – something ridiculous, a handkerchief she had embroidered for me to thank me for my kindness. I was touched, I suppose; and she looked at me with those great blue eyes, all trusting and expectant, and somehow – well, you can imagine, I suppose.'

'She saw you as a hero, I suppose,' said Eveline.

'God knows why; I had done nothing, except try to be kind. And then I did the most unkind thing I could have possibly done; I got her with child myself. I did not force her, Eveline, but what a fool I was; what a cad.'

Eveline could only agree.

'She came to me, and told me, and this time I said that she must be wrong, that she had been wrong before, and I had been careful, and – well, I did not know what to do, really, but to hope against hope that it would turn out another false alarm. Then Louisa saw me talking to her one day; saw more than that, I fear, a kiss, which I meant to be consoling – and although I denied everything, by that time it was beginning to be clear, if one looked, what her state was. In the morning, she was gone; Louisa would say nothing, except that she was getting a new maid. I made a few discreet enquiries, but no one knew what had become of her, and I was relieved, I suppose, that Louisa had taken care of it for me. I persuaded myself that Hannah would find another situation, and I would not be found out.

'But then, last month, a letter arrived from her. She had no mother or father; her only relative was a cousin in London, and she had made her way to Limehouse, to stay with the cousin, who seems a kindly woman, and has taken her in. By then Hannah was within a few weeks of her confinement. But there was no money. She wrote to ask – so humbly, it broke my heart! – if I could send her just enough for some clothes for the child. I spent a day wrestling with my demons and at last I determined that I would go to her and stay until the child was born. That I have done; I have another son, a fine child. He was born two days ago, and he and his mother both look set to thrive, thank God. I have given her enough money to keep them both for a good while, and I will send more – I mean to send her money until the boy is grown, and beyond that, indeed, for her whole life. It is the least I can do. I bought her a wedding ring, too, and she is to say that her husband was killed while working on the railway, which has at least a very small grain of truth in it.'

'And where have you lived, Bevis? Have you stayed with Hannah and her cousin?'

'No; I have lodged here, in this tavern. It is noisy, and cramped, and none too clean; but they are only a street away, and I can see them every day, and do what I can to help. God knows it is little enough.' He groaned. 'I suppose you think me a monster, Eveline.'

'No, of course I do not. I would not judge you so. I am sorry for you, Bevis; though not as sorry as I am for my sister, or for Hannah, or for the baby. And will you come back to Louisa, or will you stay here? Have you chosen what you will do?'

'Of course I will go back. I had determined to return at the end of this week, now the child has arrived. Hannah does not imagine that I will stay. I pray that she will forget me, and find some good man to marry. But I will make sure she is provided for, whatever happens in the future.'

'She is hardly likely to forget you, Bevis,' said Eveline. 'It sounds to me as if she were very much in love with you, and she will have the little boy as a reminder. Does he look like you?'

'Perhaps, a little. He just looks as babies do, you know.'

'And what is he called? Does he have a name yet?'

'Hannah wanted to name him after me, but I did not want that. I have asked her to call him after your father, Eveline, a man I admired and liked very much. The child is to be called John.'

* * *

The hansom cab rattled its way back from Limehouse to the broader streets and the grander buildings. They had agreed that on Eveline's return home, she would say only that she had met Bevis, that he would be back within the week, and that all was well. 'Say only that I had to go the aid of a friend,' Bevis had said. 'It is true, in a way; and when I am back, I will tell Louisa everything. At least then she will have the truth, and she may forgive me, and if she does not, I will only have myself to blame.'

Tomorrow, then, she would leave London. It seemed that she had lived there for weeks: the streets, at first so strange, now seemed familiar, no longer alarming, but exciting, and the Charing Cross Hotel felt almost like home. She paid the cabbie and stepped back through the hotel entrance; it was a world away from Limehouse and the dark smoky tavern she had just left. She collected her key, and turned towards the lift, which she was still finding a delightful novelty, when the desk clerk called her back and handed her a note. Her head was too full of what had happened that day, and Bevis's story, to pay it much attention; she put it on the dressing table while she went along to the bathroom, and ran a deep, luxurious bath, marvelling at the wonders of the modern plumbing, and rather regretting that back at home she would be returning only to a hip bath filled by hand, and not these taps, which magically gushed steaming water. It was only when she was dressed, and about to descend once more to find some dinner, that she recalled the note, and opened it.

My dear Eveline, if I may call you so, (it read)
I happen to find myself in town on business, and your

respected mother has asked me to call on you, so that I may reassure your family that you are quite safe. She has given me the address of this hotel.

I shall wait in the hotel saloon this evening, and hope that you will allow me to have the very great pleasure of dining with you at whatever time may suit you.

Believe me your very affectionate friend,
Charles Sandham

Charles, here, in London! How very extraordinary. What could her mother have been thinking of, to tell him where she was, after all her concerns lest anyone outside the family should know what she was about? She had a moment's exasperation: was she not even to be trusted with this little taste of freedom, but that a man must be sent to check she was safe? Still, go and meet him she must, it seemed; and she went down to the great saloon, which was all gilt cherubs and candles and mirrors, and walked, with some hesitation, into the room, and looked about her. Charles was sitting in a chair directly opposite the door, a bottle of wine at his elbow. He put down his newspaper and sprang up, instantly. He seemed immensely pleased to see her, and said how well she looked, and that London air must suit her, and how he hoped she was contriving to pass her time here agreeably.

'Yes, thank you,' she said. 'But I am very sorry my mother should have put you to the trouble of calling on me; as you see, I am perfectly well.'

'I would not, though, have forgone the pleasure of seeing

274

you, since I had the chance. You will, I hope, tell me about your time in London. What have you been doing? Have you found it delightful, or overwhelming? You have not been used, I know, to the city life. It must seem astonishing to you.'

'Charles,' said Eveline, 'I am much too hungry to talk about anything now. Until I have eaten, I shall not wish to talk at all. I am going to the dining room.'

'Of course; forgive me! You will allow me the pleasure of dining with you?'

'If you wish, of course,' said Eveline, although she would have much preferred to be alone.

Dinner was ordered, and once the crayfish soup had been drunk, and a couple of roast fowls were set before her, Eveline began to revive. Charles had ordered champagne, and he raised his glass to her with an air of gaiety that she felt hardly able to match.

'May I propose a toast?' he said. 'To meeting in London!'

She clinked her glass against his, her head full of the other meeting she had so lately had with Bevis, and took a sip.

'You seem distracted, Eveline,' he said. 'Will you not tell me what you are thinking of?'

'Oh, it is nothing,' she said. 'I am tired, I dare say, that is all, and I will be travelling home tomorrow, so I must pack my clothes tonight.'

'I will not keep you talking late, then,' he said. 'May I accompany you on your journey home? Your mama was anxious, I think, that you should not travel alone, and she was kind enough to say that she hoped I might go with you.'

'Did she?' Eveline began to wonder what else her mother

might have said. 'Did Mama tell you why I had come to town, Charles?' she asked, cautiously.

'She said merely that it was a family matter.'

'Yes,' said Eveline, 'exactly. I cannot discuss it, you understand.'

'No, of course not. I would not wish to intrude. Have you had a chance to see the sights of London, while you are here?'

'Oh, yes,' she said vaguely, 'some of them. But Charles, will you be able to travel back tomorrow; will you have concluded your business here?'

'My—? Oh, that; yes, done this afternoon.' He drained the last of the champagne, and then caught the waiter's eye, and ordered a bottle of Burgundy. 'Which train will you catch? Not too early a train, I hope. We may make a leisurely start, may we not?' He gave her a look she could not read. 'Let me pour you a glass of this wine.'

'No, thank you; I will take some coffee, and then I really must go to bed, Charles. Thank you for dinner. I am sorry not to be livelier company.'

'You could never be anything but the best company,' he said. 'Just a mouthful of this rather excellent Burgundy? Let me persuade you.'

'No, really. Just the coffee.'

'I shall have to finish it myself, then,' he said, giving her the charming, rueful smile. 'And then I will see you to your room.'

'There is no need,' said Eveline, beginning to feel exasperated, although trying her best to remain polite; but he would insist, and handed her into the lift and out of the lift as though she were incapable of managing that feat alone. They reached her door, and she took out the key.

'Well, goodnight, Charles,' she began, but before she could put her key into the door lock, he slid an arm around her waist, and was aiming a kiss at her mouth, his breath unpleasantly hot and smelling of drink and cigars. She turned her head, and the kiss landed damply on her cheek.

'Please, no,' she said; but he grasped her arm with his free hand, and pulled her to him.

'Come on, Evie,' he said, breathing heavily. 'Don't be coy,' and he began to kiss her, and moved the hand that had been around her waist up to cup her breast. She managed to bring both her hands to his chest, and pushed him away from her as hard as she could.

'You are right – not in the corridor,' he said, 'let's go inside – have you the key?'

'I do,' she said, beginning to feel frightened, 'but you are not coming inside, Charles. I think you are a little drunk. Go to your own room, please.'

'Oh no,' he said, resuming his grip on her, 'no, no, no; here we are in London, where no one knows us, and we may do as we please. This is too good a chance to miss.' He tore the edge of her dress off one shoulder, and she felt his wet mouth on her skin, and then he sank his teeth into her neck, and she let out a gasp of pain, and tried to push him away again. He was too strong, and his grip tightened.

'Now then,' he said, 'you like rough play, do you? Let me into your room, Evie, and we will have a little more, eh?' and he pushed her backwards hard against the door, and tried to wrest the key from her hands, his fingers sinking painfully into her flesh. She struggled to free herself, panic rising within her, but he pressed himself against her so that she could not escape. In desperation she kicked wildly at his shin, he gave a yelp of pain and momentarily released his grip – and then he brought up his hand and swung a violent blow at her face. A flash of pain went through her eye, and her jaw, and she cried out with the shock.

'So you are a prudish miss, after all,' he said nastily. 'All that flirting, and hints about nakedness, and you are just a cock-tease, not a modern woman, at all.'

He lunged towards her once more; but just at that moment a chambermaid appeared at the far end of the corridor, clattering a tray as she did so, and began to walk towards them. His head turned for a brief moment, and Eveline, her hands shaking uncontrollably, managed at last to push him so that he lost his balance, and staggered slightly, and in that moment she unlocked her door, stepped swiftly inside, and turned the key. She sank down, trembling, onto the bed, her face throbbing with pain, and her breath coming in ragged gasps. Charles banged on the door, and shouted incoherently; but at last he stopped, and cursed, and she heard his footsteps as he staggered away down the corridor.

Chapter Twenty-Seven

The Journey Home

By six o'clock the next morning, Eveline was walking swiftly across Waterloo Bridge, with the small portmanteau which was her only luggage. The first train for Southampton left at half past six, and she found a compartment with one other occupant, a stout, comfortable-looking woman, who nodded at her, but mercifully did not look at her too closely, or seem inclined to talk; and she subsided into a seat, and tried very hard to read her book. Her hat – and now, for once, she had reason to be grateful for it – had a half-veil, which she had pulled down across her face, to hide the livid bruise around her eye, and her gloves covered the dark marks around her wrist.

She was shaken, and tired, but most of all furious. Cutting things that she would like to say to Charles Sandham kept coming into her mind, although on the whole, she thought, never seeing him again for as long as she lived would be preferable even to the satisfaction of seeing him wilt beneath her exquisitely vengeful remarks.

The train was on time, and the journey smooth, but the steamer was delayed, and she was obliged to kick her heels for an hour and a half while she waited for it. When at last it chugged into view, and tied up, she was heartily relieved to get aboard, take some deep breaths of sea air, and find herself a seat. Very soon she would be home; but then, exasperatingly, the boat still did not leave port, and there was speculation among the passengers as to the reason: a fault with the engine, perhaps, or with one of the paddle wheels; and still they did not pull up the gangway, and another group of late passengers seemed to be trooping on. At long last, there was a shout of *all aboard!* and the engines started, and the hiss and clatter of the wheels began. She sighed with relief, and opened the newspaper she had bought at the port, and began to relax for the first time in hours.

'Eveline.'

She looked up. Charles Sandham stood before her, with the rueful smile that she had once thought charming.

'I caught the boat with just a minute to spare,' he said, as though nothing had occurred between them. 'May I sit down?'

'No,' said Eveline. 'No, you may not. Please go away.'

He sighed extravagantly and sat down anyway.

'I may owe you an apology,' he said. 'I might have spoken a bit rashly, Evie. Had a bit to drink, I suppose.'

'I do not want to talk to you,' she said. 'And don't call me Evie.'

'Did I behave so very badly?' he asked. 'Just a misunderstanding, you know. I misread the signs, I suppose.'

'The signs?' said Eveline. 'You seem to be suggesting that unless a woman is completely ignorant, or affects to be so, she is inviting whatever attentions or abuse a man may choose to inflict on her.'

He was silent.

'Did you really have business in London?' she asked. 'Or was it just that you thought it was worth coming up to town in case I was waiting to fall into your arms?'

'Shush,' he said uneasily, as one or two of the other passengers looked round. 'Your mother did ask me to see you, you know, and to escort you home. When I called, and you were not at home, I did begin to think you might have gone to London for some reason. Your questions about hotels were none too subtle.'

'So you manufactured some excuse about business, and my mother took the bait?'

'I suppose so. She seemed rather pleased at the prospect of my finding you and travelling back with you.'

'Presumably she would not have been pleased had she known your exact plans. I hardly think you were about to propose to me, were you?'

'Well, no.' He looked uncomfortable. 'I'd as soon marry you as anyone, of course, but I'm not really in a position to marry at all, just at the moment.'

'Good. At least no woman will be made miserable by you in the immediate future.'

He leant forward, and said in a low voice, 'If I had proposed marriage to you, would you have let me come to your room last night?'

'If you had proposed marriage to me, I would have refused. You seem to regard marriage as a sort of bargaining chip, but that is not the kind of marriage I would even consider. Now go away, and leave me alone.'

'Oh, come, Evie – Eveline. Don't be so missish. You know how fond of you I am. You can't be so very surprised that I should want to – to show my affection.'

'Your *affection*?'

She raised the little veil, and looked at him squarely in the face. 'Look at me, Mr Sandham. Is this a sign of affection?'

Other passengers looked round, and were beginning to take an interest. He flinched, a little.

'No, well – you should not have been such a cat.'

'A cat! Ah, a term always used for women, but never for men, I think. What term would you choose for your own behaviour, may I ask? A fine fellow, perhaps? A sporting gentleman? *A bit of a dog*?'

There were a few gasps from those people within earshot, and one or two of the women looked very shocked. A thickset man sitting close by half-stood, and looked at Charles with a menacing glint in his eye. Charles scowled, but at last he got up, and slouched away. Eveline raised the newspaper, and tried to concentrate on reading, though her face was hot with outrage as well as with pain, and her hands were, annoyingly, still shaking violently, and did so for the remainder of the voyage.

* * *

282

When the steamer docked, she stood up, and moved towards the doorway. Waiting to disembark, she found to her dismay that Charles had reappeared at her elbow.

'May I carry your portmanteau, at least?' he asked.

'I am quite capable of carrying it myself.'

'As you wish,' he said; but he walked by her side as she made her way down the gangway, for despite her efforts to hasten away from him the crowd prevented her from doing so, although his proximity made her shudder with revulsion.

She walked as quickly as she could into the little courtyard where people were waving, and calling, and waiting to meet each other. Impatiently she tried to shake him off, but still he pursued her, attempting to take her arm; and then suddenly, directly ahead of her she saw Thomas Armitage deep in conversation with Mr Watson and two other men. Thomas was standing, hands in pockets, looking serious and intent; and then he looked round, and saw her, and for a moment a smile lit his face, bestowing that sudden youthful warmth that was so often hidden beneath his serious manner. He half-raised a hand in greeting, and for a brief moment his eyes met hers; and then he saw Charles Sandham walking close behind her, and his arm fell, and the smile was replaced with an unmistakable look of the utmost disdain. Mr Watson looked round then too, and smiled, and nodded at her. She shook Charles's hand from her elbow, but Thomas had turned away, and was no longer looking at her.

'I will walk you home,' said Charles.

She swung round. 'No, you will not,' she hissed. 'I will walk alone. And if you follow me, I promise you, I shall scream in the most *missish* way imaginable, and the whole town will hear me.'

It was late afternoon when she walked into the drawing room, where Mrs Stanhope and Louisa were listlessly drinking tea. Both sprang to their feet.

'Evie, my love!' exclaimed her mother, embracing her. 'Oh, how thankful I am to see you! But are you alone?'

'Whom did you imagine would be with me?'

'Charles,' said her mother, at exactly the same time as Louisa said 'Bevis'.

Eveline went to Louisa and took her hands.

'I found him; he is well,' she said. 'He will be home in a few days.'

'Oh, Evie!' said Louisa, tears springing to her eyes. 'You are a heroine, truly! He is well, he is coming back to me; oh, how can I ever thank you? But tell me, what was it? How could he just go, in such a way? Please, tell me everything!'

'He will tell you himself; I cannot,' said Eveline gently. 'You will have to wait, Louisa; it is his story, not mine. But he loves you, Louisa; you may be sure of that.'

Louisa, after a few more protests, had to accept that Eveline would not enlighten her further; but their mother was not satisfied.

'That will not do,' she said. 'Eveline, you must tell us everything. Do not keep secrets from us,' but Eveline only shook her head, and said no more. Louisa, red-eyed, although looking more cheerful than she had for weeks, declared that she was exhausted, and would go to rest before dinner. As soon as she had left the room, Mrs Stanhope turned to Eveline with an air of delighted expectancy.

'Well, my love? Did Charles find you – did he come to the hotel?'

'Yes,' said Eveline woodenly. 'He did.'

'And escorted you home, I hope; the dear man!'

'We travelled on the same steamer, certainly.'

'And so? Evie, surely you have news for me? Are you engaged? Oh, tell me straight away; did Charles propose?'

'Did he say to you that he planned to, Mama?'

'Not in so many words, but he was so anxious to see you – so delighted to have your address in London, and so gallant in hoping he might meet you there, and be able to escort you home, that his intentions were very clear – oh, he is all charm!'

'Why did you tell him I had gone to London, Mama? I thought it was all to be secret – a family concern. You did not want anyone else to know, and I agreed with you; it should have remained a private matter.'

'Oh, I did not tell him about Bevis, and all those dreadful goings-on; though you have so cleverly sorted things out, now, and thank goodness that poor Louisa will be happy again, for she has cried every day, and been so sad. No, my sweet, I just said that you had a fancy to visit London; and it turned out that he had planned to go up to town anyway, on business; nothing could have been more fortunate!'

'So it was just Charles that you told – no one else?'

'I dare say I might have mentioned it to one or two others – Mr Watson, and the Debournes, perhaps – but nothing could be more natural, than that you should go to visit some smart shops once in a while. I may have said that you were ordering clothes; yes, I did say that. I thought it rather a clever notion, for everyone will see now how timely that would be.'

'Ordering clothes? Why would I be doing so?' asked Eveline. 'Oh – no, Mama, please tell me that you have not been saying to people that I was buying wedding clothes?'

'And why should I not?' said her mother. 'It was clear that dear Charles was simply longing to see you, and I knew it would not be long until you needed some. Oh, Evie, how delightful it will be, to tell all our friends! We will be ordering those clothes in earnest, very soon, my love!'

'I do not think we will,' said Eveline. 'I will not be needing wedding clothes, Mama. I have no plans to marry.'

'But, Eveline! Charles; sweet Charles! Whatever can you mean?'

Eveline at last removed her hat and veil, and revealed the purple bruise that disfigured her face.

'I mean, Mama,' said Eveline, 'that I would not marry Charles Sandham if he were the last man on earth.'

Chapter Twenty-Eight

An Announcement

Mrs Stanhope was mortified. She refused, at first, to believe that Charles Sandham could have behaved in such a way, so dearly held had been her dream of Eveline's marrying him; and then when the evidence of what he had done was impossible to deny, she began to insist that Eveline must have provoked him beyond the limits of what any reasonable man should be expected to bear. She wept, and reproached Eveline, who refused to discuss the matter any further; but Louisa, when she saw her sister's face, and the marks of violence that still showed there, was very shocked indeed, and remonstrated with her mother over the day that followed, and when Mrs Stanhope finally accepted that the bruises on Eveline's face and wrist and neck really had been caused by Charles Sandham, she became vehement in her outrage against him, and very tender to her youngest daughter, begging her forgiveness for ever having suggested that Charles Sandham might be a suitable match, blaming herself for the horrible events in London, and lamenting again and again that she had ever let Eveline venture to the great, wicked city all alone.

'It was not being in London that was dangerous for Evie, Mama,' said Louisa. 'It was being with Charles Sandham.'

'Do not mention that man's name any more, I beg you. It is all too dreadful. My poor, poor little girl! I shall never forgive myself, never. I actually told him where you were staying! How wrong of me, how very foolish and trusting I have been!'

'That is absurd, Mama,' said Eveline. 'It is not your fault, or mine, but his. How were you to know what sort of man he is? None of us did. I have survived; and I shall take very good care not to be alone with him again, under any circumstances.'

Mrs Stanhope's mortification, however, was not confined to her own sense that she had failed in her maternal duties. 'I shall be the laughing stock of the town,' she said. 'I am afraid people will say that we have tried to get him and failed. Everyone was expecting you to return as a bride-to-be; I must be thankful now that you did not, but it is very hard to feel that people are regarding us with pitying glances, or sniggering behind their hands.'

'Well, Mama,' said Eveline wearily, 'if you have told your friends that such a thing is likely, you may tell them now that you had made a mistake.'

'I shall maintain a dignified silence. That is all one can do. People must think what they will, and I shall merely hint that he – that man, I cannot say his name – was not nearly good enough for my daughter.'

Eveline thought it unlikely that her mother would be able to maintain a dignified silence on the subject, for her indignation was too strong, and her love of gossip was not easily subdued; but for once, she felt it might not be such a bad thing for Mama to be indiscreet. Rumours were powerful things in a small society such as theirs, and if such a rumour alerted other women, then Charles Sandham might be prevented from doing further harm. Perhaps she also hoped that some word might reach Thomas Armitage that there was no engagement, that she did not care for Charles Sandham in the slightest; not, of course, that an engaged man such as Thomas would have any interest in whether or not Eveline was affianced to someone herself. It was merely that she despised rumours, and untruths, and would be glad that the truth be known by all her acquaintance; that was all.

August had brought cold winds, and rain. Eveline divided her time between the kitchen and her photographic studio, and by so doing managed to avoid her mother's stricken looks and tender fussing care for a good deal of the time. Her bruises faded, and Louisa and her children departed for their own home, in the expectation of seeing Bevis arrive within the week; and Eveline had every hope that her sister would come to forgive him, once she had heard everything, and would be made happy again by his return. No sooner had one sister left, however, than another arrived; Beatrice and Arthur were announced on the following morning, to ask if Kitty might stay for a few days.

'You know she loves being with you all; she still talks about the crabbing she did with Aunt George and the Angell,' said Beatrice, 'I know you will not mind, Mama.'

'Of course,' said Mrs Stanhope, 'we love to have Kitty. Eveline has nothing to do; she will mind her.'

'We are going away, for a holiday,' said Beatrice gaily, 'just a short one. It has been an age, really. It was a surprise, too – I knew nothing at all until yesterday, when Arthur told me. Oh, Eveline, there you are! What have you done to your face? Is it true, as Mama said last week, that you are practically engaged to Charles Sandham?'

'No, it is not,' said Eveline. 'Mama was quite mistaken.'

'Oh, that is a pity; I had told all my friends, for Mama was so sure it was true!'

'Not such a pity,' said Arthur, 'I am not sure I wanted him as a brother-in-law.'

'I cannot bear to speak of it,' said Mrs Stanhope tragically. 'Come with me, my sweet Beatrice, and we will see to the nursery so that Kitty may be comfortable there.'

'This is good news, Arthur,' said Eveline, when they were alone. 'A holiday! How delightful; and Beatrice looks so very pleased.'

'Yes; I grasped the nettle, you know, and asked her what was making her unhappy, and at last she did tell me – oh, well, some things not for other ears, you know, but also that she felt cooped up here, sometimes, and dull, and bored, and that I was forever down at the sail loft, and we never went anywhere. So I made a plan, and we are to go on the train to Brighton, and stay in some fancy hotel; and I did listen to the things she said, Evie, just as you mentioned, and I mean to try to make her happy.'

'I am sure you will, Arthur; and I hope she makes you happy too, for you deserve it. And when you said you would rather not have Charles Sandham as a brother-in-law, I was very glad, for you never will, you may believe me, despite what Mama has been saying.'

'I am mightily relieved to hear it. I contrived to meet the man last week – asked him for a drink, on the pretext of talking about horses, but really because I had one or two things to say to him.'

'You did?'

'Yes – to warn him to stay away from my wife. He is all smiles and charm, I know that, and used to having women melt under his gaze, but I have had enough of his hanging round Beatrice, and after a few drinks I told him so – said if he wished for a wife, he had better find one of his own. Well, he had drunk quite a bit by then, and his tongue was loosened, I suppose, because then he said that he was here for that very purpose, but she must be a rich woman, for he had more debts than he could pay, and his uncle looked set to live for another twenty years, so there was nothing for it but to find a wealthy bride. He is sure that there will be heiresses by the dozen here for August, and he will find one before the summer is out.'

'Debts? But everyone thought he had a fortune of his own. Is that not so?'

'He had a reasonable fortune, it seems; but it has gone, on travel, and cards, and horses, and who knows what else. Tried to touch me for a loan, on top of everything – infernal cheek. It seems that because of his debts he could not stay in London any longer, so he has come down here to live at his uncle's expense, and find a wife who will pay his debts and make him independent again.'

'Poor woman, whoever she may be,' said Eveline.

'Yes; I have no doubt he will succeed in his plan, though – he is the sort of man who always does. Meanwhile, he has been kicking his heels in his uncle's house, with nothing to do but to flirt with the prettiest women he can find. I hope very much he did not make you fall in love with him, Evie.'

'No, I am not in love with him, nor have I ever been,' Eveline assured him. 'Have you told Beatrice this?'

'Yes, I have; and I said that if I see him trying to make love to her again, I shall knock him down. I sincerely trust that it will not come to that, for I am no fighter, and I expect I should come off worst; but Beatrice seemed mighty pleased with the notion, and I am a hero to my wife, at least. Brighton will be just the thing, I fancy: a change of scene, and all sorts of fashionable shops and so forth. As long as I can prevent her spending our entire income on hats, I shall be satisfied.'

Kitty's visit brought a welcome distraction to the Stanhope household. Eveline did her best to amuse and entertain her little niece, teaching her to make saucer cakes, and cinnamon biscuits, and strawberry tarts, and to feed the chickens, and collect their eggs, and to arrange the eggs carefully in a basket in the larder. Aunt George and Miss Angell gave her lessons, and Eveline took her down to the beach to collect shells and pebbles whenever the weather permitted, glad to have the chance to escape from the house.

Not feeling able to face having to undeceive her friends regarding Eveline's not being engaged, Mrs Stanhope was not at home to callers for very nearly a week, and declined several invitations herself, which went much against the grain. At last, however, Mr Watson called, and was admitted, for she could hardly deny such an old friend; and then she found she must tell him everything, and he listened with such kindness and patience that at last she was in a better humour than she had been for many days, and came to the point where she was able to say that she had made a dreadful mistake regarding Charles Sandham, and even that she supposed Eveline one day must have some say in the matter of her own marriage.

'But I hope you are not very much distressed, Eveline?' asked Mr Watson. 'I am deeply shocked by what your mama has told me. I would take the young man to task myself, but she thinks that would only lead to more of a scandal. And then, of course, it is not at all a pleasant thing for a young woman to be talked about, and I fear many people did believe you to be engaged. I myself, I am afraid, made that assumption when I saw you step off the packet steamer arm in arm with Mr Sandham, since your dear mama had thought it so very probable.'

'Everyone will think the very worst, I know,' said Mrs Stanhope. 'The women in this town are nasty, spiteful cats, the whole pack of them. Augusta Sandham is the worst of them, too; and in fact I think she is very much to blame, for having such a dreadful man as a nephew.'

'Well, there we are,' said Eveline. 'I will be considered either a jilted maiden, or a scarlet woman. Either way, I do not much care. Perhaps people will leave me alone, and I may get on with something more interesting.'

'No, no,' said Mr Watson soothingly, 'it will blow over. People will talk for a few days, until the next piece of news, and then it will all be forgotten. Why, even Tom said to me—' and then he stopped, in some confusion.

'What?' asked Eveline, 'what did he say?'

'Why, only that – when we saw you, in the Fountain Yard, you know, by the steamer – that it was up to you, what you did, and you were able to make your own choices, and if you liked Charles Sandham enough to go to London with him, then that was no one else's business.'

Mr Watson looked as though he hoped this reported remark would be comforting, but in this he was to be disappointed, for Mrs Stanhope began to lament afresh and Eveline found it so peculiarly irritating, for reasons she would have been hard-pressed to explain, that she excused herself from the discussion, and went outside to walk up and down very briskly, and let the air cool her face. And once in better command of herself, she went to find Aunt George and Miss Angell, who were helping Kitty to build a tree house in the garden. Eveline soon became engaged in the project – 'You will find a tree house the very thing if you should need ever to escape, or to find a place of your own,' she said to Kitty, who wholeheartedly agreed. The chosen tree was an oak, which had fine stout branches growing low enough to be easily climbed; and with some wooden planks, which had been left over from the new potting shed, a section of garden trellis, and an old Mackintosh coat for a roof, the house began to take on a very fine aspect indeed. All four were so absorbed in this creation, that they scarcely noticed the time passing, and when at last it was declared to be finished, and certainly the finest tree house anyone had ever seen, the light was fading from the sky.

'Heavens!' said Miss Angell. 'We have missed dinner, I suppose. I wonder we did not hear the bell. I hope your mama is not unwell, for she would have sent out for us, would she not, being as she is very particular about mealtimes?'

'And I have not had my tea,' said Kitty, 'though I don't mind not having bread and milk. Perhaps I can just have cake instead.'

'Well, we had better see what is amiss,' said Eveline, and they trooped back to the house.

Mr Watson's coat and hat were still hanging in the hall.

'Good heavens!' said Eveline, 'he is making a very long visit. I hope he is not inveigling Mama into investing in the next railway scheme.'

'Well, we shall have to interrupt him, whatever he may be doing, or we shall all die of starvation,' said Aunt George, and opened the door to the drawing room. Mr Watson and Mrs Stanhope were there, as Eveline had left them; but both now had a glass in their hands, and a slightly furtive air.

'Ah!' said Mr Watson. 'Please, join us – Miss Georgiana, Miss Angell, Eveline, will you take a glass of champagne with us?'

'Delighted,' said Aunt George, 'naturally; are we celebrating something?'

Mrs Stanhope looked at him, and smiled, and nodded.

'We are indeed,' he said, 'for I am the luckiest man in the world. This lady has done me the honour, the very great honour, of agreeing to become my wife.'

There was a moment's silence, and then everyone began to congratulate Mr Watson, and embrace Mrs Stanhope, and generally exclaim at the news. Another bottle of champagne was brought up from the cellars, and toasts were drunk, and the cork was dabbed behind Kitty's ears for luck, and she was allowed a little glass of her own. Mrs Groves, having despaired of dinner ever being required, sent up a cold ham and a chocolate cake, so Kitty had her wish after all, and the whole party grew quite merry.

'I am so happy for you, Mama,' said Eveline. 'It had never crossed my mind before, but now I see that you and Mr Watson will be a perfect couple. How long have you felt that this might be? Or was it a surprise?'

'Oh,' said her mother, looking round to make sure that her husband-to-be was not within earshot, 'when Mr Watson proposed to me this afternoon, I believe he took himself by surprise; but truth to tell, I was quite prepared.'

'You are very naughty, Mama,' said Eveline affectionately.

'And do you truly not mind, Eveline?' asked her mother, a little anxiously.

'How could I mind?' she said. 'It is delightful. He will spoil you shamelessly, and you will make sure he is never dull.'

'I am very fortunate,' said Mrs Stanhope, 'and if I could but see you married too, Evie, my happiness would be complete.'

'It is possible to be happy without being married, Mama. Let us enjoy this moment, without fretting over anything else. Tell me, when is the wedding to be?'

The marriage of Mr Watson and Mrs Stanhope was fixed for late September – only a few weeks away, but what was there to wait for? as Mr Watson asked; and it would be a quiet affair, with only family there to witness the occasion.

'There is just one important thing I wish to do, before my wedding,' said Mrs Stanhope to Eveline. 'Heavens, how strange it seems to be saying that! But, Evie, I will need your help, I think.'

'Of course; anything, Mama.'

'It is the rose, for the churchyard; do you remember? The rose in memory of my little boy?'

'I have asked Aunt George and Miss Angell about it, already. They have found one, a sweetly scented rose, with little flowers; the buds almost green, and then turning purest white as they open.'

Tears misted Mrs Stanhope's eyes. 'That will be perfect. And we may plant it soon, do you think?'

'I will speak to the rector, and arrange it all.'

Eveline was as good as her word, and she called on the rector that afternoon, her head down against the drizzle of that chilly August. He was glad to help when he heard the melancholy history that she related, and they walked into the churchyard together to see the place where the rose might be planted. Her father's grave lay to the side of a tall yew tree, neat and cared for, but with the marble headstone now a little mossy and streaked with rain.

'Here, I thought,' said Eveline, 'just at the side of the plot. My aunt will bring the rose, and I will help her plant it; will this get a little sunshine, do you think, enough for the rose to thrive?'

'I think so, yes,' said the rector. 'These things help us, sometimes; a place, or an object, to help us think about those we have lost. Shall I leave you now, Miss Stanhope? You will want a moment alone, I expect.'

Eveline stood by the grave, and thought about her father, and how often the things he used to say still came into her head; and then she thought of the little lost baby, who had been her brother, and whose memory her mother had carried so secretly in her heart for all these years. She turned away, at last, and walked down to the sea. It was cold, and grey, and relentlessly the waves broke, and retreated, and broke again on the pebbled beach. She began to walk away from the town, as fast as she could, not caring for the rain, which fell on her face, and soaked her clothes; and she only turned when the surging tide prevented her walking any further.

Chapter Twenty-Nine

Out Into the Night

Even for the quiet, modest, simple wedding that Mrs Stanhope insisted she would prefer, there were, it seemed, a thousand things to be done. Food, and clothes, and flowers, were all to be thought of; a notice to be placed in the newspaper, the banns to be published, and naturally a photograph to be arranged to commemorate the occasion. Eveline said that she would take a likeness of the happy couple, if they wished it, but Mrs Stanhope had already determined that a formal picture of the wedding party would be required, and that was certainly the province of Mr Fry. Her decision may have been influenced by the understanding that he would then display the picture in the window of his studio, for the town to see, and indeed it would have been a great pity for such an elegant group of people, dressed so beautifully, not to be seen by the wider world.

Mrs Stanhope was anxious that, without a lady's maid, she would not be as lovely as the intended of a gentleman as handsome as Mr Watson should be. So Eveline took to curling her mother's hair each day, and Mrs Stanhope herself ironed and starched her lace caps; but she need not have been so concerned, for her happiness conferred beauty enough. The food was planned – 'Nothing too elaborate,' said Mrs Stanhope, rather to the surprise of her daughters, 'for Mr Watson likes simple food, he says, and we will have as much as we can from the garden, with just some cold sirloin and a raised game pie,' although she later decided that a wedding cake was essential, and Mrs Groves and Eveline found themselves with yet another task in producing something adorned with as many scrolls and festoons of icing as physically possible. The days flew by in a whirl of preparations. Beatrice, returned from her holiday with roses in her cheeks and a new lightness in her step, volunteered to be responsible for choosing the wedding clothes, and she and her mother spent many happy hours at the dressmaker's, looking at silks, and velvets, and lace, so that the train journey to Newport, which had seemed a matter of weeks ago to be a grand adventure, was now no more unusual than a ride in the carriage had once been, and a great deal less trouble, after all.

Eveline managed to be excused from the almost daily

visits to Madame Delphine, even though Mr Watson's kind insistence that all the dressmaker's bills must be sent to him meant that, as Beatrice said, she might have had any amount of new clothes; but she said that she trusted Beatrice to choose something for her – 'as long as it is not a crinoline, Bea, or anything with frills' – so that when, one morning, a note arrived from Theodore Fry, begging that Miss Stanhope would call into the studio at her earliest convenience, she was free to throw on a cloak against the drizzling rain, and walk down into the town, with no one to protest.

Mr Fry and Jennie were there, looking out of the window for her, and when she walked into the shop, they were both barely able to contain their excitement; for there was a letter from the Photographic Society to say that two photographs had been chosen by the committee to be exhibited in London. One was a picture taken by Mr Fry of a locomotive entering the railway station, emerging through the clouds of steam like some great mythical creature, magnificent and terrible; and the other, Eveline's likeness of Aunt George. The pride and delight felt by Eveline at this news was so great that she was quite overcome; and they all three embraced, and exclaimed, and laughed, and in the absence of champagne toasted their success in gin, of which Mr Fry happened to have a bottle in case of emergencies. As if the honour of having their photographs accepted were not enough, it seemed that there was a prize for each of ten guineas, bestowed by some generous patron of the arts.

'The first money I have ever earned!' said Eveline, in wonder. 'Actually earned, myself! Now, I wonder, Mr Fry, how much would a small camera cost? I shall put this prize money towards one; something portable, that I could take about with me. I saw so much in London that I longed to photograph: the faces, and streets, the river – oh, to be able to capture what one sees, to look, really look, and get the way the light falls, or the expression in someone's eyes!'

In such happy speculations an hour passed; but then Mr Fry had a customer, and Eveline prepared to leave. Jennie stepped out with her onto the street, to bid her goodbye. The rain at last had stopped, and from the west clearer skies showed.

'There will be a full moon tonight,' said Jennie. 'I might swim; would you care to come with me, Eveline? To swim by moonlight is magical!'

'I should like that very much,' said Eveline. 'But do the bathing huts open at night? Surely not?'

'No; I was thinking, rather, that if you do not mind the walk, we would go along the shore, all the way past Ned's cottage – there is a little bay there, hidden away. It is half-sand, half-shingle, and the beach shelves very steeply, but you are a strong swimmer now, and it is very private. No one ever goes that far along, I think, except that sometimes Ned takes a fishing boat out from there.'

'That sounds infinitely preferable to a bathing hut.'

Jennie looked suddenly doubtful. 'Although your mama may not allow it, perhaps?'

'I shall come, in any case,' said Eveline, firmly. 'I have

done with trying to be respectable. It does not seem to be my forte; so I think I may as well just do as I please.'

It was easy, now, to slip out of the house, and through the side gate in the grey wall. The sea was inky black, and the moonlight made a trail of silver across the surface. Tiny ripples broke on the shore, but otherwise it was still, and calm, and apart from the moon, and a handful of stars, the only light was just a pinprick from some small fishing boat too far away to distinguish.

'I did bring both our bathing dresses,' said Eveline, opening the bag she had lugged all the way along the shore, 'though I wish we had something less heavy to wear. A man's bathing suit, now; that would be the thing! They are so much more sensible.'

'Or,' said Jennie, 'we can swim without any bathing suits. Would you think it very shocking, Eveline? There is no one to see us, you know, in the dark.'

'You are so sensible, Jennie,' said Eveline. 'That is a far better idea,' and they both undressed, and folded their dresses and petticoats and underclothes and stowed them under a rock. The night air was cool and soft as they stepped cautiously across the beach, and into the dark, softly surging sea. It was cold, shockingly so, as she waded deeper, and she took a deep breath, and plunged into the water. It closed over her shoulders, and she ducked her head beneath the surface, and rose up again gasping at the shock, and then swam as hard as she could away from the land. At last, she stopped, and turned on her back, floating luxuriously, and feeling the water like satin on her naked skin. Jennie surfaced a few yards away from her, and swam over towards her, to ask if she was too cold, or too tired.

'Never!' said Eveline, 'this is so delicious – I have never felt so free – it is magical to be part of the sea, like this, as though we were fishes, or mermaids,' and they both gazed up at the night sky, letting the waves lift them in a slow, lazy rhythm; and then swam again, until they were so cold they could no longer feel their toes, and they reluctantly swam back to the shore, and wrapped themselves in the Turkish towels that Eveline had brought.

'Is that boat coming closer?' asked Eveline, watching the little light glowing in the distance.

'It is probably Ned, coming back from night fishing,' said Jennie. 'We had better dress, I suppose,' and they did, struggling into their clothes as best they could, so that by the time the little boat was nearing the shore, and a tall figure jumped out to haul the boat onto the beach, they were both looking respectable and demure once more (although Eveline had decided she would not try to get into her stays and chemise and drawers, and had merely pulled on her dress, which made getting dressed in the dark while still chilly and damp from the sea a good deal easier).

'Ned?' called Jennie, 'Is that you? Have you made a catch tonight?'

'A few mackerel, that is all; but enough for a supper, we think.' Two figures materialised from the darkness: first Ned, carrying a dozen mackerel in a basket, their scales gleaming silver; and then with a little shock Eveline realised that the taller man behind him, who had pulled the boat up onto the beach, was Thomas Armitage.

Thomas nodded at them both. 'We thought we'd build a fire and cook the fish here,' he said, laconic as always, as though it were nothing surprising to find two young women, their hair falling in damp tendrils down their backs, alone on a beach in the night. 'Are you hungry? It will not take long to make the fire.'

'I am extremely hungry,' said Eveline, 'Jennie and I have been swimming. I think the idea of some supper sounds an excellent one,' and Jennie wholeheartedly agreed. The fire was made, and the fish was expertly gutted by Ned and Thomas, and threaded on sticks, and grilled over the flames; and it turned out that the two men, with some foresight, had left a few bottles of ale neatly hidden beneath an old lobster pot higher up the shore. Eveline, eating the hot smoky fish and drinking the cold bitter ale, feeling the warmth of the fire on her face, and the cool of the night against her back, thought that she had never been happier in her life. The four young people ate, and drank, and talked, as the moon sailed slowly across the night sky; until at last, Jennie said that she must go, and Ned that he would walk her home. Ned and Jennie said goodnight, and went hand in hand towards the town.

'I, too, should go, I suppose,' said Eveline reluctantly. She had a sense that this night had given her something, some delicious moments of freedom, that she feared she might never have the chance to taste again. With a sigh, she began to pack the rest of her clothes and the Turkish towels back into her bag, while Thomas put out the fire, and raked the sand over its ashes.

'Do you want to go now?' he said. 'I will walk with you, if you do.'

'I must, I suppose,' said Eveline. 'It's very late, Thomas.'

He did not move, for a moment, and then took a step forward, and stretched out his hands.

'Or we can stay here, just for a while,' he said, and she looked at him, his face shadowed and unreadable in the darkness, and then she walked towards him, and into his arms, and he drew her close, and bent his head to kiss her. His mouth tasted of salt.

'You are shivering,' he said, and pulled her closer still, and kissed her eyes, and her throat, and then her mouth again. She felt herself dissolving with bliss.

'Eveline,' he murmured, his voice deep. 'Oh, Eveline, I want you so much—' and his arms crushed her to him. She could feel the hardness and heat of him through her thin silk dress. Her hands slid around his waist, and she touched his skin beneath the loose shirt. From that moment, she was lost; they both were lost. He caught her up and pulled her to the ground.

There was a moment, when he drew back, and muttered, 'This is folly – I must not compromise you—' but she only pulled him closer, and then he entered her, and she arched her back beneath him, with a sharp cry of pain and pleasure, and knew her life had changed irrevocably.

* * *

306

Later, they lay side by side, looking up at the stars.

'You are very lovely,' he said. He propped himself on one elbow and looked at her. 'A goddess, in fact.'

She smiled. 'Really? A goddess?'

'Certainly a goddess.' He nuzzled her shoulder, found she was cold, and wrapped her once more in his arms.

They dressed, when they grew too cold to stay there any longer, and walked back towards the town, his arm around her shoulders, hers around his waist. Their steps matched; it felt the most natural thing in the world to walk by his side, silent, and every now and then turning towards each other as if impelled by some mutual unspoken force to kiss. When they reached the road that led up to Eveline's house, she kissed him once more.

'Goodnight,' she said. 'Goodnight; I shall never forget this.'

He caught her to him again, and held her there.

'Tell me you are not engaged to Charles Sandham?' he said. 'Watson says one thing, Ned another; it is driving me mad, Eveline.'

'No,' she said, 'no, I am not engaged to Charles Sandham, and never have been.' He sighed with relief, and tightened his hold.

'And you?' she asked, dreading his answer.

'No,' he said, laughing, 'I am not engaged to Charles Sandham, either.'

Suddenly, she could not bear the thought that he might tell her about the woman he truly was engaged to, and that the evening would end with regrets and explanations that she did not want; so she laughed, and said as lightly as she could, 'He is not nearly good enough for you, anyway, Thomas,' and then before he could stop her she shook herself free of his embrace, and ran lightly up the sloping street, and left him standing alone, looking after her, with the moonlit waves still breaking on the shore behind him.

Chapter Thirty

Half-sick of Shadows

Sleep was a long time coming that night. When the doorbell rang, early next morning, Eveline was alone in the kitchen whisking egg whites for meringues; and she started, and the blood rushed to her face, for that was surely Thomas! And she rushed up the stairs, her heart thumping uncomfortably, before Mary could get to the front door; but it was only Mr Watson, bearing a sheaf of flowers for his beloved. She did her best to compose her face into a smile of welcome.

'Mama is in the morning room,' she said, 'worrying about sugared almonds.'

'Really?' he said. 'I thought we were to be having a very

simple wedding; I do not recall sugared almonds being mentioned as essential.'

'You may be surprised,' said Eveline, 'at what is now essential, apparently.'

'Then sugared almonds we will have,' he said. 'But are you well, Eveline? You look a little flushed, my dear. I hope you are not exhausting yourself with all this wedding business. I should be mortified if you were to make yourself ill on my account; that would never do. You young people do dash about so; you would do better to take a rest, now and then. That is what I tell Tom, but he never heeds me. I dare say I was the same at his age.'

'Is that so?' asked Eveline, rather faintly.

'Indeed; and he has had to go off first thing this morning, rushing off up to London, it seems.'

'London?' said Eveline blankly. 'Mr Armitage has gone to London?'

'Yes, for a meeting, or an interview, or some such thing. His work here is nearly done, you know, and we do not know if we will ever get another line here, for the landowners are very much against it; so if he can secure work elsewhere, then he must.'

'Yes, of course,' said Eveline, 'of course he must.'

Mr Watson went to deliver the flowers, and reassure his bride-to-be that she should have as many sugared almonds as she wished, and Eveline, her mind a whirl of desolate thoughts, trudged back downstairs to finish the meringues before the egg whites fell. She discovered that her hands were shaking uncontrollably. So he had gone; gone to

London, in pursuit of his new work and his new life, and she would never see him again. What had she expected? she wondered bleakly: Thomas beating on her front door, full of declarations and proposals? The magical disappearance or tragic (yet convenient) demise of the mysterious fiancée? Absurd, ridiculous notions! She drew a deep breath and tried to quell the shivers of shame and delight that rose inside her at the very thought of him. Yesterday had been a moment of madness, which he had no doubt already half-forgotten; but for her it could never be forgotten. And now a cold fear began to sweep over her, as she thought of what she had done, and she began to wonder whether her life even now lay in ruins. To give herself so shamelessly! To court such danger! Such disgrace, such humiliation – and then, if the worst happened, her family would share in that disgrace – it was too terrible to contemplate. And who was there to turn to? She could not share her fears with her sisters, still less with her mother; it was unthinkable. She felt a prickling of tears behind her eyes, and a sense of desolation, as though her world had turned grey, and bleak, and empty, and the day dragged on, while she tried to maintain an appearance of normality, and make conversation, and generally behave as though the world had not shifted on its axis.

After another sleepless night, she arose pale and drawn, and her mother, alarmed at her pallor, was all for her resting in bed – 'For how am I to manage, Evie, if you are not well?' she demanded. 'There are still a thousand things to be done before my wedding, and only three days to prepare!' – but Eveline begged that she might be allowed just to go for a walk.

311

'Some fresh air, Mama, will clear my head, I am sure. I will only walk into the town and back.'

Mrs Stanhope regarded her suspiciously.

'You are not up to any mischief, Eveline, are you?'

Eveline blushed hotly as she thought of what her mama might say if she knew exactly what sort of mischief she had been up to.

'No, no, Mama – of course not—'

'And now you look a little feverish. Whatever can be wrong? Have you caught a chill, I wonder?'

'Really, it is a slight headache, nothing more.' She sought desperately for some excuse that might distract her mother. 'You know, Mama,' she said, 'I might look to see if they have any new napkins at the draper's, for you said, did you not, that you might like some new ones for the wedding breakfast?'

'Oh, that is a thought! White linen, I think – or should we have damask? I like the sort with drawn-thread borders, you know. Very well, go for your walk, but be sure to come straight back, my love.'

Eveline, lost in a daze of fearful thoughts, walked as quickly as she could towards the town. There was, perhaps, after all, one person she might confide in, for she would, she thought, go quite insane if she did not share her anxieties with someone she trusted. She reached the door of Mr Fry's shop, and stepped inside. Jennie was there.

Could Jennie be spared for half an hour? Yes, naturally, Mr Fry was all smiles, for no doubt the young ladies would be discussing important matters such as dresses, which an old fellow like himself had no knowledge of! Yes, yes, they must go, he was not busy, there was no rush, and the sea air would bring the roses to their cheeks. The young women walked down towards the shore; Jennie looked enquiringly at Eveline, but said nothing until they were away from the bustle of the town, and out of earshot of anyone else.

'Are you quite well, Eveline?' she asked at last. They had stopped to sit on a low wall, looking out to sea. 'You look pale – worried – do tell me what is wrong.'

Eveline took a deep breath.

'I hope you won't be shocked, Jennie,' she said. Jennie smiled at her, and took her hand. 'I don't think that is likely,' she said, 'whatever it is. My life has not been like yours; I was not born a lady.'

'When you hear what I have to say, you may not think me very ladylike,' said Eveline, and began to tell her, briefly and haltingly, what had happened after Jennie and Ned had left her and Thomas alone on the beach that night.

'So you see,' she said, 'I am frightened, Jennie. He is gone, and I might be . . . might be—' She could not say the words; tears overcame her.

'Might be with child?' Jennie said gently. 'Oh, it is always the way; men can take their pleasure, but women pay the price.'

'No, no, it was not like that,' said Eveline earnestly. She mopped her eyes. 'I cannot blame Thomas; at least, I am as much to blame as he.'

'I do not think so,' said Jennie darkly. 'He should not be doing such things when he has a woman of his own in the north. I am surprised at him! I had thought him a good man, but there, men are all the same, my mother always said.'

'He is a good man, truly – at least, I thought – oh, well, the thing is, Jennie, I have been so wicked, and foolish, and now I am so afraid.' She dissolved once more into tears.

Jennie thought for a few moments.

'Can I ask – how near your monthly time are you?'

'Oh – very close – but why?'

'Something else my mother told me, along with men being all the same, and a thousand other pieces of advice. If you are near that time, you might well be safe. The few days before, she says, are your best chance of safety. Perhaps all will be well.'

'Really? I did not know – oh, Jennie, if you think that is so, how fortunate, how wonderful!'

'I do not think it is by any means certain,' said Jennie, 'but I hope it may be so.' She put her arm around Eveline's shoulders. 'You have always been so kind to me, Eveline, and if it were not for you, I would not have my work with Mr Fry. I will pray that I am right.'

'I am so grateful, Jennie. You have given me some hope. I suppose I must go and buy napkins for Mama, now. Thank you, thank you.'

Later that day, she slipped into her father's study, and after some searching found the book she was looking for. The heavy tome was leather bound, and in gold letters on the spine were the words *Domestic Medicine*. It was, she supposed, one of the few of her father's books she had not read cover to cover during the years since he died. She leafed through it, hoping wildly that no one would come in to interrupt her search, and at last found what she was looking for: *Advice to Women*, it read, and feverishly she scanned the chapter. At last she closed the book and replaced it carefully on the shelf. It seemed that Jennie's mother and the distinguished doctor who had written the book were in agreement. She heaved a sigh; oh, that it might be so!

The next day, her immediate fear was over; she was not with child, and she experienced a giddy, light-headed relief. How free, how thankful she felt; yet very soon that relief faded, and was followed, irrationally, by an even deeper melancholy, for there was still no word from Thomas, and now, at last, she knew her own heart. She had thought that he might send a note, or a letter, but there was nothing. His absence, his silence, was, she supposed, a clear enough indication that he did not feel the same as she, and she felt his loss as though it were a physical pain inside her. *My heart aches*, she whispered to herself: *my heart aches. So sad, so strange, the days that are no more. Dear as remembered kisses. He cometh not. I am half-sick of shadows.*

This is what the poets write about, she thought. This is why they write.

Chapter Thirty-One

The Wedding

Eveline was not even to find solace in being alone, for there was still a great deal to be done before the great day dawned, and her family were all in a state of high excitement, and there was much coming and going, deliveries and tradesmen calling at all hours, and she was constantly called upon for opinions and assistance.

'You look far too pale, Eveline,' said Beatrice critically. It was the eve of the wedding. 'Quite washed out! Does she not, Mama?'

'A little; yes, a little,' said Mrs Stanhope, absently. 'Would some extra lace at the wrist have been too much, Beatrice, do you think?'

'I think we were right to keep the sleeves very plain, Mama, so that the elegance of those delicious gloves can be seen. But Evie, really, you should make more of an effort for Mama's sake. You have a distinct want of complexion. Go to bed and get some beauty sleep. If you look no better tomorrow, I think you will have to wear a touch of rouge, for you look positively haggard, you wretched child.'

So Eveline, rather to her relief, retired early, and was at last alone. For a while she tried to read, but the words danced before her eyes, and slid from the page, and became meaningless, and at last she gave up, and sat in the window seat to gaze out into the darkness. Ragged clouds scudded across a gibbous moon. She rested her forehead against the glass, and told herself firmly that she must be strong; must carry on however her heart was aching, for it would be quite wrong to cast even the slightest shadow on her mother's happiness. It would take all her resolve, all her strength, but she would not be selfishly thinking of herself and her own heart. She would, at least, as well as she could, appear happy.

The day of the wedding dawned clear and bright, and Mrs Stanhope looked most charming in pale dove-grey, with velvet ribbons, the tiniest of veils, and a pair of very lovely pearl and diamond earrings, which were the bridegroom's present to his bride. ('The dear man!' she had exclaimed, 'sometimes it is as if he can read my mind, you know.') Louisa and Bevis were there, with Henry and Daisy, and if Bevis seemed a little subdued, he was at least by Louisa's side, and when she turned to him to say something about the children, he raised her hand to his lips, and kissed it most tenderly; and Eveline was glad for her sister, and welcomed Bevis with real affection, although she thought of Hannah, and the little boy, and hoped very fervently that their lives would not be too hard.

Beatrice and Arthur, too, looked content, as the wedding guests left the church, and walked back to the house. There was a moment's consternation that the party would be too crowded in the dining room, for it turned out that Mr Watson had invited one or two friends, after all, to witness his wedding, and balance the numbers a little; but with remarkably quick thinking, he persuaded his new wife that the wedding breakfast might be brought outside, and eaten as a picnic.

'I have seen a delightful photograph of our own dear queen, with the late Prince Consort, God rest his soul, and all the precious princes and princesses, sitting outside in the sunshine; so natural, and yet so regal!' he said. 'I think we may do the same, with all the family gathered around us.'

The new Mrs Watson was instantly delighted by the notion; Eveline could only admire his methods. Bevis and Arthur carried rugs, and chairs, and a table for the food, and all the dishes were brought out, with the wedding cake at the centre of all.

'Aha!' said Mr Watson, as the first champagne cork popped, 'and here, just like the royal family, we have our own photographer to record the scene,' and there, all smiles and bows, was Mr Fry, accompanied by Jennie. Glasses were pressed into everyone's hands, and a toast to the happy couple was very gracefully proposed by Bevis. The wedding party was then arranged for the photograph, and held its collective breath as the seconds ticked by, until with a flourish the Professor declared himself satisfied. Mr Watson prevailed upon him and Jennie to stay for the celebration, and everyone disposed themselves about the lawn to eat, and drink, and be happy. The children, giddy on lemonade and cake, rushed about, and turned somersaults, and took second helpings of everything into Kitty's tree house; Aunt George and Miss Angell complacently pointed out the glories of the late summer borders to an admiring rector; Mr Jones from the railway board paid Jennie roguish compliments; Louisa and Beatrice talked of clothes, and Bevis and Arthur of horses; and Eveline wheeled out her camera, which she had, to the Professor's admiration, loaded onto an old perambulator chassis for ease of transportation, and took a photograph of her mother smiling mistily at her husband, with the new earrings catching the light.

The house, next day, was very quiet. The newly married couple had left for a short honeymoon in Eastbourne – 'Just for a few days,' said Mrs Watson, 'and we are to go to Paris in the spring' – Eveline's sisters and their families had all departed, and Aunt George, and Miss Angell, and Eveline, were left to return to their own lives, and to eat cold beef and wedding cake; and in Eveline's case, to think ceaselessly of Thomas Armitage. She had tried valiantly to drive such thoughts away, but it was hopeless; his face, his voice, his touch, were in her thoughts at every waking moment, and in her dreams at night. It was over a week now, since he had been gone. Mr Watson had said he had travelled to London for a meeting, or an interview, or some such thing; well, that would certainly explain his absence for a day or two, perhaps even three; but for so long? No, surely not. He had gone to London, and then what? He had not rushed to return, to find her, even to make some sort of awkward goodbye, let alone to swear undying love. And yet . . . of course, something might have detained him in town. If he was seeking a new position, as Mr Watson had seemed to suggest, it might perhaps take longer than she had first thought. Of course, that was it; such things could not be settled in a day. Her spirits rose a little, and hope began to revive. He might even be on his way back now. He might, in fact, be calling at the house at any moment.

She determined that she would, of course, be busy when he arrived: it would not do to look as though she had nothing to do but wait for him; and after all, it was high time that the books and ornaments in the morning room (which happened to overlook the front door) were dusted and arranged. For a whole day, therefore, she conscientiously busied herself with cloths and brushes, moving objects from one shelf to another and back again, and thereby unconsciously offending the servants, who took it as a direct reflection on their work, and shook their heads crossly every time they passed the room where Miss Eveline was so unaccountably determined to spend her time. Every now and then, however, she found herself, duster in hand, standing at the window and looking out, in case a tall figure, loose-limbed, with a long, graceful stride, should suddenly appear. Every footfall, every voice, made her jump, and made her heart beat a little faster; but he did not come.

What could he be doing? What was he thinking? The clock ticked. A fly, trapped between the window and the blind, buzzed ceaselessly, and she opened the sash to free it. And suddenly, as she stood gazing at the empty gravel drive in front of the house, a thought came to her. She recalled Thomas's face when he had seen her, as she stepped from the steamer, with Charles Sandham walking so close beside her. His look of disdain, of disgust, even, was still clear in her mind. Of course: that look was not for Charles; it was for her. He had thought her just returned from some illicit excursion accompanied by that horrible man. He would have thought the very worst; indeed, he had thought so, for Mr Watson had virtually said as much. And now, she had proved to him that she was, indeed, as her mother might have said, no better than she should be, for she had given herself to Thomas, and of course he had assumed that she had already given herself to Charles too. Of course he had; why should he not assume that? *Your reputation!* her mother had said, *your reputation!* and then she had thought that rebuke merely the stuff of old-fashioned convention. She had not cared for convention, or for what her neighbours thought; but she did care, infinitely, for what Thomas thought, and in his eyes, she now realised, she was beneath contempt. She had fallen in love; while he had merely taken an opportunity, as men did. She felt cold, and sick inside. She sank to her knees, and rested her head on the window sill, and at last the tears came, and with no one to hear her, she sobbed in anguish. It is over, she thought. There is no hope. It is over.

* * *

In the days that followed this bitter revelation, she cried for many hours, but always in the privacy of her own bedroom; and at last, she scolded herself into resolving that she should at least, although desolate and heartbroken, try to be busy and useful. She visited Mr Fry, and helped at the studio for a few hours, grateful for the distraction of work and the old companionship.

'Come back tomorrow, Eveline, if you can,' he said, 'I have heard of a second-hand camera that I think you might enjoy – quite portable, and modern. I will have it sent here, and you can try it, perhaps, to see if it is what you would like.'

The camera was indeed suitable; it had its own leather travelling case, and a folding tripod stand, and a separate lens in a black velvet pouch. Eveline for the first time in many days, felt that life might still hold at least a little purpose. She spent a morning experimenting with it in Mr Fry's studio, and it was all she could wish for. What better way could there be to spend that treasured prize money? All was agreed, the price was acceptable, and it would be delivered to her the next day.

Lost in contemplation of the opportunities the new camera would present, she walked back via the harbour, and paused to gaze out to sea, wondering if she might make a series of photographs of the sea in different lights. The same view, perhaps, from the same spot, but taken at varying times; in rosy dawns, or sunsets, or blue skies, or storms, with huge ragged clouds casting shadows on the water. She was so absorbed that she very nearly walked into Sir William, gesturing expansively towards his yacht while in conversation with another man, and there, close by, to her dismay, was Charles Sandham, standing next to a young woman. All three men were dressed identically, in white trousers, blazer and peaked cap, as though they were overgrown schoolboys from the same school. The lady on Charles's arm wore a huge crinoline, trimmed with a great deal of lace and ribbons, and a bonnet with what seemed to be an entire bouquet of flowers adorning it, and she and Charles seemed to be engaged in a dispute of some sort, perhaps as to the advisability of boarding Sir William's yacht in such a costume. Eveline hoped fervently that she might walk by unseen, but Sir William hailed her, and she was obliged to smile, and greet him, and to be introduced to Mr Lyle and his daughter. The gentleman had a prosperous look, well fed, and sleek, with a huge cigar clamped between his teeth; and Miss Lyle had a small, pretty face, marred by a sour, petulant little mouth, and a sulky expression, although whether that was a permanent feature or merely due to her dispute with Charles was hard to say. She shook hands rather limply with Eveline, gave her an appraising, dismissive glance, and immediately turned away to begin a complaint to her father about having been misled by her friends into wearing quite the wrong thing for the afternoon, and how selfish they had been, thinking only of themselves, and not really caring for her at all; her father did his best to soothe and placate her, but she continued to rail against the so-called friends in a voice that steadily rose in stridency, and Charles stepped aside for a moment, to smile ruefully at Eveline.

'Ah, Eveline,' he murmured. 'Where is the life that late I led?'

'Where indeed?' she said, with icy politeness. 'Your new friend does not seem happy, Mr Sandham. You had better go to her.'

He sighed. 'Yes, I had. She is not easy to please.'

'But wealthy, perhaps?'

'Oh, very wealthy; her papa is something in the city.'

They both turned to look at the lady. She was still haranguing her unfortunate parent, her voice resembling nothing so much as the incessant yapping of a small but vicious dog.

'I think she will suit you very well,' said Eveline. 'I hope she is everything you deserve,' and she began to walk away; but then she stopped, and turned back for a moment. 'And by the way,' she added, 'if I should ever see or hear the slightest evidence that you have mistreated her, or any other woman, I shall blacken your name beyond anything you have thought possible. I know what you are, and my family know too. Do not forget that, Mr Sandham. Do not *ever* forget it.'

Chapter Thirty-Two

The Watsons Entertain

The happy couple were returned from their honeymoon, and Eveline had been so used to seeing Mr Watson at their house, that it hardly seemed odd that he was now there for breakfast as well as dinner. It had been decided that Mr Watson would move into the Stanhope residence, and he seemed perfectly content with the arrangement, and quite amenable to joining the ready-made household if that was what his wife wished; and indeed she was absolutely determined that she would continue to provide a home for her sister-in-law and for Miss Angell. They were so much beloved by the entire Stanhope family, that anything else was unthinkable; and here they were so settled, so very content, and absolutely devoted now to their poultry (a pair of Indian Runner ducks, acquired recently, was their latest enthusiasm. 'Not the best of layers, it must be said,' observed Aunt George, 'but they do have a very sweet nature, and they look so charmingly ridiculous.') The garden, too, in all its beauty and profusion, was entirely their creation, and it gave everyone such delight; and if that made Augusta Sandham gnash her teeth with envy, well, that was quite incidental.

'Eveline,' said Mr Watson, on the day after their return, 'I wonder if I might consult you? Your mama runs the household, of course, and I would never interfere, but I do wonder if we might not engage a new kitchen maid. You have been working hard, I know, cooking and cleaning and whatnot . . .'

'I am glad to help,' said Eveline.

'But you may not always be here, my dear. I do not think you are the sort of girl to stay quietly at home for the rest of your life.'

'No, I hope—that is, I do not plan to. So yes, a kitchen maid, certainly, although . . . that is, I do not know how much Mama had told you of our finances, but we have had to be making some economies.'

'But I am here now, and you must allow me to be at least an equal partner in the household. We men have our pride, you know.'

Eveline gave in. 'I suspect Mama would really like a lady's maid, too. My hair-curling is not up to standard, I know. But let her be for Mama alone; I would prefer to go on as I am.'

'And a carriage?'

'You must ask Mama that.'

Mrs Watson was certainly delighted at the prospect of a new lady's maid, and a kitchen maid, and Mrs Groves hardly less so. But rather to everyone's surprise, she did not think that she wished for a new carriage.

'Oh, I am quite used to travelling about by train, now,' she said airily. 'I do not want to go back to the old days, rattling about in a coach, like poor Augusta Sandham; so old-fashioned, I think!'

Eveline smiled to herself a little at this; but she was truly delighted to see how happy her mother was with her new husband. Mr Watson's presence, it seemed, only added to the comfort and cheerfulness of the family, as well as to his wife's own happiness; and naturally it was very pleasant for the new Mrs Watson to feel that her friends and acquaintances were rather envious of her ability to capture a new husband at her time of life, and such a charming and eligible one at that. In fact, she was even now planning a sumptuous dinner, a dinner which would clearly demonstrate the elegance and style in which they now lived, and to which she planned to invite her family and closest friends.

'Yes,' she said graciously, 'even Augusta and Sir William, for I shall not let it be said that I bear a grudge, although I shall never allow that dreadful Charles over my doorstep again. In any case, I hear he has gone back to London with that silly rich girl, and they are to be married within a month. Well, I wish her the joy of him!'

'And he of her,' murmured Eveline.

'It was very fortunate, as things turned out,' said her mama, 'that you did not accept him, Eveline, was it not? For as well as being a bad man, he had no money after all. You were very sensible, my love.'

'Thank you, Mama,' said Eveline. 'I am glad to have done something sensible, for once at least.'

The dinner was to be held in the grandest style. Aunt George and Miss Angell redoubled their exertions to provide the most delicious produce from the garden, and the hens were laying so well that soufflés and meringues and custards were created in abundance. There were to be oysters, and fried sole, and red mullet; a shoulder of mutton, and a *fricandeau* of beef; and a haunch of venison, which Bevis had sent over from his estate, along with several brace of pheasant, which was positively magnificent. Eveline brought in some late roses to make a centrepiece, the table was set with the best china and the new linen napkins, and the glasses and the silver were polished until they glittered. As well as the Sandhams, Louisa and Bevis, and Beatrice and Arthur, were, naturally, to attend; Aunt George and Miss Angell had been persuaded to be part of the occasion; the Debournes were of course to be there, and Eveline had suggested, more in hope than expectation, that her mother invite Mr Fry.

'Otherwise, we will be thirteen at dinner,' pointed out Eveline. 'You have always said that is bad luck, Mama.'

'But, you know, my love, he is trade, after all,' said her mother. 'A very pleasant man, of course, and clever, in his way, but still, what will people think?'

'Do we care what people think?' asked Eveline. 'Mama, Mr Fry is a friend. That is all that matters, surely?'

Her mother was still wrestling with this question, when Mr Watson came to the rescue.

'I myself like Theodore very much,' he said genially. 'Of course, the more old-fashioned, and, dare I say it, *philistine* among our neighbours may not appreciate him as we do, even though it is surely the wish of any enlightened person to encourage the arts.' He sighed. 'But you may be right, my dear; some people will not see his true worth.'

A glint came into his wife's eyes.

'Yes,' she said thoughtfully, 'how perceptive you are, my dearest! Augusta, for example, has hardly read a book in her life, you know. She is shockingly old-fashioned, too; I have always said so. Do you know, I think it is positively our duty to cultivate the artists in our little society. I see that I shall have to encourage poor Augusta to become a little more enlightened in her outlook.'

Thus Mr Fry was admitted to the exclusive list of guests, and on the evening itself Eveline managed to arrange the seating plan herself, so that she could sit next to him, and thus be assured of interesting company. They had a great deal to discuss as to Eveline's latest photographs, and an idea she had for a set of portraits of the fisherfolk, taken not in a studio but with their boats, on the shore, hauling the fish in baskets, or mending nets; and then there was the excellent news that Mr Fry had secured a commission from the Railway Company to take a whole series of pictures of locomotives, following his success at the Photographic Society.

'I have been most fortunate in that, for it is a project that I look forward to immensely, from the artistic point of view as well as the commercial; and Jennie is the perfect assistant,' said Mr Fry, accepting a glass of the late Mr Stanhope's excellent claret with an appreciative nod. 'She has a good eye herself, and is so meticulous in all she does, and so pleasant with the customers, that I believe the business has never been so good.'

'I am glad to hear you say so,' said Eveline, 'for Jennie is a dear friend, and I know she in turn is very happy to work with you, Mr Fry.'

'I only fear,' said he, 'that soon she will marry her young man, and then she will be lost to me.'

'I expect she will marry Ned, certainly,' said Eveline, 'they have set a date, I think, for the spring; but that need not stop her working, surely?'

'It is quite out of the question for any married woman to work,' pronounced Lady Sandham, who had been following this conversation from her place across the table. 'A woman's place is in the home, I have always said. No woman of any refinement would ever let her thoughts stray from her own home and fireside.'

'But men work after they are married,' said Eveline.

'That is quite different,' said Lady Sandham severely.

'I do not see at all why it should be different,' said Eveline, studiously ignoring her mother's warning stare. 'Jennie is very skilled at her work; if she wishes to continue, why should she not?'

'And I very much hope she will,' said Mr Fry, 'nothing would please me more, but it is just that, in the way of things, once married, she may find that she has *other duties*.'

'Exactly,' said Lady Sandham, 'I did not like to mention such a delicate topic at the dinner table; but you understand me, Mr Fry, I can see,' and she bestowed on him a slightly alarming smile, half-condescending, half-flirtatious, which made Mr Fry take another glass of claret with extreme haste.

'You mean she will have a baby, I suppose,' said Eveline. Lady Sandham gave a delicate shudder and pressed her lips together.

'Really,' she said faintly. 'In my day, no young woman would have mentioned such a thing. But there, I dare say I am a little old-fashioned in my ways.'

'Do not reproach yourself, Augusta,' said Mrs Watson kindly. 'You cannot help being old-fashioned, I know. Do take some more of this pheasant – Bevis shot it himself.'

Lady Sandham, momentarily silenced by her hostess's remark, and quite unable to think of a suitable riposte, allowed herself to be distracted by the pheasant, and Eveline turned back to Mr Fry.

'Jennie might not necessarily have a baby,' she said thoughtfully. 'At least, not straightaway. She is clever, you know, in all sorts of ways.'

Mr Fry nodded, cheerfully, if uncomprehendingly. 'We can but hope so,' he said. 'This claret, Mr Watson, is remarkably good; oh, yes, thank you, just another glass would be *most* acceptable.'

The food was perfectly delicious, and the hostess received the many compliments on the excellence of her table with great satisfaction; although, however modern her outlook these days, she still drew the line at disclosing to her friends that her youngest daughter was at least partly responsible for the dishes before them.

'This venison is really very fine,' said Mr Watson. 'Bevis, old man, you are too kind. Luckily, I have just taken delivery of a rather fine French brandy, so I shall be able to repay your generosity after dinner with a glass or two, eh?'

'That sounds like a bargain,' said Bevis. 'Thank you, sir.'

'Just one glass, though, Bevis,' said Louisa, giving her husband a warning look.

'Of course just one, my sweet,' he said, and took her hand. 'Be it never so fine, Watson's brandy can have no charms for me when you are near. *Leave a kiss but in the cup, and I'll not look for wine.*'

'Oh, really, Bevis,' said Louisa, blushing. 'You are absurd,' but she smiled back at him with a look that was very close to adoration, and allowed him to raise her hand to his lips, and to lean over and whisper some sweet nothing into her ear, which made her blush even more rosily than before. Bevis, thought Eveline wryly, would always have the ability to charm his way through life; but if he was now making her sister happy once more, he must, she supposed, be forgiven.

Arthur, seated on Eveline's other side from Mr Fry, then claimed her attention.

'I have hardly seen you, Evie, since we were back from Brighton,' he said. 'It's a ripping place, Brighton; you would like it, I think. Sea bathing is all the rage there.'

'I should love to visit Brighton,' said Eveline wistfully. 'To travel; to get about the world, and see new places – that is what I long for, Arthur.'

'Well, Beatrice and I could take you to Brighton next summer, perhaps,' said Arthur. 'Bit of a holiday. What do you say?'

'Would you?' asked Eveline. 'A holiday! How very delightful that would be. Now I have something to look forward to; oh, thank you, Arthur!' She turned to her sister. 'Bea, should you mind?'

Beatrice looked rather coy, and peeped at her husband through her lashes.

'Arthur, my love,' she said, 'I am not sure we will be able to take Evie anywhere next summer.'

'Won't we?' he asked, blankly.

'No, because . . . well, because I may not be in a condition to travel by then.'

'Not in a . . . ?' Arthur continued to look mystified.

'Not in a *condition*,' said Beatrice patiently, 'to travel, or anything else, really.' She raised her eyebrows helplessly at Eveline.

'Oh, Bea!' said Eveline, laughing, despite seeing her promised holiday vanish almost as soon as it had been proposed, 'do you mean you are to have another baby?'

'Yes,' said Beatrice complacently, 'I am; that is, we are.'

'Good God!' said Arthur, staring at his wife. 'Another baby! I say, Bea, that is marvellous news! When did—that is, Brighton, I suppose . . .'

Poor Lady Sandham, the conversation having once more taken so deplorable a turn, looked quite stricken; but the rest of the party began to exclaim, and to congratulate Beatrice and Arthur, and toasts were proposed, and drunk, and there was much talk of how pleased Kitty would be to have a little brother or sister. Bevis leant over to thump Arthur on the back; Mr Watson, kind and courteous as always, was the picture of pride and happiness as he urged his guests to refill their glasses once more; and Mrs Watson, presiding over such a gathering, and now in receipt of this delightful news, felt herself to be extraordinarily blessed.

'A new grandchild!' she said. 'Beatrice, my love, you must take very good care of yourself, now.'

'You must have no fears on that score,' said Arthur. 'I shall be taking great care of her, you may be sure.'

Eveline looked around her. Her sisters' faces were glowing in the soft light of the candles; Mama was beaming tenderly upon Beatrice, clucking gently about cradles, and caps, and new drapes for the nursery; her aunt was discussing the latest news of the shocking war in America with Mr Watson; Mr Fry was explaining chromatic daguerreotypes to the Debournes; and even Augusta Sandham, her feelings soothed perhaps by a third helping of Eveline's raspberry meringues, looked almost cheerful as kind-hearted Miss Angell, taking pity on her, was making a most generous offer to visit her in the near future to advise upon a new scheme for the gardens at Sandham Park. *I am very fortunate*, thought Eveline, *to be part of this family. I must count my blessings; I am surrounded by affection, and good humour, and warmth; I am safe, and cared for, and immensely privileged. And yet . . .* and yet. Try as she might to forget, her thoughts would stray back to the spring, which seemed so long ago now, and the evening party – so like tonight's in many ways, so different in others – when she had first been introduced to Thomas Armitage. He had seemed so cold and forbidding, she had flared up – she could hardly remember why, now – and the coming of the railway had promised, then, to be an outrage and a disaster. How many changes had come since that evening! Changes for the island, for this little town, for her family, and for her own heart. Laughter rose around her; the warm murmur of conversation rippled on; the candlelight danced, the crystal and the silver sparkled, and the ruby wine flowed. Eveline smiled, and listened, and nodded; but somewhere inside she felt empty, and desolate, and filled with a longing for a certain face, rather stern in repose, often sardonic, yet with a smile that had once made her heart turn over. It would have been very selfish to wish this happy evening at an end, and she subdued her restless thoughts as well as she could; but when the last farewells had been said, she found herself to be weary beyond measure, and heartily glad to find solitude once more.

Chapter Thirty-Three

Different Sorts of Freedom

Despite the very fine brandy with which he had regaled his guests late into the night, Mr Watson departed, as he always did, at nine o'clock the next morning, for the railway offices; although soon his work there would be done, he said, for the line was complete, everything running smoothly, and the last hitches overcome.

'But I do not wish to be late this morning, for I must bid Tom farewell; he leaves today, and I have a silver cigarette case to give him by way of a small gift – it is nothing, really, when I think of the fine job he has done,' and with that he closed the door behind him. Eveline was rooted to the spot: so Thomas was here – had returned from London, but had not come to see her – was leaving today. Well, that was certainly the end of any faint lingering hopes she might have entertained that she would ever see him again. He did not want to see her, that was plain, or he would have been at her door, surely, or sent a note; but there had been nothing, nothing at all, and now he was leaving this very day.

She would keep busy, that was the thing – but Mrs Groves had nothing much for her to do today, save to feed Autolycus, and Aunt George and Miss Angell were entirely wrapped up in some vigorous pruning, and after half an hour trying to concentrate on developing a print, which turned out to be hopelessly overexposed, she suddenly made her mind up to walk to the railway office.

'I shall just say goodbye to him, that is all,' she said to herself, 'for once we were friends. We must shake hands, at least; then it really will be over.'

She did not stop to put on her hat, or to question her own motives, but half-walked, half-ran as fast as she could through the town, trying not to catch the eye of acquaintances who might delay her, and weaving her way through the people who stood idly about, talking and stupidly blocking the way as though they had nothing else to do. She walked so fast that by the time she reached the station she was breathless, and knocked on the door with her heart pounding. Mr Watson received her.

'Eveline, my dear – is all well? Is something wrong? Not your mama, I hope?'

'No – oh, no – it is just that I thought I would say goodbye to Mr Armitage, as I was . . . as I was passing,' she said, feebly.

'You have just missed him, I am afraid,' said Mr Watson. 'Gone to collect the last of his things from his lodging, though he will be back very soon. You are most welcome to wait, of course; in fact, I think he may have said that he hoped to see you before he left. Yes, I am sure he said something of that nature. But you do not look altogether well, Eveline. Here, sit down, and I will fetch you a glass of something.'

Eveline sank gratefully into a chair, as Mr Watson disappeared into the recesses of the building. This will not do, she said to herself firmly. Practically fainting in such a feeble, female way! How absurd. It was merely that, after all, Thomas did want to see her! A wild hope seized her, and something very like joy surged through her. She took some deep breaths, and stood upright, steadying herself against the long table that stood against the wall. A few letters lay in a tray on its surface, waiting, she supposed, to be posted, and her eye fell upon them. The top envelope, of thick cream-coloured paper, was addressed in a strong, clear hand, and the direction leapt out at her: *Jane Armitage, Moortown House, Leeds*.

For a moment, her mind refused to comprehend it. Who could Jane Armitage be? Thomas would not address his mother so. Or an aunt, or a grandmother. She dropped back into the chair. He had been away, now, for long enough to travel back to the north. Mr Watson had said he thought Thomas had gone to London, but the man was so vague and forgetful, that meant nothing at all. It drove into her heart like a knife: Thomas had already returned to Leeds to marry. He had gone to the north, the wedding had taken place, he had come back here to collect the last of his possessions, and this letter was to forewarn his bride of his imminent return. He was married; he had left Eveline's arms and gone straight to his wedding with another woman. With this vile Jane.

She stood up and began to walk towards the door.

'I have some brandy, here,' said Mr Watson, reappearing. 'Now, this will do you the world of good. Stay, Eveline, you are not leaving? Tom will not be too long, I am sure. Will you not wait?'

'I cannot wait,' said Eveline. 'It does not matter. I have nothing to say to him, after all.'

She had no recollection of how she got home. The streets were a blur, the people ghosts. How he must despise her! She had given herself to him, and it had meant nothing at all, except a light diversion before he became a married man. Horrible phrases rushed into her mind: *a last fling – wild oats – a bit of muslin* – and no doubt a thousand other revolting epithets of which she was mercifully unaware. How he must have congratulated himself on his good fortune, to find a woman so ready to throw herself at him, so freely, and on the eve of his wedding! How he must have laughed as he regaled his friends with tales of how women in the south, even those of respectable families, were of conveniently easy virtue. Yet she had thought, truly thought, that he too had felt something deeper as they lay together in the moonlight. The memory flooded back, and she pushed her knuckles into her mouth to stop herself from uttering a cry of pain.

* * *

Her aunt and Miss Angell were, as always, in the garden. The day had all the glory of autumn about it, fresh and chill, the grass soaked with dew, and the light golden. The two ladies were sitting together on the bench by the border.

'How melancholy you look, my dear,' said Miss Angell. 'Will you come and sit with us? Whatever is wrong, you know, being in a garden is always a salve to the spirit.'

'Thank you, you are kind – but I need to be alone, I think. Forgive me.'

'That tree, then,' said her aunt, 'you had best have some time there, my love.'

'My tree! I did not know you knew about that.'

'I have only glimpsed you there, once or twice; your secret is safe with me.'

'It is absurd, I know, to be climbing trees; it has always felt like a place I can be free, that is all,' she said.

'Freedom is something you have always sought, Eveline, is it not?'

'I suppose it is. But there are different sorts of freedom. I had ridiculous ideas, I think, about how I could change things, and not be bound by convention, and get about the world. I have more modest ambitions now.'

'We have found freedom, of a kind,' said her aunt, and she took Miss Angell's hand.

'Yes, I know you have,' said Eveline, 'and I am so happy for you. One day, perhaps, I shall say the same.'

She kissed them both, and then walked across the lawn, and around what used to be the rose garden, and climbed onto the old wheelbarrow, and then the wall, and the roof of the shed, and up onto the old familiar branch. The beech leaves were turning to amber, and the first of them had fallen to the ground. Soon, she would not be able to hide here any more.

The pale yellow woods were waning
The broad stream in his banks complaining
Heavily the low sky raining . . .

She knew the poem well enough by now; had spent the summer learning it. Well, there was no point in being so ridiculously romantic: she had looked down to Camelot, but here she was, still alive, and there were no curses, or cracked mirrors, to haunt her now. She closed her eyes, and thought about a new series of photographs: not her family in fancy dress, but honest portraits of the people she had met, and was yet to meet, with all their wit, and cunning, and honesty, and dishonesty; all their hardship, and their struggle, and their sorrow, and their merriment, written in their faces. She might submit other photographs to the society; she might travel, and capture scenes in lands she had never seen; she might even establish a studio of her own, one day. She would be strong. There would be a way.

'Miss Stanhope.'

Her eyes flew open: Thomas Armitage was standing below her, looking up.

'Your aunt said I might find you here.'

Her heart gave an absurd leap.

'Mr Armitage.' She struggled wildly to assume an air of

polite indifference. 'I . . . I thought you were gone. Mr Watson said you had left.'

'Yes, Watson told me you had called at the office. I was coming to find you anyway, you know. May I come up?' and without waiting, he climbed easily up to where she was sitting, and swung himself astride the branch, facing her.

'I am on my way to the steamer; I have an hour, that is all.'

'And you are going back to the north.' She managed, she hoped, to keep her voice steady.

'Indeed. To Leeds, to say farewell to my family; and thence to Liverpool, for the ship.'

'You are going on a voyage?' She had some dull premonition that he would be taking his bride on a honeymoon journey; to Europe, perhaps.

'Yes; a voyage to America. I have secured a post there, as chief engineer to a railway company – the railroad, they call it. It is a vast country, and there are tens of thousands of miles of railroad to be built – out to the west, right across the continent, through lands that are still wild and unknown.'

'America! Then you may not return, I conclude, for many years?'

'No, perhaps not. I am just back from meeting a representative of the railroad company who is in London; he and I had much to discuss, but we have come to an agreement at last, and we have done a good deal of planning already. There is a war, you know, in the southern states; we are agreed that the railroad is of vital importance now. I am to go out there for a few years, at least.'

Eveline swallowed, and said with as much resolve as she

could muster, 'Your new wife – she will not mind leaving her family behind? She must be a patient woman, and a brave one.'

'My new wife? What are you talking about, Eveline?'

'I saw the letter, Thomas. I was not spying. I merely happened to see it.'

'The letter?' He sounded grim. 'What letter is this?'

'The letter to a Jane Armitage. Your wife. Who else?'

Astonishingly, he started to laugh.

'The letter to Jane? I will probably be back in Leeds before the letter gets to her – but I was writing to my sister, to expect me soon. My sister, Eveline, not my wife.'

'Oh!' She felt the blood rush to her cheeks. 'A sister! I did not know you had a sister.'

'I do. She is very dear to me; it is she I will miss the most, when I go.'

'I am sure she is delightful,' said Eveline. A sister – a sister, of course, a sister. Jane! What a perfectly charming name. She felt light-headed with relief; but all at once she recollected her former fears.

'You do have a sweetheart, however, I believe,' she said, as coldly as she could.

'A sweetheart? What now? For God's sake, Eveline, stop concocting this nonsense.'

'Ned and Jennie said – they told me – that you had a sweetheart. At least, they thought so.'

'A sweetheart? Well, I do not know what Ned was thinking. He is not generally given to fantasy and gossip.'

'They said – Jennie said – that you had mentioned a new

life. That you were saving money for that – for a wedding, for a marriage, they thought . . .' Her head swam, for a moment, as she took this in. 'I suppose they jumped to a conclusion, then?'

'Clearly, they did.' He looked into her eyes, very serious. 'My new life is this work I had been hoping for, in America. I have been saving money for my fare, and to have enough in my pocket when I start my new work on the railroads there; that is all.'

'So you will be travelling alone to America?'

'Yes. Unless you will come with me.'

She stared at him, her heart beginning to thump.

'Come with me, Eveline. Marry me. It may not be an easy life, but what new worlds we will have to discover, what things we will see! You would like that, my lass, would you not?' He leant forward and kissed her. 'Will you, Eveline? Will you marry me?'

She caught her breath, and the world spun around her.

'Of course,' she said. 'Yes, Thomas, of course I will marry you.'

'We could be married on board ship, apparently,' he said, 'if you don't mind the lack of fuss.'

She started to laugh. 'What, no lace? No orange blossom?'

'Would you mind?'

'I should be heartily relieved.'

'Then can you be at the Liverpool shipping office one week from today? I will have a ticket for you. Do not bring too much luggage; we may have to travel long distances once we are there.'

'I shall have to bring my camera, though. How many new

faces, and sights, I shall have to capture!' She flung her arms around him, and kissed him so fiercely that they both very nearly overbalanced.

'Come on; we had best get back to earth, sweetheart – I have a boat to catch,' he said.

On the ground, he pulled her into his arms, and kissed her again and again, with long, deep kisses that made her knees weaken beneath her. At last she sighed with happiness, and rested her head on his shoulder.

'Thomas,' she said, 'you did not think that I ever had any fondness for Charles Sandham, did you? I did not go to London to meet him, you know; I travelled there for a quite separate reason, and he found me. It was all a horrible scheme on his part.'

'I was riven with jealousy,' he admitted, 'that day when I saw him with you. I told myself that I must give up hope of winning you, for he seemed so much more suitable than I to be your husband, and your family must have thought so too. And then Watson was certain it would be a match; said as much, at one point. Yet somehow I could not give up hope – could not quite believe, once I had come to know you, that you would want him. The man is a snake. I thought so the first time I met him.'

'He is,' said Eveline, 'and he is nothing to me, nor ever has been.'

'I should hope not,' said Thomas. 'Or I would be obliged to kill him.'

'There is no need to kill him,' she said, smiling, 'he has found a fate worse than death already, I am glad to say.'

'Good.' He kissed her once more. 'Do not fail me, then, Eveline,' he said. 'One week from today.'

'I will not fail you,' she said. A thought occurred. 'Oh, but, Thomas, how am I to get to Liverpool?'

He laughed. 'The steamer, then the train to London. There are trains from London to Liverpool, pretty regularly. You are an experienced traveller on the railways, now, are you not?'

'Of course; the railway.'

'Does the journey alarm you?'

'Alarm me! No. I love the railway,' she said, smiling.

He took out a penknife, and cut one of the last of the crimson roses still blooming beside them, and neatly removed the thorns. Then, smoothing the dark curls back from her face, he tucked the rose behind her ear.

'We have an adventure before us, do we not, my love?'

'We do,' said Eveline. 'We have the adventure of a lifetime.'

Acknowledgements

I would like to thank Rosie, Josh, and Alice, for their enthusiasm and their input, and all my dear family and friends who have been a source of support and encouragement throughout.

Special thanks are due to Paul Atterbury for his expert advice on Victorian railways. Thanks also to the staff of the Classic Boat Museum in Cowes, and of the Isle of Wight Steam Railway.

Eveline's adventures in photography were inspired by the work of Julia Margaret Cameron in her studio on the Isle of Wight. *Julia Margaret Cameron* by Helmut Gernstein, and

Immortal Faces by Brian Hinton, were invaluable sources of information, as were *The Isle of Wight Central Railway* by R. J. Maycock and R. Silsbury, *The Isle of Wight Railways* by Michael Robbins, and *The Victorian Home* by Kathryn Ferry.

Finally, my most grateful thanks to my marvellous agent, Sarah Such; and, most of all, to my partner, Terence Hart, for his unfailing patience, inspired suggestions, and willing participation in bizarre excursions in the name of research.

The Cowes to Newport Railway, on the Isle of Wight, did open on June 16th, 1862. Everything else in this story is fiction, and any mistakes are my own.

Heather Cooper
Cowes, 2018

HEATHER COOPER grew up in the north of England and has fond memories of corresponding with writers P. D. James and Seamus Heaney during her time working at Faber & Faber. She later worked for the National Trust and the NHS, and now lives on the Isle of Wight with her partner.

heathercooperauthor.co.uk

To discover more great books and to
place an order visit our website at
allisonandbusby.com

Don't forget to sign up to our free newsletter at
allisonandbusby.com/newsletter
for latest releases, events and exclusive offers

Allison & Busby Books
@AllisonandBusby

You can also call us on
020 3950 7834
for orders, queries
and reading recommendations